D0205889

DUCKETT & DYER

Dicks For Hire

All characters and events in this book are fictional.

Any resemblance to actual events or persons living or dead is coincidental, but would be pretty cool, to be honest.

ISBN: 978-1-7338943-1-9

SSN: 113-85-921— wait... no. Disregard that.

10 9 8 7 6 5 4 3 2 1

To my Grandfather, without whom I never would have started.

To my friends, without whom I never would have finished.

DUCKETT & DYER

Dicks For Hire

A NOVEL

BY

G.M. NAIR

PROLOGUE

So This Is How It Ends . . .

"Listen, it's not the worst idea I've ever had. And it certainly won't be the last," Stephanie Dyer said, just moments away from her death. The energies of the rip in multidimensional space-time crackled behind her, silhouetting her body and casting a shuddering, uneven blue pallor across the hardwood floor. Pushing her fringe of hair out of her eyes, Stephanie surveyed the living room one last time. It was a bit different than she remembered it. It hadn't been that long, had it? A calming sense of nostalgia warmed her chest as she took stock of the scuffed, scratched floors and the body of the old woman that lay, unmoving, by the overturned armoire.

As she turned to face the swirling blue abyss, the other conscious occupant in the room stirred. Clutching his side, Stephanie's oldest friend Michael Duckett struggled to remain on his feet by bracing himself on the back of the armoire. Michael looked tired. Not as tired as she was — not by a country mile — but tired nonetheless. She couldn't blame him. It had been a long road, and it would have to end here.

"Please," he said, "We have do this together."

"No, Michael," she refused to meet his gaze, "I need to do this alone. I started this loop and I need to close it. And to do that, I need you to trust me."

"Steph—"

"I know I haven't given you any reason to, and I'm sorry. I wish I could go back and fix that. But I tried and look how that ended up," Stephanie chuckled before composing herself. She turned to him and their eyes met for what felt like infinity, "So for once, can you just pretend that I know what I'm doing?"

The room around them stood quiet. There was no movement aside from the rotating portal that hung in the middle of room over the toppled coffee table.

"I'm sorry," he continued, attempting to push up the glasses that had been lost long ago. "I'm sorry I called you an embarrassment."

Stephanie felt the hint of a grin form at the corner of her mouth. "But I *was* an embarrassment."

"Yeah. But you're not supposed to *say* that," Michael returned a tentative smile that left before it could fully form. He looked away. "But you've always been my best friend. And . . . and you were right, too."

"About what?"

"It was kinda fun to play detective with you. Just like it used to be when we were kids."

Stephanie could do nothing but nod, with words caught in her throat. She couldn't bring herself to explain what this meant to her. It would be too complicated. It was always too complicated. She didn't understand it most times.

"I . . . " Michael sputtered a bit. "I don't want you to die."

"Neither do I! You think I'm doing this for my health?" Of course, trying to lighten up dour times with a joke was Stephanie's natural instinct, and her last moments were no exception. But, to her credit, she pivoted right back into earnest sincerity. "You're my best friend, too, Michael. I'm trying to help you, like you always did for me. Just think of this as my way of saying thank you."

"For what?"

"For putting up with me," Stephanie winked and let out a small sigh before turning to the portal, which had begun to emit a low, angry hum. She didn't know what lay on the other side but, in her heart, she knew that the next jump would be her last. The story couldn't end any other way. And it she had to try to end it. It had to be her.

So Stephanie leapt headfirst into the roiling tides of the space-time continuum, letting the blue energies wash over her body one last time. As she left this universe and this time behind, she closed her eyes, all too ready for the inevitable.

It may have been the end, but at least it was a pretty badass way to go.

CHAPTER ONE
Hot Date With Destiny

Michael Duckett was a young man with a decent head on his shoulders and a crippling anxiety that prevented him from ever using it. He had just slogged his way through another day at work, punching numbers into a computing box for no reason besides enriching his corporate overlords. It was a dreary, soul-crushing job that left his bank account only a little less than empty and his body a lot more than tired and drained every night. Tonight was no different, aside from the fact that it was Wednesday and that meant it was laundry day.

A holdover from his childhood, the "Wednesday-Laundry Day" mantra had been championed by his micromanaging mother. Despite the fact that she—now in her self-dubbed "sexy sixties"—was immersing herself in whatever horrifying bacchanalia they got up to in Boca Raton and was not around to badger him, Michael had the laundry day itch branded onto his soul. Not to mention a myriad of other more socially debilitating neuroses he had yet to work through.

Still, Laundry Day had its share of perks. That is to say, one perk in particular that went by the name of Terri Bradshaw. In a rare stroke of luck, Terri and Michael happened to have the same laundry schedules. She had introduced herself some weeks ago over the folding tables, and Michael found her very easy to talk to, which, for someone who used to suffer minor panic attacks before making phone calls, was an even rarer godsend.

"So, do you come here often?" Michael had asked.

She chuckled and turned back down to the jeans she was folding. Her auburn hair swished to cover her face and a smile. "Nice one."

"Uh . . . yeah," Michael wasn't sure what joke he had made, but he leaned into it. For the first time in a long while, his innate fear of being judged unfit by the opposite sex was nowhere to be found. This was an opportunity he refused to miss, so he leapt on it. "I'm Michael. Michael Duckett."

"Terri. Nice to meet you." Terri placed her jeans neatly into her laundry bag. "So, Michael Michael Duckett, what do you do?"

Michael deflated a little. The mere mention of his boring job sent his stomach into an involuntary stress gurgle. He hated being asked about it almost as much as he hated the job, "Oh, I'm an Analyst . . . at The Future Group."

"Oh, you work for The Future Group?" Terri leaned back a bit, eyebrows raised. She was still interested. "My brother works there! Do you know Jacob?"

"Jacob? I love that guy. Of course I know Jacob!" Michael did not know Jacob. In fact, as unlikely as it seemed, Michael had never met anyone named Jacob in the 24 years he had skulked about this Earth. The Future Group employed over 7,000 people. Perhaps one or more could have been named Jacob. He didn't really know. Either way, he'd gotten himself in deep already, so he just smiled and nodded.

"He loves working there," Terri continued. "Says it's the best job he's ever had!"

Michael did not share Jacob's assessment. He fidgeted with his glasses, running his fingers along the thin frames. "Yeah, uh, it has its ups and downs."

"Hah, well Jacob doesn't stop raving about it."

"Yeah, that's ol' Jacob. He's always . . . always . . . raving . . . " Michael trailed off. He had no idea what else he could say about Jacob, besides the fact that he had good taste in sisters. Luckily enough, the conversation took a turn and Jacob was never mentioned again. And so it went with Michael and Terri sharing a good time amongst the fumes of noxious chemicals synthesized to mimic the pleasant scent of spring meadows.

As the weeks passed, they spoke more about their days (usually uneventful), their old college roommates (the worst), their favorite wines (hers rosé, his a dry pinot grigio), how Haagen-Dazs made the only good kind of chocolate ice cream (it was sweet, but not overwhelmingly sweet, and thus a delight to the palate, even when re-purposed for Rocky Road), and other topics Michael assumed normal people talked about.

Terri had a habit of good-natured ribbing, which Michael found endearing. Their rapport was fun and flirty, but Michael still possessed the underlying fear that it could turn on him at any moment, so he never asked her out, of course. Each subsequent Wednesday, he hoped it would be the day he would overcome the mental programming that had held him back since high school, but it never was. Today, though, this today would be that day.

Right?

Carting his wet clothes from the washer to the dryer, Michael thought of Terri, whom he had not yet seen today, though his time at the laundromat was half over. It broke with the tradition they had established. Well, he had established, anyway. The wet slops of seven identical powder-blue button-downs slapped against the porous metal cavern as he moved on to his unmentionables and inserted a handful of moistened boxer briefs, all gray.

After his clothes were safely spiraling into a state of dryness, Michael bussed his cart over to a set of hard plastic chairs that had been designed for maximum lumbar injury. He sat for a while, shifting his weight into increasingly painful positions, figuring the distraction would keep him from obsessing over Terri. Meanwhile, the television hanging above him spoke dire warnings of missing persons. A local doctor had mysteriously disappeared from his bedroom in the middle of the night and the police, as usual, were baffled. All that and what an upcoming spate of thunderstorms would mean for his weekend would follow after a few messages.

Michael's attention, however, was drawn to the irritating fact that a single piece of clothing remained in his cart: another pair of underpants that had camouflaged against the side. This one, however, was conspicuously dry. The corner of his eye twitched with the impotent rage associated with the thought of having missed a single item of laundry. But perhaps it was unwarranted. Maybe it was a clean pair that had stowed away with its filthy brethren. Only one way to be sure. Michael raised the underpants to his nose and gave them a cursory sniff. He was met with the fading scent of faux mountain air. His suspicion was correct: they were quite clean.

What Michael had inconveniently forgotten was that he was in a public laundromat. Public laundromats tend to be occupied by people, and this one was no different. Michael was sucked back into the moment by a short burst of stifled laughter. Across the way, Terri leaned against the detergent vending machine, wearing a green top and a knowing smirk.

"Nice one, slick," she shook her head.

"Yeah, well, they were clean!" Michael removed the underpants from his nose and tried to sound authoritative, but his declaration ended with a sort of yelp as he walked towards her.

Terri giggled. He could marry that giggle. "I'm sorry, did I embarrass you?"

"Um . . . no. No! Not embarrassed at all. How're . . . you?" Michael pushed his glasses up the bridge of his nose.

"I'm alright," she said, loading her washing machine. "Just a bit late today."

"Oh, are you?" Michael pretended not to have noticed. He feared the implication that he had been keeping track of her schedule and their usual rendezvouses. He had, but still. Also, he didn't think his joke about a "laundrez-vous" would land. His jokes rarely did.

"Hey, listen," Terri looked away, "I'm in a bit of a rush today, so I'll just cut to the chase and ask: do you want to get dinner sometime this week?"

Alarms went off in Michael's brain, signaling a code blue. Never having had a code blue before, there was no plan of action in place. So all that came out of his mouth was a slow, droning "Uh . . ." followed by ". . . dinner?"

"Yeah," Terri smiled and Michael's heart quickened to a pace just short of a serious medical emergency. "Do you have a place you like? I could do anything."

"I know a great Italian place down on Concord Street! Let's go there!" He wasn't certain how he knew of it, but, similar to the way a surfer's life might flash before their eyes before a shark attack in an attempt to glean information that could prevent their death, Michael, in a more mundane application, recalled a slew of reviews he had seen on the internet. A restaurant on Concord Street stuck out as the only place that was infestation free after last month.

Terri smiled again and her hazel eyes sparkled. "I can meet you there at 6:30 tomorrow. Does that work for you?"

"Great. That's great!" Michael's grin froze on his face and began to hurt his cheeks as time passed. Had that really worked? As his mind wrapped itself up in questions, he hardly noticed as a full half-hour sped by. Still transfixed and, honestly, confused by what had happened, he folded and packed his dried clothes and slung his bag over his shoulder. He waved goodbye to Terri as he slipped out the door. The smile persisted. If it continued for four hours or more, he would have to call his physician.

* * *

It was dark outside by the time he left. Michael couldn't see his watch, but it was definitely around 9:30. He walked down the street past a row of cars, neatly angle parked. At the end sat Michael's 1982 Mercury Zephyr, a car that he lovingly referred to as "the Garbagemobile." The otherwise red car had a canary yellow passenger's side door that failed to function since its previous owner had opted to weld it shut for undisclosed reasons. Still, the trunk worked well enough. Michael thumped his fist on the corner and it popped open, allowing him to toss in his laundry. Or was it clothes, now? When did your laundry stop being "laundry" and become "clothes"? When you folded it? When you brought it home? Or when you put it in your dresser? Michael enjoyed this pointless line of questioning brought on by the euphoria of his potential date with a beautiful woman, as it distracted him from overthinking about said date.

Michael slammed the trunk shut and turned to find the crazed blue eyes and wild hair of an entirely different, entirely angrier woman who had definitely not been there a second ago. He jolted backwards and tumbled onto the asphalt. A jeep whizzed by his head at what felt like 50 miles per hour, but was probably more like 5.

"Oh my God! What the hell, lady?" A situation in which panic was natural. Michael almost felt at home.

"You're Michael Duckett!" The woman declared in a voice so far from Terri's melodic tones, it would need a GPS to get within striking distance.

"Uh . . . yeah?" was all he could muster. "How do you know my name? Who are you?"

"I need your help!" She seemed less interested in his questions than her own agenda, whatever that was.

"You need . . . my help?" Michael pulled himself to his feet by leaning on the Garbagemobile's rear bumper, which shuddered against the rusty nails holding it on. "For what?"

"I saw your ad. I need to hire you. It's urgent."

"Sorry. My ad? I think you have the wrong guy. I'm not for hire." Michael brushed himself off and, being certain his life was no longer in any significant peril, took stock of the situation. He sidled past the woman, who was wearing medical scrubs beneath the folds of a long brown coat, and onto the sidewalk. If she had escaped from a mental hospital, killed an orderly, and stolen his clothes, that would explain the scrubs. It was a bit of a reach, but not an unreasonable conclusion given the circumstances.

"I have a case for you," she said. Her eyes had a cold fire behind them that complemented the harsh red lipstick that popped against her dark olive skin. She would have been beautiful if she hadn't been completely off her rocker.

"Yeah, a . . . nut case," Michael winced. Another joke that didn't land tonight, but there really wasn't much time to workshop it. "Lady, I can give you bus fare or . . . uh . . . whatever you need. But I'm pretty sure you have the wrong person."

"No. I definitely don't. You're the detective!" Despite her manic motions, the woman's frizzy, curly blast of bright blonde hair refused to move very much.

"Detective? What the hell are you talking about?" Michael inched toward the door of the Garbagemobile. "I'm not—"

The woman slapped her hand on the door, blocking his escape. With her other hand, she removed a smartphone from her purse and thrust it at him. "I recognized you from your photo."

Michael left the smartphone in her hand and awkwardly scrolled down with a single finger. It was not often that Michael got to use a fancy smartphone. His own was an elderly flip affair with a creaky hinge. The screen on this one was brighter and boasted a higher resolution which allowed the bold black headline to leap out of the bright white background in all-caps, silently yelling at him:

"MICHAEL DUCKETT AND STEPHANIE DYER – PRIVATE EYES FOR HIRE – NO CASE TOO TOUGH, NO CASE TOO CRAZY – REASONABLE RATES – ANY TIME DAY OR NIGHT."

It was a simple internet classified ad—the Hail Mary of desperate schlubs seeking used leisure suits or unlikely missed connections. Below the headline was a picture of him and his oldest friend - and roommate two years running - Stephanie Dyer, standing side by side. It was cropped to focus only on their chests and heads, so Michael couldn't place where or when it had been taken. Stephanie was making overenthusiastic gun fingers at the camera, while Michael seemed aloof in an attempt to appear cool. It had not worked.

"What is this?" he asked, even though a sneaking suspicion was already forming in his mind.

"This is your ad," she pushed the phone into his face, "I found it on the internet. I want to hire your services as a detective."

"I'm sorry, lady," Michael stood up and gently guided her away from the car, "This is a fake ad. I'm not running a detective agency." The very idea of him being a detective was ludicrous. Except for the one time in grade school when he and Stephanie had tried to solve the case of who had been sneaking cookies from the cookie jar. It had been his dog. No charges had been filed.

"But, then who do I go to for help?" She continued, "My fiancé is—"

"Whatever it is, you should probably go to the police. I'm sorry for wasting your time. So if you could just—" Michael had been taking silent steps back toward the Garbagemobile. Upon reaching the door, he wrenched it open and slipped in, with one swift motion.

"Nff! I ndd tuh hurr yu!" The woman's voice was muffled by door, window, and labored chugging of the car's engine. Michael waved a half-hearted goodbye as the Garbagemobile lurched out of its parking spot and out into the night.

As soon as Michael saw the ad, he knew what was up. He'd have been stupid not to recognize another dumb scheme in a long line of dumb schemes from the mentally regressive couch potato he'd been saddled with. He grumbled to himself, tightening his grip on the steering wheel, "Stephanie . . ."

CHAPTER TWO

Duckett & Dyer

Michael carefully inched the Garbagemobile between two cars across the street from his apartment building. Since he had parked on a hill with an angle of greater than 25 degrees, Michael made sure to place the brick he kept in his trunk beneath his rear tire before leaving the car unattended.

When Stephanie and Michael had first decided to rent the place, he was enamored with the listing's description of exposed brick walls in the bedrooms. What the listing meant to say was that the landlord, an angry Greek man with a nigh unpronounceable name, had neglected to put up drywall, and the exposed brick was quite literally the only thing between the tenants and the elements. One had fallen out of the wall in his room, and the hole now served as a makeshift air vent. The brick had found its new home beneath Michael's right rear tire.

Sighing, Michael balanced his seventeen pounds of laundry on his back and trudged up the stairs to his apartment, each step straining with a groan so drawn-out that they had to be faking it. As one could have expected from the so-called exposed brick, the entire complex had seen much better days. It had been advertised to him as a pre-war building, but the agent had conveniently forgotten to mention which war. Michael's best estimates put it somewhere between Franco-Prussian and Spanish-American. Merely running one's fingers across the wall caused flakes of mint-colored paint to flutter to the ground. Yet, with Stephanie's unfortunate habit of perpetual unemployment, it was the best apartment they could afford. Michael had several fights with the landlord where he argued that, given the building's conditions, he shouldn't have had to pay rent at all. However, Mr. Dupopolous—neither Michael nor Stephanie were sure of his real name—felt the exact opposite.

Five flights of stairs later, Michael was finally able to set his bag down. He fumbled with the keys for a moment before swinging the door open to reveal Stephanie sitting where he had left her: on the collapsed cushions of the dusty, stained couch with her dusty, stained feet up on their dusty, stained new coffee table—the previous one had been destroyed in a "mysterious accident" weeks earlier. Stephanie refused to claim responsibility.

Stephanie still wore her high school-era green army jacket that fit like the skin of a recent liposuction patient and, slumped back in the couch, it was difficult to tell where the jacket ended and Stephanie began. Two slight hands emerged from the cloak-like sleeves and gnarled themselves around a video game controller. She made no attempt at eye-contact. "Sup, Mike?"

Michael and Stephanie had met in elementary school, after Stephanie had saved him from a gang of bullies. Michael remembered only one bully, but the number of violent kids present rose every time Stephanie retold the story. When they met, Stephanie had been under the care of her aunt and uncle—her parents had died a few years prior—but despite this, she was a carefree or, more accurately, careless girl, constantly acting out in the most oddball ways, making her a bit of an outcast. Michael had gravitated to her, as he, too, wasn't particularly popular, but for completely different reasons.

Michael had fond memories of their playdates, inside jokes and the mutual understanding that comes with long-term friendships. For someone as prickly and anxious as he was, Stephanie had provided him a certain measure of comfort that leveled him off, protecting him from himself. And she—Michael hoped—appreciated his rational thinking when she went off the rails. It had been a perfectly balanced ecosystem. But, somewhere along the way, the scales tipped disastrously.

If he were to really think about it, Michael would say the backslide started during Stephanie's ill-fated high school goth period where she spouted nothing but nihilistic clichés. Michael knew this was probably a short-lived phase likely due to some repressed feelings about her parents. Time proved him right, as Stephanie soon found the whole shtick depressing. That, and she had never been great at applying the makeup.

Michael did still find a certain sense of camaraderie and support from her during high school. No one knew him like she did and, even though she put up walls, Michael felt he knew her as well as he could.

But, once they began striking out on their own, Stephanie's insistence on how life was chaos and nothing really mattered morphed her into a lazy, devil-may-care couch potato with a tenuous grasp on the idea of responsibility. If nothing really mattered, Stephanie figured she could be free to do whatever it was she felt like.

So, while Michael grew up, went to college and got a job—albeit one that he hated, but a job nonetheless—Stephanie embraced a philosophy that she thought sounded good on paper, but did not translate well to the real world. She always managed to find her way into trouble, despite her refusal to do anything productive. She often used the death of her parents as an excuse, but Michael could never tell if she was serious.

Still, he stood by her, and kept her afloat, because of his desire to protect her from herself as she did for him and in the hope that one day things between them would be as good they used to be. Besides, she was the only friend Michael had to count on. But count on for what, he couldn't really say.

"Is this what you've been doing all day?" Michael lugged his laundry in and closed the door, sending chips of mint green floating down from the ceiling. The lead content of the apartment's paint had yet to be determined.

"Nah. I watched a little TV. Got some groceries," Stephanie curled her bare toes toward a small, unopened can on the coffee table. "Bought some of this great new meat spread. You want some?"

Michael squinted in the direction of the coffee table. "Steph, I think that's dog food."

"Nuh-uh. The guy at the store said it's made from real meats."

Michael grabbed the can and rotated it so Stephanie could see exactly what he could. A smiling cartoon Dalmatian waved its over-sized black and white paw at the viewer from a pleasant yellow background. "There's a *dog* on the label!"

She hit a button on her controller and the laser noises from the television stopped. "Oh. Well, I guess it's a good thing I didn't eat any then," Stephanie did her trademarked shrug-and-grimace. The thick mane of hair atop her head flopped lazily over the shorter sides. The laser noises resumed and her eyes returned to more important matters. "By the way, Mr. Dupopoloose came by today. Wanted to talk to you about the rent."

"That greedy bastard probably wants to hike it up again. I'll deal with him later," Michael speed walked down the hall and into his room to grab his laptop, but yelled loud enough to ensure that Stephanie could still hear him, "But first you and I have to have a little talk!" Michael returned to the living room, just in time to catch Stephanie approaching the window. She often used the fire escape as a means of egress when Michael needed something from her. She would be gone for the better part of the day before returning, successfully dodging the issue. This time, she wasn't so lucky. "Sit your ass down. You're not going anywhere."

Stephanie rolled her eyes and plopped back down on the couch. "Do we need to do this now? I'm a very busy lady with a lot of important . . . appointments."

"Oh, yeah? With who?"

"So many people. You wouldn't know them," Steph began to rise.

"Name one."

"Spider Johnson," she fired back, too quickly.

"There's no way that's the name of a real person."

"Spider is too a real person. And Spider does *not* like to be kept waiting. So if you'll excuse—"

"Sit," Michael popped open his laptop and searched the internet for "Duckett & Dyer." The classified ad that crazy woman had shown him popped up almost immediately—third after an independent tie-dye T-shirt shop and the website for Duck Dynasty. He turned the screen to face Stephanie. "Would you mind explaining to me what this is?"

Stephanie squinted at the screen and enunciated each word. "Michael Duckett and Stephanie Dyer . . ." Her eyes lit up as she finished the last phrase. "Private Eyes for Hire? Whoa. That's pretty badass, Mike. Sounds fun. I've always wanted to be a detective."

"No!" Michael clamped the laptop shut in front of Stephanie's nose. "Not fun! What the hell were you thinking putting up an ad like that? Some woman accosted me outside the laundry today because she said she had a case for me!"

Stephanie sat up straight. "And you didn't take her up on it?"

"Of course I didn't. I don't know the first thing about being a detective."

"Aw, man. Where's your sense of adventure, Mike?"

"And where's your sense of being a normal human being? I have a life and a job. I can't run around helping some lady's murdered fiancé!"

"Her fiancé was murdered?"

"Well, no," Michael faltered, "I don't know. Maybe? He might still be alive. I didn't stick around for the details. The point is this is wildly irresponsible. You can't just put out random ads because you think we'll have fun reliving our childhoods."

"I get your point, Mike. Really, I do," Stephanie nodded. "But there's one thing I'm confused about."

"Really, Steph? What could possibly be confusing about this?"

"Well, uh . . . I didn't put up that ad."

Michael had his mouth open, as he anticipated an easy rebuke, but had not expected that response. "What?" was all he could come up with.

"Yeah. Wasn't me."

"Well, it certainly wasn't me!"

"I dunno what to tell you, Mike. But, whoever it was, it sounds like a hell of an idea," Stephanie smiled and leaned back against the fading couch cushions with her hands behind her head. "Maybe it's the universe's sign that I *should* be a detective! And you could be my sidekick."

"Nope. Nope, nope, nope!" Michael pushed the coffee table away and got up. "I've been after you to get a real job. A paying job! Not playing detective. And there is no way in hell that I'd be your sidekick. You can barely tie your own shoes."

"I can tie my shoes, Mike," Stephanie groaned, "Don't overreact."

"Really? Is that why your feet are so dirty? Did you or did you not go to the grocery store without your shoes on?"

Stephanie paused before rebutting. She glanced down at her filthy feet, then back up at Michael. "The foot is nature's shoe."

Michael glared at her. "Be that as it may, we're ending this whole thing right now. I'm going to email this website and have this ad deleted. It's some sort of dumb prank. Or worse, we're being set up by one of those online killers. Who knows who put it up?"

"Now isn't that one heck of a mystery?" Stephanie raised her eyebrows and put on an infuriating smirk. "Ah? Eh?"

"No. No mysteries! I don't have time for this. I've got a date tomorrow and—" Michael clasped his hand over his mouth, but the damage had already been done.

"Oh. My. God." Stephanie's eyes lit up. She shot up out of her groove in the couch and smushed Michael's cheeks together before he knew what was happening. "My Little Mikey has a date! Give me the deets! All of the deets."

"Ugh." Michael wriggled out of Stephanie's grasp, "I don't want to make a big deal out of this. It's nerve-wracking as it is."

"Sorry, Mike. I'm just so happy you're finally getting yourself out there. Long overdue, I'd say. So how'd you trick this one?"

"What? I didn't trick—" Michael narrowed his eyes. "I didn't trick her. She asked *me*."

"Whoa. How desperate was she?"

"Thanks," Michael deadpanned. "Anyway, I invited her to dinner tomorrow night at that Italian place down on Concord."

"Oh, Scarantino's? Nice! Great date spot. But always super crowded. I know a guy there. He can hook you up with some free breadsticks," Stephanie nodded. "So, tell me about her."

"Well, she's the girl from the laundromat I told you about."

"Oh shit, buddy. The Laundry Girl? That's adorable. Way to go. What's her name again?"

"Terri Bradshaw."

Stephanie scrunched her face up, "What, like the football player?"

"No. Not like the football player," Michael pinched the bridge of his nose, pushing his thin-rimmed glasses up his forehead.

"Yeah, I guess he's more of a commentator now."

Michael slumped into the couch, occupying the groove that Stephanie had vacated. "Steph, I'm really stressed out about this date. It's been a real long time and I really like her and I just want everything to go perfectly. And you're not helping. Neither is this detective nonsense."

"Okay, okay," Stephanie slid down beside Michael and patted his shoulder. "Don't worry about a thing. I'll call my breadstick guy over at Scarantino's and make sure he gives you some extra special treatment."

"Really?"

"Yeah."

"What's the catch?" Michael side-eyed her.

"Catch? There's no catch."

"You're not going to do anything crazy, are you?"

"When have I *ever* done *anything* crazy?"

Michael stared blankly at her, but Stephanie actually seemed to be under the impression that the answer wasn't "all of the time."

"Besides, ain't no one able to make a rezzy at Scarantino's unless you call a week in advance. But my breadstick guy will hook you up."

"You could do that?" Michael's heart softened and his shoulders slumped. "For me?"

"Of course. I know you've been really stressed out lately about your job and stuff, and I haven't been the most useful, so consider this my way of helping out a bit," Stephanie smiled and Michael's heart grew three sizes, although that could've also been attributed to the stress. "Besides, you're my best friend and I love you," she paused, "But not in the sexy way. That'd be weird."

Michael knew that to be true.

"So don't worry about a thing," Stephanie slumped back into the couch. "Any special requests?"

"Rosé. She likes rosé."

"Pfft, typical," Stephanie sneered before realizing her mistake. "I mean—no problem! Rosé it is. Top shelf. I'll get them to give you the best seat in the house, too. What time are you looking for?"

"Could you maybe get something for 6:30 tomorrow?"

"Consider it done."

"Thanks, Steph." In order to successfully woo Terri, Michael needed to ensure total success. Who knew when he would get another chance to woo? But with Stephanie's help he might just be able to pull this off. Michael got up and grabbed his laundry bag from where he had dumped it near the door. A warm twinge occupied Michael's chest. Stephanie had actually promised him some genuine support and not some sort of dumb joke or wacky scheme, as she was wont to do.

Michael was ashamed to admit to himself how annoyed with her he had been for the past few months. But, maybe she was finally starting to take some things seriously. Maybe she had started to realize how her behavior affected him. And maybe things were on the upswing and it would be back to the good old days soon enough. Michael smiled. "I really appreciate you helping me out."

"No problem. You can count on me," Stephanie said. But before Michael was down the hallway out of earshot, she added, "Just one question, though."

Michael leaned back into the living room, as the faint patter of rain began to tap on the window. "Yeah?"

Stephanie squinted. "How hot is she?"

CHAPTER THREE

High Voltage

Detective Rex Calhoun slumped in his seat, cradling a large bottle of malt liquor. He took a sip and pulled down his hat, hoping the other passengers on the train wouldn't see him wince. The stuff tasted like piss and looked like piss, so at least it had that little synergy going for it. He let out an exasperated groan as he took another sip and wrapped his tattered thrift-store jacket tighter around himself. Maybe if he really leaned into his hobo disguise, no one would approach him.

His target was Tobias Wilkes: an enforcer and dealer for the city's most insidious drug pushers, known on the streets as the Trick Ponies. Calhoun had put together a small narcotics task force that had been chasing them for the better part of two years. But now he was nearing the end. According to an anonymous tip, Wilkes was due to attend a clandestine Pony meet-up in a particularly unsavory area of the city known as "Squalor's Wallow." Tailing Wilkes would be the key to taking the Trick Ponies down, and Calhoun was determined to do that himself. So much so that he'd declined any assistance on this stakeout, out of the fear of spooking Wilkes.

Station after station, the crowd in the train began to filter out as they approached the darker, danker side of the city. Each person unfurled umbrellas as they exited. The drizzle outside was steadily increasing. By the time the train made its way into Squalor's Wallow, Calhoun was alone, wallowing in his own faux squalor and the roar of rain outside. He leaned against the train wall and pretended to sleep. Two stops hence, his quarry arrived. Tobias Wilkes stepped through the sliding doors and, after giving the car a quick glance or two, sat down at the far end, a good distance from Calhoun's disgusting hobo character that had taken up residence in the other corner. Wilkes looked younger in person. Handsome, too, if Calhoun had swung that way and wasn't an angry, bitter 49-year-old man. Wilkes carried no blemishes except a small scar through his left eyebrow.

Calhoun, his eyelids cracked a smidge, made sure his snores were only loud enough to be believable. He saw Wilkes for the young gun he was: calm, measured and all too cocksure, leaning on his knees.

Five stops further, deeper into Squalor's Wallow's industrial district, Calhoun noticed that Wilkes began to shift in his seat. This was it. He was close. So close, he could taste it. It tasted of low-grade malt liquor.

Wilkes got off at the next stop, the only disembarking passenger not to have opened an umbrella. Calhoun remained seated until he saw Wilkes' figure disappear down the station stairwell. Immediately,

Calhoun jumped up and slid perilously between the closing subway doors, which clamped around the tail of his ratty disguise. The train began to pull out with his coat in its metal grasp, but Calhoun ignored it and turned back to the matter at hand. Pressing himself up against the station wall, Calhoun listened to Wilkes' footfalls fade down the stairwell and out through the bottom of the station. He ran down the stairs to ground level, eager to keep a respectable distance. Hiding in the copious shadows beneath the overhead tracks, Calhoun watched as Wilkes moved down the street, opting to stay beneath the railway bridge and out of the torrential rain.

Calhoun tailed him tightly, but not too tight, opting to pause and hide behind each concrete pillar of the elevated train tracks. Calhoun ducked back just as Wilkes glanced over his shoulders and peeled off onto a side street into the oppressive rain. Calhoun gave himself until the count of ten before continuing the chase.

He emerged from beneath the safety of the tracks and was immediately soaked to the bone. Dashing through ankle deep puddles, Calhoun crossed the street onto the sidewalk. Wilkes was nowhere to be seen.

Shit, he cursed to himself as the nagging fear of losing his last two years of work began to creep up on him.

Calhoun pushed through the sheets of rain and the poor visibility it afforded him. Either Wilkes had booked it straight down the street or had turned the corner around the nearest brick flophouse. Calhoun breathed. He could still do this. That was when he felt the rain shift.

A fist flew at his head as Wilkes leapt out of a hidden blind alley. But despite his aged frame, Calhoun was too quick, ducking beneath the punch and pushing Wilkes out into the middle of the street. He'd lost the element of surprise, and Wilkes certainly wasn't going to lead him to the Trick Ponies meeting now, but if he could corral and book him, maybe they'd be able to get something out of him at the station. Calhoun drew his gun out of his coat and pointed it at Wilkes, even though shooting him was out of the question.

"Freeze! Police!" He said, as if that wasn't obvious.

Wilkes only smiled as a large truck rounded the corner and drove between them, sending a wave of rainwater up onto the sidewalk as he made his move down the street.

Calhoun cursed again—this time audible if it hadn't been for the rain—holstered his gun and gave chase through the roaring downpour and through the burning in his lungs and knees that he would be feeling for weeks. Wilkes sprinted across the next crosswalk, jumping over the hood of a lone blue car inching forward through near zero visibility. Calhoun diverted around the car and continued to pursue the retreating thug. Wilkes looked back with a frightened stare as he saw that Calhoun, teeth gritted, was gaining ground.

Close enough to see Wilkes' deep navy letterman jacket, Calhoun took a chance and pounced, catching Wilkes' legs and tackling him to the ground. Wilkes was relatively unfazed and the two tussled across the sidewalk, collecting scrapes and bruises that would no doubt affect Calhoun's aging body more.

Wilkes was faster and scrappier than Calhoun, his glancing blows packing a wallop, but Calhoun managed to get a few lucky shots in the face and gut. It had been a while since Calhoun had gotten in a good, proper street fight. Truth be told, he was afraid those days had been behind him, and was a little glad that he had been wrong. Calhoun kept up the pressure, until he managed to shove an elbow into Wilkes' sternum and sent him sprawling across the wet concrete.

Blood streamed down Calhoun's cheek and into his mouth, the sharp iron taste diluted by the rain, as he pinned Wilke's torso down with his knees. Blocking a few more blows with his forearms, Calhoun caught each of Wilkes' wrists in his grip in quick succession. Calhoun smiled, but it felt more like he was baring his teeth as the storm's lighting flashed above them.

"Tobias Wilkes," Calhoun said through his teeth and over the rumbling thunder. It was not as satisfying an arrest as he would have liked, but at least it wasn't a complete write-off. "You have the—"

Calhoun felt nothing, but heard everything as his world turned a bright blue-white and his ears flooded with the resonance of a deafening explosion before he passed out.

*　*　*

The honks of a car horn were the first things to pierce the fog that surrounded Rex Calhoun, but they were minor blips of sound in the haze of white noise that flooded his ears. Calhoun gurgled and spat out mouthfuls of dark water from the pothole puddle he found himself face down in. His head was on fire, and he struggled to remember how to breathe. Pushing himself up with his hands, which were overwhelmed with pins and needles, Calhoun found that trying to get up was a bad decision and wobbled back down onto his knees.

Looking up, Calhoun filtered the overpowering glare of the car's headlights through his fingers. The streams of light were only making his headache worse, allowing him to feel the blood pounding through his eardrums. The driver of the car lowered his window and started to yell something, faint and unintelligible. In response, Calhoun felt around for his gun, and, upon finding it on the ground nearby, simply waved it around in the air. This shut the driver up and he rolled up the window and drove around the waterlogged detective.

Calhoun blinked twice. His vision and hearing were still impaired, but based on the vague chugging of the car's engine and the persistent heavy patter of the rain around him, he hadn't gone completely deaf. What had hit him, though? It had felt like a bolt of lightning. But if it had been a lighting strike, both he and Wilkes would have been dead.

Wilkes.

A surge of adrenaline tempered Calhoun's body issues as he spun around looking for his quarry. He noticed that whatever hit the two of them had thrown him twenty feet from where he had Wilkes pinned to the ground, near the aluminum shutters of an abandoned storefront. But Wilkes was nowhere to be found.

Calhoun's enraged "Dammit" was lost to both his ears and the rain as he pounded his fist against the metal shutters. How could he have escaped? Surely Wilkes had to be as dazed as he was. Or maybe it had hit Wilkes directly. But then why wasn't there a charred smoking corpse on the ground? He would've at least been satisfied with that. What the hell happened?

As if his thoughts had been heard, a single, yellow piece of paper flitted down from overhead, jostled by the impact of rain drops until most of it was soaked enough to plummet to the ground beneath Calhoun's feet. Squinting, Calhoun dropped to his haunches and picked it up.

Despite his still bleary vision, Calhoun could clearly read the black marker that scrawled its way across the yellow, dissolving paper.

SORRY ABOUT THAT. TOBIAS IS GONE NOW. BUT WASN'T HE A BAD GUY, ANYWAY?

Calhoun shot to his feet and craned his neck up to survey the darkened rooftops. All he could see was the dark black of the night sky and the interminable rain. But, when a—thankfully far away—bolt of lightning zigged and zagged through the sky, the silhouette of his mysterious messenger was thrown into sharp relief against the oppressive gray of the cloud cover. Calhoun could barely make out the form of a long, dark trench coat and the brief glint of goggles covering his eyes.

"Freeze! Police!" Calhoun shouted for the second time that day as he drew his gun. Another flash of lighting illuminated the sky, casting more light across the figure's black coat as it twisted and swirled out of sight. Calhoun rushed to the side of the building. The rusty fire escape ladder had been lowered, and he slipped several times in a mad scramble to the top of the building. But Calhoun, despite his aching bones, managed to pull himself up across the stone lip of the roof. Scanning the adjacent rooftops, he found that the dark messenger, much like Wilkes, was long gone, melting into the dead of night between the curtains of rain.

However, sitting in a puddle on the black asphalt shingles before him lay another drenched sticky note. Calhoun picked it up and it, too, began to dissolve in his hands, but not before delivering its infuriating message.

WHOOPS. TOO SLOW! BUT I'LL SEE YOU AGAIN SOON.

Calhoun snarled. He stood alone, in the rain for a good long while, allowing his failure to seep into every nook and crevice that the rain had already soaked into.

CHAPTER FOUR

The Best Laid Plans . . . (Well, "Best" Is Generous)

Time at The Future Group trudged by way too slowly for Michael's taste. Attempting to concentrate on work with his date on the horizon was a fool's errand. Michael could barely concentrate on his work on normal days, so this was hardly surprising. Instead, he busied himself by drumming his fingers on his desk and watching the time. It was 1:36. Letting out an extended groan, he ran his fingers through his hair and attempted to get to work, but found himself drowning in magical daydreams about Terri. A millennia of romantic bliss passed in his head and was veering into vaguely creepy territory until someone knocked on his cubicle wall. Michael swiveled around and his silky afternoon reverie vanished, sending his smile tumbling into frown territory.

"Heyo!" Ravi Shah, a co-worker from three cubes over, stood before him with a coffee cup in his hand, an elbow on the drab taupe cubicle fabric, and a smile on his face. Michael had grown to hate that smile. "How's it going, Mike-ster?"

Michael hated being called "Mike-ster". Anyone would. It was a stupid nickname. It didn't even roll off the tongue. "Not bad, Ravi. How about you?"

"Oh, y'know. Just squeezing by," Ravi danced his way into Michael's personal space, adding too many e's to the word "squeezing" in the process. "Wanted to see how things were going. You coming to Brianne's party tonight?"

"Oh. Uh . . ." Michael saw enough of these idiots at work every day. Why in the world would he voluntarily hang out with them after hours? He had given into peer pressure before and ended up having as lousy a time as he had imagined. Luckily, today he had an excuse. Michael knitted his brow in faux disappointment. "No, sorry. I can't. Busy tonight. Got a date."

Ravi, on a vowel kick, let out an "oooh" with far too many o's. "Very sweet, Mike-ster. You're moving up in the world."

"Yeah. I guess. Ha ha." Michael's laugh was more of a flat cough.

"So who's the lady?"

"Met her at the laundromat. Her name is Terri Bradshaw."

"Like the football player. Cool," Ravi began to nod, and probably wouldn't stop until he left the cubicle. "That's a sexy name. You gonna get down with this girl?"

"It's . . . a first date, Ravi," Michael wished he had gone through with his plan to install a door on his cubicle. He thought Ravi was a useless waste of space. But today, his irritating, incessant office socializing might be of some use. Maybe he'd know Terri's brother. "Say, Ravi. Do you know a Jacob?"

"Sure. Jacob Westphall? Jacob Smiley? Jacob Hawthorne? Jacob Renfro? Jacob Washin—"

"Jacob Bradshaw," Michael cut him off at the pass, as Ravi would have gone on forever. Given the sheer number of people at The Future Group, it was a near certainty that there'd be too many Jacobs, and that Ravi would know all of them. "Terri says he's her brother."

"Oh, ol' Brad Boys II?" Michael should have known Ravi had a ludicrous nickname ready. "Yeah, I know him."

"Yeah. Perfect. That's great," Michael sped up his speech, as his top priority at the moment was finding Terri's brother. Maybe he could get some inside info on how to impress her. And if he could do that while simultaneously getting Ravi to remove himself from the area, it would be the height of convenience. "Maybe you could go see if he's around or not."

"That's a great idea! I'll head on over right now," Ravi, still nodding, couldn't leave the cubicle fast enough.

"You do that," Michael muttered. He swiveled back around, as aggressively as one could swivel. Despite the how much the conversation had irritated him, it had at least pushed him closer to the end of the workday. Michael returned to his workstation and looked down at the tiny clock in the corner of his monitor. He adjusted his glasses. It was 1:37.

"Goddammit."

*　　*　　*

It was only two hours later that Michael's intense anticipation crossed the line into a more familiar sense of intense anxiety. He began to realize that he had placed his faith in Stephanie Dyer to coordinate and make a reservation at a popular restaurant. Stephanie Dyer: a woman whose entire breadth of knowledge was limited to obscure '80s trivia and the name of a "Breadstick Guy" that Michael still wasn't sure really existed. After slipping into the bathroom and checking under the stall doors, Michael flipped open his phone and, despite the cracked LCD display and a missing 7, called her.

"Go for Steph," Stephanie's smug charm came through the speaker. "Who may I ask is calling?"

"You know it's me," Michael whispered a shout. "Every phone has caller ID!"

"Oh, hey, Mike. What's up?"

"Have you talked to your breadstick guy yet?"

"No. Of course not. It's 3:30. I'll give him a ring in an hour. Trust me. It's on my list."

"Your 'list'?" Michael whipped off his glasses. "What else is on your list?"

"Play video games. Buy a women's tuxedo t-shirt. Nap. Eat a sandwich. Call Breadstick Guy," Stephanie paused. "Should I go on?"

"Fine. Fine," Michael regretted asking. "Do whatever you need to. But just make sure everything is perfect for the date, okay?" Michael leaned his head against his arm and his arm against the oddly warm stall door. "This needs to go well."

"Relax, Mike. You worry way too much. I'll get everything you want done."

"Reiterate all my demands back to me."

"Chill out. I won't let you down. This is going to be perfect, just like you wanted," Steph hung up.

After pacing back and forth between the sinks and the urinals for a good minute, Michael speed walked headfirst through the endless rows of cubes that covered the 35th floor like bland, beige Savannah grass. Reaching his own tiny 6x6 box, Michael found, to his chagrin, Ravi and a second person he didn't recognize, standing within. Irritatingly, both were smiling. "Can I help you?"

"Hey, Mike-ster. This is Jacob."

Michael took two steps back. Something was clearly wrong. For one, this Jacob was about 20 years older than Terri. And secondly, he was Vietnamese. "This is Jacob Bradshaw?"

"Sorry, Mike-ster," Ravi said. "Wrong Jacob. This is actually Jacob Duong. He's the database manager on the 29th floor. I was looking for your Jacob, but as luck would have it, the two of us got to talking. Seems like he's in a bit of a pickle."

"I'm in a bit of a pickle," Jacob parroted.

Ravi continued unabated, "A bunch of his team is out this week, and he needs to fill some spreadsheets by EOD. You seemed like you were free when I stopped by, so I volunteered you. Shouldn't take you more than a few hours. Sound good?"

Michael seethed with nervousness that began to burn into impotent rage. "Gee. Thanks."

Ravi turned to Jacob. "See? I toldja. What a great guy."

"Thanks, Mike-ster!" Jacob gave Michael a pat on the back, which did nothing to assuage the fury over Ravi's stupid nickname now infecting another human being. "I owe you one. I'll send the files over right quick. This should only take you an hour or two. But I need this done urgently, so get it to me ASAP."

"No. Problem." The gaps between Michael's teeth were likely to get bigger, were he to keep forcing all these words through them.

"Thanks in advance!" Ravi and Jacob echoed the infuriating phrase all Future Groupers were fond of when asking about work, before sauntering off towards their respective desks.

"But what about Jacob Bradshaw?" Michael called out, but Ravi was either out of earshot or could not hear him over the cloud of smug self-satisfaction that swirled around his head.

Michael took a deep breath before sitting down at his desk. It was just some data entry. It wouldn't take too long. He could get it done and still make it to Scarantino's before Terri got there. This might still work, as long as he got the data in time. Maybe things would go exactly as planned.

*   *   *

Things didn't go exactly as planned. Jacob sent the data an hour later. In a desperate frenzy, Michael produced the most slapdash work of his career in . . . whatever exactly it was his career was in. By the time he had put all the nondescript inputs into their little gray boxes, it was 6 p.m. After firing off an email to Jacob WhatsHisName, Michael grabbed his coat and dashed out of his cube before anyone could ask him for one last thing. He ran past several of his co-workers, still tapping away at their desks. They had an unfortunate penchant for staying late. It would have made Michael feel bad, if he had cared.

The elevator bell dinged and Michael burst out into the marble lobby of The Future Group's enormous midtown tower. He gave a quick nod to the girl at the front desk, yanked the polished metal handles and slipped out the glass doors. He sprinted across the courtyard towards the parking deck, donning his coat one arm at a time, but ultimately inside out. Bounding up the ramps, he reached the third level and found the Garbagemobile within striking distance. Unfortunately, also within striking distance was the crazy woman who had accosted him outside the laundromat. She leaned back against the Garbagemobile, her frizzy blonde dye-job popping out over the rusted red paint. Still clothed in hospital scrubs, she gave Michael a particularly harsh brand of stink-eye.

"No. No. No. No. No! C'mon!" Michael's fury came out as more of a petulant whine. "Why are you here? How do you know where I work?"

"I just want you to hear me out. You haven't answered any of my emails. My fiancé—"

"Oh my God, I don't care. Rrrgh!" Michael stifled a guttural roar and reached out with his hands in gnarled claws halfway toward the lady's neck, before dropping them. "I don't have time for this, lady. I seriously do not. I'm not the guy you think I am. I haven't received any of your emails and I definitely don't give a flying crap about your fiancé. So if you'll excuse me. I'm kind of in a rush, so if you could . . ." Michael fished around for his car keys but the woman slapped them out of his hand. They skidded across the gravel. "Hey! What the hell, man?"

"You're running a real shitty business, Michael. Here I am trying to hire you and you're not letting me get a word in edgewise!" The woman's nostrils flared and her blue eyes burned in a terrifying mix of fire and ice. If looks could kill, she would be the Ted Bundy of looks. "I need help. This. Is. My. Life."

"And this is mine!" Michael scooped up his keys, ducked, and rolled beneath the slight, yet ferocious woman, clearing the gap between himself and the car. He felt like he was in an action movie, but probably as the bad guy. "Sorry, but I have to go. I hope you get the help you need. Professional or otherwise."

Michael slipped into the Garbagemobile and slammed the door, while stabbing his keys into the ignition and cranking them with more torque than necessary. The engine roared to life before petering out into a pathetic sputtering. Another crank produced the same result. "You have absolutely got to be kidding me."

A knock on the window drew Michael's attention back to the eyes of the woman as their daggers pierced the smudged, dirty glass. He offered a weak smile and rolled down the manual window. It caught a few times on the way down and shrieked for the last few inches as it was lowered. Michael bit his lip as he looked up at the woman. "Hi."

"Listen here, Buster Brown."

"Buster Brown?"

"My future marriage is at stake here," her hands slotted over the edge of the window and locked in place. "And I need you to stop and listen to me."

"Okay," Michael wasn't sure if the woman could shatter the window with her bare hands, with the strength of her grip and the general crappiness of the car. In any case, he didn't want to take that chance, so Michael tabled his frustrations, took a deep breath and proceeded with caution. "I hear what you're saying, but I really need to be somewhere right now. Prior engagement. And I'm running late."

"Fine," her hands released his car from their kung-fu grip and stepped back. "But I'm not waiting anymore. Sit down with me on Friday. I'll come to you."

"Sure. Whatever. Fine. Bye!" Michael turned the key a third time and the Garbagemobile emitted a strained chugging noise he had never heard before followed by a loud whooping as it came to life.

"Piece of crap," he muttered and jammed his foot on the accelerator, screeching away.

CHAPTER FIVE

Back in Business

"Well, if it isn't Ace Ventura: Wet Detective."

Word of Calhoun's failure had quickly made it around the station, and Detective Alexander Brook was taking full advantage of it. He leaned back on his desk chair with his arms behind his head and a shit-eating grin across his face when Calhoun trudged in in the morning.

"If I had been witcha, he wouldn't have gotten away, y'know. And maybe you wouldn't have had to dry clean your gabardine." The fact that Brook was the only other member of Calhoun's limited narcotics task force made things worse. The entire station believed Squalor's Wallow and the Trick Ponies were a lost cause, but, in the interest of putting forth the bare minimum of effort, they'd given Calhoun a limited budget that would support two cops. Brook certainly wasn't Calhoun's first choice for support, but he was his only choice. No other subdivision would take his Brook's smart ass given his reputation for outstanding incompetence. One particularly notable incident featured a state's witness under Brook's protection being drowned in a gas station toilet. Calhoun had only taken him on since he thought two heads would be better than one, but his days of backing that theory were rapidly coming to an end.

"Up yours, Brook," Calhoun grumbled, taking solace in the fact that he had his own office, away from Brook's irritating presence in the bull pen.

"So what's next, Calhoun? Should we track down that lightning bolt for questioning?" Brook called as Calhoun stomped away, making a beeline for his office. The other officers in the pen looked up from their work, but didn't dare say a word. "I heard it knocked over three convenience stores on its way outta town!"

Calhoun cracked open his door, slid in and slammed it shut behind him. He sighed angrily to himself and removed his hat and coat, hanging them on the rack teetering behind the door and then gingerly made his way across the morass of overflow papers, records, and cases from his 25-year career that streamed out of the green filing cabinets that hogged most of the room. Calhoun's office just barely surpassed the lower limit to be legally considered an office space, and was a few square inches larger than the upper limit of a storage closet, which was what it had been previously. He shimmied through the two-foot gap between his desk and another cabinet and fell into his creaky wooden seat. A folder with surveillance photos of Tobias Wilkes lay open on the desk, aching to be closed and placed with its filed brethren. But today, it was not to be.

The sting of defeat pierced Calhoun's chest as he stared down at Wilkes' young face. He jerked his desk drawer open until it hit the wall behind him two inches later. After several tries, he managed to extricate a thin green bottle, little bigger than a flask. Boar's Head made better deli meats than they did whiskey, but theirs was the only distillery that made a bottle thin enough to fit through his drawer gap. He turned the bottle around in his hands, realizing that, if he ever mentioned the absolute insanity that was the disappearing sticky note messenger from last night, it could be evidence that he was occasionally drunk on the job. He hadn't been. Wilkes and the Trick Ponies were his white whale. They were too important and he was too determined to be their Ishmael. Or Jonah. Whatever. The name didn't matter.

Still, there were times when the nature of the job beat you down so hard that a little nip now and then was necessary. This was one of those times.

The sticky note man's long coat and shiny goggles flashed in Calhoun's head as he began to unscrew the top. He couldn't have been with the Ponies. His note had made that quite clear. Some sort of vigilante, maybe? Had he used the lightning strike as a distraction to murder Wilkes?

Calhoun stopped himself as a stray, dumb idea crossed his mind.

Obviously, he didn't call down the lightning. This wasn't one of those damn comic book movies. What a ridiculous thought to entertain. Calhoun hadn't even started drinking yet. But he'd soon fix that.

The bottle neared Calhoun's lips, and was stopped by a sharp rapping against his door. Calhoun took a quick swig anyway and dashed the whiskey back into his drawer.

"Yeah?" He croaked past the Boar's Head burn.

He slammed the drawer shut with a clang as the door to his office opened a slight crack large enough for a girl's face to peer in. "Uh . . . Detective Calhoun?"

Calhoun raised an eyebrow. The girl was young enough that it was plausible that she'd gotten lost from a school trip. How she knew his name was beyond his understanding.

"What is it?" He snapped. "Who're you?"

"Hi, yeah—" The girl started as she pushed the door open, only for it to slam stuck against the rickety wooden chair that had taken up residence behind it. She struggled for a few minutes, attempting to gain more purchase, but eventually gave up and slipped her slight frame through the crack. "Hi."

Calhoun eyed the girl. She was young, yes, but she was drowning in a CSI windbreaker, which implied that she did indeed belong in the building, but not necessarily in his general vicinity.

"What do you want?" Calhoun asked gesturing around at the random papers and files that blanketed his office, leaving it one U.N. resolution short of a warzone. "Can't you see I'm busy?"

"Yes, sir. Uh, sorry about that," she tiptoed her way around his coatrack and toward his desk. "I just wanted to ask . . . did you lose a suspect to . . . uh . . . lightning?" She winced as she said the last word.

Calhoun groaned and rubbed his eyes. "Did Brook send you in here? Because you can tell that little shit to go fu—"

"No, no," she waved the accusation away. "I actually need your help."

"Help? What do you mean 'help'?"

"Carrie McDermott. CSI," the girl extended her hand.

Calhoun did not take it. His lip curled. "How old are you?"

"Old enough."

"You look twelve."

"I skipped a few grades," McDermott responded without missing a beat. She dropped her hand. "I've been working for Detective Hobson on a missing persons case."

"Hobson? At the 35th?" He knew Kiara Hobson. Their paths had crossed once in a while. Good detective. A little too full of herself for her own good. That was a trait he only liked in himself. "What does she want with me?"

"Two weeks ago a doctor from City General by the name of Coleman Supirn went missing," McDermott said. "Wife and him go to bed. Next morning, she gets up, finds he's missing. Gone without a trace."

"Yeah. I heard about that," Calhoun said. He'd picked up rumblings about the case, but it was pretty cut and dry to him. Guy got sick of his wife and took off. Hobson should have just closed it and moved on. "I don't see why you have to bother me about it."

"The wife reported waking up to a strange smell. Burning air. Ozone. Consistent with the after effects of a lightning strike."

"That could be anything. Ever smell a burning computer?" Calhoun had never figured out how to make the damned things do what he wanted them to.

Still, McDermott didn't back down. "The wife reported hearing thunder and seeing bright flashes of light during the night. She thought nothing of it, but there was no storm activity at the time."

"Listen, kid," Calhoun leaned on his desk. "I lost a suspect in a thunderstorm. And I'm kind of sore about it. Some doctor running out on his wife in the middle of the night doesn't interest me. I have plenty of my own shit on my plate."

Ignoring that he accidentally implied that he defecated on his own dinnerware, McDermott let out a sigh and slammed her hand on his desk so hard that Calhoun almost jumped back. When she withdrew it, he stared at what she had left behind: an evidence bag containing a single, yellow sticky note. The black chicken scratch across it spelled out one word.

SORRY.

Calhoun's eyes narrowed and darted back and forth from the note to McDermott's face. "Where did you find this?"

"Under the victim's bed," McDermott leaned back and smiled. Calhoun knew that she knew that she had him.

"Any fingerprints?"

"I wish," she said. "So I'm betting you have one of your own?"

He bit his lip so hard he'd be tasting blood for the rest of the afternoon. "It was raining. It dissolved."

"Acid rain a big problem around here?"

"Okay, kid," Calhoun folded his arms. "Tell Detective Hobson that she has my attention. But I don't know how she knew to send you to me."

"She didn't," McDermott muttered, with a grim finality. "Detective Hobson's gone missing, too."

"What?" How had he not known about this?

"For the past three days. I went to her apartment this morning. Had the super let me in. Nobody there except half-eaten Chinese take-out and the smell of ozone," McDermott said. Calhoun could see that she was hurt, loyal, and, best of all, determined. He wished his own daughter would've turned out like her. But she had opted to be more like his scumbag ex-wife. That damned harpy just couldn't leave well enough alone—

"And then there was this," McDermott added, interrupting Calhoun's day-mare. A second plastic baggy emerged from her windbreaker. This one she slid across Calhoun's desk. Yet another sticky note, this one face down.

"Huh." Three missing people in the span of two weeks. All potentially hit by lighting. And, if the notes were any indication, the same dark asshole was responsible. And now a cop was involved. "So if Hobson's gone . . . why'd you come to me?"

McDermott gestured at the note with her chin and a piercing glance. Calhoun turned the bag over to see the message.

TELL DETECTIVE CALHOUN I SAID "HEY."

His fists clenched but he said nothing, staring at the note for long enough that it might have caught fire in another second.

"Detective Calhoun?" McDermott once again forced her way through Calhoun's fog of rage.

He blinked twice and looked up her. Whoever this sticky note bastard was, he'd just made Calhoun's shit list. Wilkes and the Ponies would have to wait. There was a new white whale in town. A whiter whale. There were no laws against someone having two white whales. And if this second could lead him to the first, well that was a lead Rex Calhoun was damn sure going to take. And he was going to need help. Proper help.

"Kid," he looked up at McDermott, "I'm gonna need you to go outside and talk to Detective Brook."

"You want me to call him in here?"

"Oh, hell no. Tell him that he's off my task force effective immediately. And you're in," Calhoun smiled. "Then flip him off."

CHAPTER SIX

Dinner for None

Thanks to a staggering amount of traffic, Michael coaxed the struggling Garbagemobile down Concord Street a full 45 minutes late. He had texted Terri about the delay, but had received no response, which terrified him further. Hopefully she wasn't mad at him.

Michael's fears subsided a bit when, for the first time today, luck smiled upon him as he sidled into a parking spot right in front of Scarantino's. Since the street was on level ground, he didn't require his usual strategic brick placement, so he jumped out of the car, dashing straight into the restaurant. Or, he would have, had the door been a "push" door rather than a "pull" door. After making sure nobody saw him, Michael used his sleeve to wipe away the smudges his nose had left on the glass and entered.

Stephanie was right, Scarantino's was one of the best upper lower mid-range restaurants in the city. Its dollar-sign rating varied anywhere between two or four $s and the online reviews praised the food—classic Italian in nature—and the varnished wood décor—a welcome contrast to the road signs and assorted trash that adorned the walls of the Family Eatorium just two doors down. The reviews also had nothing but good things to say about the breadsticks. In fact, some of the comments were graphically and unnecessarily sexual in nature. All in all, Scarantino's was an undoubtedly great date spot, doubly confirmed by the enormous number of couples Michael saw seated as he scanned the restaurant for Terri. Unfortunately, there was no single woman seated alone, so Michael approached the maître d'.

"Good evening, sir. How can I help you tonight?"

"Hi, yes," Michael said, his head on a swivel, hoping to catch a glimpse of his missing date. "I have a reservation for two under Duckett . . . or maybe Dyer," he couldn't be sure how Stephanie had reserved the seat. "But I'm a little late. I hope that's okay."

"Not to worry, sir. I see a Duckett here," the maître d' pointed at the little book that sat atop a plinth. "A table for two, correct?"

"Yes, that's right. Do you know if the other party's here yet? A girl, I mean. My date. She has the most beautiful hazel eyes I've ever seen and she likes rosé and Rocky Road, if that helps."

The maître d' blinked. "Um, unfortunately, sir, we haven't seen anyone matching that . . . vague description. And no other party's asked after your reservation."

"Huh." Michael bit his lip. "Do you think she might've gotten confused and went to the Family Eatorium instead?"

"I couldn't tell you that. Sorry. But perhaps you'd like to wait at your table?"

"Yeah. Okay. Sure." Michael rubbed his arm. "Let's go."

The maître d' grabbed two menus and led Michael past a bevy of happy couples and around a few decorative wooden pillars that melted seamlessly into the ceiling. They stopped at a table located adjacent to the women's bathroom.

"This is the table?" Michael gestured towards it with an open palm. "There's got to be some mistake."

"No, sir." The maître d' lay the menus out on either side of the table and straightened his vest. "This was the specific seat requested."

"I was told I'd be getting the best seat in—" Michael stopped himself as it dawned on him that Stephanie's definition of 'best seat in the house' would be the one closest to the bathroom. "Dammit."

"Is everything okay?"

"Not really. But it's not your fault."

"Well, your waiter will be with you shortly. I hope you enjoy dining with us tonight," the maître d' smiled, nodded and marched off.

Michael sat down and placed his hands on his knees, taking long breaths in order to calm himself. Within moments his right hand was on the table, its fingers rapping against it in quick succession. Where could Terri be? Maybe she was late, too? Michael dug his phone out of his pocket and his fingers tapped against its keypad instead of the table.

"Hey. Just got here. Sorry I'm late. Work stuff. Let me know if I missed you. Thanks!"

Michael set the phone down next to his menu and looked away. Two seconds later he looked back. No response yet. That was okay. It was only a few seconds. Two more seconds passed. Still no response.

Michael read and re-read the text message he had sent as a wave of hot shame enveloped him. Why did he say "thanks!" at the end? This wasn't a work email! Hell, he never even thanked people in work emails.

Michael pushed the phone to the opposite end of the table to prevent his fingers from doing any more talking. A full five minutes passed until he made a lunge for it. He began to tap out another more frantic, more ill-advised message, but, before Michael could hit send, the server approached him.

"Good evening, Monsieur. Eet ees good to see you. Voulez-vous like to have ze wine you ordered? Uh . . . le wine?" The accent was so outrageous and completely ignorant of the fact that they were in an Italian restaurant, Michael knew that it could only be one person. He sighed and placed his forehead on the table for a good moment, wondering when his life had devolved to the level of second-rate sitcom, before looking up again. Behind the bottle of rosé that had been thrust into his face, Michael found Stephanie, wearing her tattered green jacket, now draped over a tuxedo t-shirt in lieu of her usual worn out white top. The fake mustache that clung to her upper lip was so large that it would offend a caricature.

"What . . . the hell . . ." Michael squinted in confusion with a dash of bubbling anger.

"Sup, Mike?" Steph whispered down to him, trying to conceal her true identity for some reason. "I figured I wasn't doing anything important today, so I thought I'd help hook you up on this date. No better wingman than the waiter. Ain't no one suspects the waiter. Sounded like a fun idea. I'm glad I thought of it."

"You've got to be kidding me." Michael massaged the bridge of his nose beneath his glasses. "Get out of here! Why did they let you do this? *How* did they let you do this?"

"I told you. My breadstick guy here owes me a favor. He hooked me up with all this. Where's your ladygirl?"

"She's not here yet, Steph. And thank god for that. I would hate for her to see . . ." Michael gestured to the production in front of him, "this."

"Chill out, Mike. She'll think it's cute. Chicks love dumb stuff like this."

"No. *You* love dumb stuff like this."

"And I'm a chick. So ipso facto." Stephanie looked around. "You get the breadsticks yet?"

"No. I just sat down."

"Okay, great," Stephanie yanked out the chair opposite Michael and plopped down. "Let's get a round. Yo, Mark. Mark!" She yelled. "Yeah. I'm talking to you. Sling some sticks this way!"

"What? No, Steph. Get outta here! Terri could be here any minute."

"Don't worry. I'll skidaddle when I see her coming," Stephanie grabbed the first breadstick out of the basket before a real waiter – Mark, presumably – could even set it down. "Oh, man. I love these things. They're like crack, but if you put garlic butter on crack." After shoving a stick in her mouth, she ripped it in half with her teeth and started to gobble before returning her attention to Michael. "You need to relax, Mike. You're shaking."

"You know I'm nervous about this date, Steph," Michael looked down at his vibrating right hand and used his left to still it. "Having you messing around here is making it worse."

"Here. Just have some of the rosé I got you guys, it'll loosen you up," Stephanie poured the light pink wine into Michael's glass.

"Fine. Maybe you're right," Michael grunted and took a big swig, hoping to calm his nerves, which refused to stop firing. However, as soon as the first splash of rosé hit his tongue, Michael gagged so violently that most of the wine ended up expelled onto the table cloth, collecting in an angry pink pool. Michael pushed away from the table, but it was too late, a fair amount of it had dribbled onto his pants. And, yes, it did look like he had urinated on himself. A few other patrons turned but quickly reverted back to their own business. Michael blew the remainder of the liquid out of his mouth. "Ugh! What the hell was that? It tastes like battery acid and grapefruit juice had a baby!"

"These guys were all outta rosé," Stephanie jerked a thumb over her shoulder. "So I just mixed some red and white wine together."

"And why," Michael said through gritted teeth, "is it hot?"

"Well, I accidentally left it near the oven. So that's my bad."

"Goddammit, Steph!" Michael's forehead met the stained table cloth. Small pools of mixed wine began to collect around his cheeks.

"Hey," Stephanie punched him in the shoulder. "Cheer up, bucko."

"Cheer up?" Michael's winey face looked up from the table. "This is the first date I've had in years and you've already royally screwed it up. And my date didn't even show up!"

"Maybe she's still on her way. You said traffic was bad, right?"

"She's not still on her way. She's stood me up and based on my current state, I don't blame her!"

"Whoa, Mike. Relax," Stephanie placed a supporting hand on Michael's shoulder. "You're a good dude. One of the best guys I know. And I'm sure this girl sees that, too," Stephanie smiled. "She'd be crazy not to and there is absolutely no way she's standing you up."

* * *

Two hours and four baskets of breadsticks later, Stephanie changed her tune. "Okay, maybe she is standing you up. My bad."

"Let's just go," Michael pushed himself away from the table, and slunk out of Scarantino's, avoiding eye contact with everyone and everything, including the door. Since the breadsticks were free, he didn't need to deal with the further indignity of fumbling around his near-empty wallet. He probably wouldn't be returning here anytime soon.

Michael wrenched open the door to the Garbagemobile and sat down, his butt sinking slowly into the groove of compacted seat foam that sagged in the middle. He kept his hands at ten and two and stared vacantly at the car parked in front of him, reliving every one of the failures and missteps in his life. Usually this jarring greatest hits compilation of his greatest misses was reserved for the minutes before Michael fell asleep, or at random, inopportune times during the day, but Michael felt it warranted a timely update with his latest disappointment.

Michael was halfway through a recap of his awkward pre-teen years and a particularly scarring gym class experience when Stephanie swung herself in through the open passenger window of the Garbagemobile, her typical method of dealing with the door that had been welded shut. She slammed her body down into her seat, with several extra servings of breadsticks in her lap, wrapped in a stolen napkin. She spat a few crumbs out at him, "You okay?"

"Yeah. I guess. I'm fine," Michael knew he wouldn't get any further support from Stephanie. He wished he could have one serious conversation with her. In all the years they had known each other, she had never spoken in any way that wasn't some sort of joke, bit or—in her goth phase—nihilist hogwash. She had never talked to him about what happened to her parents. Nor did she tell him when she came out as bisexual. She didn't tell anyone. For her it didn't matter. Not that it would've made a difference to him, but Michael couldn't help but feel betrayed that she hadn't at least trusted him enough to let him know. It was like nothing really mattered to her, at all. Not even stuff that would have been important to any reasonable human being. Michael was just too tired to ask her about anything she didn't want to put forward, and, in turn, he shared nothing important with her. He had hoped that their friendship would endure, but now the weak scaffolding was finally beginning to show cracks. And he was beginning to question if it was even worth the trouble.

Without a word, Michael shoved the key into the ignition and cranked the Garbagemobile into emitting a rumbly, inconsistent growl that eventually leveled out and allowed them to chug away back to their rotten apartment, so he could continue his useless existence.

CHAPTER SEVEN
Rent Control

Michael fiddled around in his pocket for his keys as Stephanie juggled her bounty of breadsticks, shoving some in pockets and others under armpits. Without a word, he pushed the lobby door open, careful not to dislodge the panes of glass that were being held in place only by duct tape and the general stickiness of the building. A dank musk—overpowering the smell of the breadsticks—flowed out of the rarely cleaned lobby. It was a lobby in name only and was more of a short causeway paved with mismatched bathroom tiling and lit by the efforts of a single dwindling bulb hanging from a loose wire.

Stephanie lagged behind Michael as he made the pilgrimage up the five flights of stairs. By the time he began to unlock their apartment door, Michael had had enough time to package up his irritation and exhale it all out in a long sigh. Maybe tomorrow would be better.

"Holy hell!" was the appropriate response to seeing a hulking, bear-like, Greek man taking up most of the space in your living room, while brandishing a menacing length of pipe. Michael delivered the line exceptionally well. Stephanie's breadsticks landed on the floor with soft thuds.

"Where is my rent?" The man slammed the pipe into the living room wall, leaving a massive dent and showering the room with paint chips and dust that Michael hoped wasn't poisonous.

"Mr. uh . . . Dupopopolous?" That wasn't his name. But that wasn't what Michael was confused about at the moment. His landlord wasn't usually this angry. Annoyed, sure, but never angry.

"The rent!" His chest, and its thicket of midnight black hair, heaved rhythmically coinciding with blasts of hot air escaping from his flared nostrils, each with their own associated thickets.

Stephanie leaned in over Michael's shoulder, "I think broheim here wants the rent."

"Rent? What rent?" Michael asked. He wasn't in the mindset to deal with this. "What are you talking about?"

"I'm away for three months to visit family and you think you can get away with not paying rent?" The landlord stomped toward the door and towered over Michael, who attempted to inch around him, but found himself slipping on the dusty living room rug. Michael's glasses grew increasingly wet with fog from his sweat and his landlord's breath.

"No, you've got this all wrong! I paid the rent. I wrote the checks. Every month." Desperately, he glanced through his peripherals at

Stephanie, who peered in from the hallway. The grimace on her face stated that she wanted no part of this. "Steph, tell him!"

"Yeah. Uh . . ." She said. "I'm pretty sure he sent 'em."

"Then explain where they are," the landlord crossed his arms over his wife beater, waiting. His eyebrows bunched into a forest so thick and dark that light had no chance of escaping its clutches. "I have seen no money. Do you think I maintain this place for free?"

"Actually, I don't think you maintain this place at all," Stephanie added, in an attempt to be unhelpful.

"I don't know what happened, I swear!" Michael had moved so far into the room that he had his back bent over the coffee table at this point, unable to stand in the face of adversity.

"Hey, bud," Stephanie crept into the room, her arms out as if trying to calm a feral animal. "My friend here's had kind of a hard day. Could you maybe back off? We can talk it over later and we'll all be happy."

"I am not going to be happy until I get my money," Mr. Dupopopolous growled. His indifference to Michael's crumbling social life was palpable. "I do not care how hard a day he had. No day is worth three months' rent."

"Listen here, Mr. Man Mountain. He got stood up by a girl he liked. You've been there, right?" Stephanie offered, even though odds were he probably hadn't. "He needs to collect his thoughts and realize there're plenty of fish in the tank."

"I will put *him* in a fish tank if I don't get my rent! Where's my money?"

"Rrrgh!" Michael, his anxiety cracking over into immense frustration, wrenched off his glasses in a clawed hand and massaged his temples with the other. "I don't know, okay? I know I paid you! Every damned month! I can get you the carbon copies of the checks!"

"I have no need for copies. I want the money," he pushed Michael's chest, using only a jab of his finger. "You get me the money by next week, or you will be out on your asses. This, I swear." And with that, he trampled across the breadsticks and left, leaving the vibrations of a slammed door in his wake, as well as a new crack that snaked down the drywall.

As soon as Michael was certain the door would remain standing, he turned to Stephanie, and enunciated his words so that he would be sure they were as clear as crystal, "Do you know anything about this?"

"No way, man," Stephanie sidled past him and flopped into her natural position on the couch, absolving herself of all responsibility. "Rent's your headache, not mine."

Michael snarled, not happy to be reminded that he was the only one who did anything around here. "Well, something happened. And now we're going to be homeless unless we can come up with three month's rent in a week! I don't get paid nearly that much. You're gonna need to get a job."

"Don't worry about it, Mike. I can do that," Stephanie clicked on the TV. "And if you must know, I already made a list of jobs I could tackle."

"Oh, your job list?" Michael mocked, but with a dash of irritated malice. "Yeah. I know about your list. Half the things on there weren't real jobs!"

"Like what?" Steph's eye's remained fixated on the TV. There were cartoons.

"You wrote down 'stunt swordsman,' 'cat scientist,' and 'Professional Batman.' Professional Batman? What even is that? These aren't things you can *be*."

"Why? Because I'm a woman?" Stephanie tilted her head and pursed her lips in accusation.

"Because you're not a *cartoon character*!"

"All I need is a grappling hook and a few hundred billion dollars. And I already ordered the hook off the internet. Also, if you don't remember, my parents are dead. It's perfect."

"How can you even joke about that?"

"Hey, they're my dead parents. I can do what I want. And now I can be a real Batman and jump in on that detective thing from yesterday," Stephanie thwacked the remote against her palm as she became infatuated with another idea. "Ooh. Maybe I should buy a fedora and a trench coat! Hey!"

Michael grabbed the remote out of Stephanie's hands, and along with it, her attention.

"Listen. To. Me," Michael enunciated. If the buck wasn't going to stop here, it had better be pumping the brakes. "Stop blowing off real life like it doesn't matter. Just because it doesn't matter to you, doesn't mean it doesn't matter to me. I need you to take some actual responsibility and not dress up like a goddamn waiter or a superhero, because, believe it or not, that doesn't help!"

Stephanie stared at him blankly before extending her hand for a futile grab at the remote.

"Enough," Michael threw the remote onto the couch. "Y'know what? I don't care. I don't have the energy to deal with this right now. I'm going to sleep. In the morning, I'll call the bank about these checks and see if they can help me sort out the raging dumpster fire that is my life. Good night, Steph." Michael stormed down the hallway and slammed his door.

"Alright, Mike. You win! I'll get a job," Steph's voice echoed from outside, over the din of the television. "I won't let you down."

"That'll be the day," Michael sighed as he crawled under the covers in his wrinkled, sweat-and-wine-drenched clothes. An easterly wind carried the patter of rain through the missing brick in his wall, delaying any sort of restful sleep.

CHAPTER EIGHT

Kicked in the Teeth

In an attempt to organize their investigation, Calhoun and McDermott had spent the first part of the day cleaning his office. Papers were swept away to reveal thick sheets of dust, which were then swept further away to reveal a nice hardwood floor. Files were put back in the cabinets where they belonged and the cabinets themselves were shuffled to one side. The door-blocking, rickety chair was turned into McDermott's assigned rickety chair. When all was said and done, the office was still suffering from its lack of square footage, but it now allowed a moderate amount of mobility.

The second part of their day was spent undoing the first by spreading out papers, records and other evidence surrounding the disappearances of Dr. Coleman Supirn, Tobias Wilkes, and Detective Kiara Hobson. Once the floor was again invisible, they managed to slap a cork board on the wall, with the sticky notes and other pertinent documentation attached, most recently a rough sketch of the mysterious assailant Calhoun had encountered after Wilkes' vanishing. It wasn't a very good sketch and more resembled a black blob with large white eyes, but it would have to do for now.

"So you're saying you saw this person." McDermott looked at Calhoun with an intensity that convinced him that she didn't think he was crazy. So she may have been crazy herself.

"Yeah. He was on the roof of an adjacent building. I climbed up the fire escape to chase him, but by the time I got there, he was gone." Calhoun stared at the sticky notes he had recreated from memory, the originals having been washed away in the rain.

SORRY ABOUT THAT. TOBIAS IS GONE NOW. BUT WASN'T HE A BAD GUY, ANYWAY?

"Hm." McDermott rubbed her cheek. "This one seems a little apologetic. Same as the one they left with Detective Hobson. Maybe this guy has a moral compass."

"Yeah, but these other two," Calhoun pointed at the sticky notes that addressed him directly.

WHOOPS. TOO SLOW! BUT I'LL SEE YOU AGAIN SOON.

TELL DETECTIVE CALHOUN I SAID "HEY".

"It's like they're taunting you," she finished. "Like this Sticky Note Specter wants you to catch him."

"If he wants to be stopped, that would fit in with your morality angle. But what the hell is going on with this lightning? It can't be a coincidence."

"Maybe he's a wizard," McDermott said with a smile.

"Don't be ridiculous. If there was some sort of magic moron in my town, I'd know about it. Maybe he's got some sort of portable lightning rod and collects the corpses after they're fried."

McDermott winced. "That's incredibly dark."

"You stay on the force long enough, McDermott," Calhoun would've tipped his hat, had he had it on, "you'll see a lot worse."

McDermott ignored the comment and turned back to the corkboard, "Well, whoever he is. He's got some sort of weird vendetta against you. Can you think of anyone who would? Anyone you've sent away that would hold some sort of grudge?"

Calhoun chewed on a pencil as he flipped through the dusty rolodex of his mind. He'd put away plenty of people that would've gladly have done him in, but they were all either dead, still locked up, or, in one notable case, the assistant manager of an unsuccessful noodle shop in southeastern Kentucky. And none of them showed any proclivity to shooting lightning out of their butts.

"Hm," he muttered. The rolodex slowed down and Calhoun got a better look at some of the cards. He didn't remember anything in particular, but a thought struck him.

"You know someone?"

"Nope. Not at all. But there is something . . ." Calhoun used his toes to rock his wobbly chair back and forth. "What if this isn't the first time this . . . what'd you call him?"

"The Sticky Note Specter."

"Sure. Whatever. What if this isn't the first time he's has struck?"

"You think this guy's been active before?" McDermott asked.

"Dunno, but I've been at the scene of a few kidnapping cases back in my day. Might be worth pulling out the files to see if anything matches." Calhoun gazed at his array of metal cabinets that were quietly rusting on the other side of the room. "Could take a while."

"No kidding." McDermott placed a slight hand on her stomach, which had begun to audibly gurgle. "But first, I might need some grub. It's almost—" she glanced at her watch, doing a double take. "Midnight? Holy crap."

A quick glance out the office window confirmed that fact. They'd been too absorbed in the investigation to notice the passage of time.

"Alright. Go grab something," Calhoun said. "I'll start doing some digging."

McDermott jumped off her rickety chair. "I'll probably hit Chub Burger. You want anything?"

"Kid, I've been runnin' on fumes for years. I'll be fine," Calhoun sighed as he made his way over to the filing cabinets. "But a chocolate shake would be nice."

McDermott offered a curt nod and was out the door. He watched her leave with a fatherly admiration of her work. She was young, but she had a certain grit he admired. Not like the other idiot kids these days—and some adults, like Detective Brook—who thought they could just fly by the seat of their pants. She had promise.

Calhoun pulled open the nearest drawer, which made an extended screech. He thumbed through files in one drawer before moving onto the next. Eventually, he brandished a pile of five different kidnapping cases he'd remembered working on. Transferring the folders to his already full desk, Calhoun began to flip through them. Each brought long hidden memories to the forefront and mugshots of criminals Calhoun had helped put away for good. Most of the victims, too, were recovered. Were he a superstitious man, he would have knocked on wood to ensure his continuing good luck. Most importantly, the perps were in the clink and there were no unexplained, electricity-related circumstances.

Then he happened upon the last file in the stack.

It was a thin one and one that he had no memory of ever participating in. The detective in charge of the case, Clarkson, had long since left his suburban precinct, and, in fact, the country, which had gotten "far too liberal" for him. He was decorated and honored by the state for the length of his service, but not necessarily the quality. Calhoun had only the most fleeting memories of the old man's farewell party. Clarkson had walked out the door in a Hawaiian shirt, hat in hand, all the while cursing something about "the women and the gays." He had never been really concerned with the actual work, which is why it did not surprise Calhoun to find that this case remained cold.

Calhoun perused the few pages in front of him, whose edges had yellowed with age and coffee stains. The report was simple and to the point. A man by the name of Arthur Finster was reported missing by his wife after not returning home after work. A black and white picture of Finster showed a large balding man whose eyes burned with a misguided authority that may have given him a bit of a temper. "Ah," Calhoun realized. Finster was a gym teacher. That made sense.

There were no eye-witness reports, but several children and other teachers at school had reported seeing him leave the school, nothing further. Calhoun squinted at the exact date of disappearance and picked up his phone. After a few rings, a bleary-voiced Alex Brook picked up.

"Brook!" Calhoun growled. "I need you to do me a favor."

"Calhoun? Why are you calling me? What time is it?"

"Doesn't matter. Running some info on a case. I need you to look up the weather on a particular date."

"Why can't you do it?"

"I'm not good with computers."

After an extended sigh, Calhoun gave Brook the date and he proceeded to search. A few minutes later, he came back with an answer. An answer that Calhoun expected.

"Says it was rainy. Thunderstorms. Happy?"

"Not really, but I'll take it."

"Fine. Is there no one else at the station?"

"There probably is."

"Then why'd you call me?"

"Because you're an asshole, Brook," Calhoun said, and slammed down his receiver. "Good night."

A thunderstorm masked Finster's disappearance. It was a reach, but it was a plausible reach. Calhoun settled back in his chair before turning over more of the case file's documents. His heart nearly stopped when he saw the telltale yellow corner of a sticky note peering out from beneath the final page. On the opposite flap of the folder was another note. It was new and showed no signs of weathering. The glue held fast to the manila flap and the black words relayed their message with an implied grin.

CARRIE WAS KINDA CUTE. I WOULD'VE KEPT AN EYE ON HER.

His ears perked up at the sound of what could have been a faint gunshot, but that Calhoun knew was thunder. Calhoun raced out of his office with little regard for the mess on the floor, leaving a swirling morass of papers in his wake. He stormed down the station steps and onto the streets as the skeleton crew working the nightshift stared oddly at him as he booked past.

The thunder had come from the northeast, he was fairly sure, so Calhoun rushed in that direction, the glow of the streetlights blurring together. Wind whipped against his face as clouds slowly began to amass above him. He skidded to a stop when the first tang of fresh ozone slipped into his nostrils and invaded his lungs. This, combined with the running, caused Calhoun to double over in a coughing fit. He always had to be reminded he was older than he wished he was.

As Calhoun hacked out his last cough, he looked up to find an empty street.

"McDermott!" He called out. Then after a while, "Carrie!"

He knew it was useless, but he had to try. His yell echoed down the street. From a window far off in the distance, the wind carried a "Shut the hell up" in his direction, but that was it.

Out of the corner of his eye, Calhoun caught the faint movement of fabric in the breeze and spun around to find someone watching him from within the glowing cone beneath a streetlight. The figure's long coat flapped in the breeze in sync with the long, wrapped scarf that covered most of his face, the rest being shielded from view by a set of dark welder's goggles.

"You," Calhoun snarled. "Where's Carrie? What've you done with her?"

The Specter only offered a playful shrug and began to step out of the light.

"Oh, no. Not this time," Calhoun reached for his holster. "Freeze!"

Calhoun attempted to draw his gun only to find that he had left it in his coat. What he had carried with him instead, was the Finster File, clutched in his outstretched hand.

"Goddammit!" Calhoun threw the folder to the ground and dashed toward the streetlight, only to find that his white whale had used the distraction to recede into the shadows from whence he came. There was no sign of him nearby, except for the rapidly fading scent of ozone.

Calhoun cursed himself for his stupidity. If he had been quicker to review the files, he could've warned Carrie, and if he hadn't forgotten his gun, he could've taken that son of a bitch down where he stood and ended this ridiculous farce. But now he was missing the only ally who would believe him and had to deal with the perpetrator slipping through his fingers. He had only one more lead to follow.

Calhoun paced back to where he had dropped the Finster case file and scooped it up, thumbing through it in search of an address. Drops of drizzle began to smatter across the sidewalk as Calhoun slapped the folder closed and shielded it within his jacket, beginning the long walk back to the precinct.

CHAPTER NINE

Ad Nauseam

Michael's cell phone alarm blared through his dreams at 7 a.m. He stared at it for a full 30 seconds before hitting snooze and going back to sleep. Unwilling to face the world, he repeated this depressing exercise again at 8 and once more at 8:30 before tossing it against the back wall. Unfortunately, being a cell phone, it was just the right size to miss the wall entirely and sail through the empty brick hole in the middle. That woke him up.

Putting on his glasses and peering through the hole, Michael spotted the plastic and silicon remains of his phone scattered across the asphalt below. If it weren't for that damn brick, currently wedged beneath his rear tire and the asphalt, he'd still have his phone. At least it was Friday.

After that minor hiccup, the rest of the day went fairly smoothly. Stephanie was either fast asleep or absent from the apartment, as the

TV was not on and Michael could eat his cereal in relative peace. After Michael worked over the Garbagemobile's engine for ten minutes, it permitted him to drive without incident. Work was as mind-numbing as usual, but, since it was the end of the week, all Michael needed to do was wait it out. As he clacked his way across his keyboard, his anxieties began to pile up. The residual heart attack of missing rent, the Terri fiasco, and, in the back of his mind, the faint trauma of being accosted twice by that crazy lady.

Only one of those things remained in his control, and in an attempt to pull his life back from the brink, Michael decided to give his bank a call. Surely they would be able to provide some answers about the missing checks. But, after navigating through an oppressive automated system, Michael found the bank's phone-based service to be completely unintelligible. At one point, he had been directed to what sounded like the mutant love-child of a fax machine and a 14.4 kilobaud modem. The end result was an irreversible twenty-dollar transaction from his account to an account located in the Korean Demilitarized Zone.

It was around 11:30 when he finally decided that no actual work was going to get done for the rest of the day, and left, managing to dodge Ravi and any other co-worker on the floor that might want to recruit him for another meaningless task. Fool him once, shame on him, fool him for the three years he had worked here . . . also shame on him. Michael slung his coat over his shoulder and slunk out the exit.

Making use of his extra time, Michael opted to hit the bank where it lived: its single, inconvenient brick-and-mortar branch downtown. His experience there was also less than stellar. After much cajoling, the assistant manager showed Michael the records she had on file regarding his recently cashed checks. She declined to help him any further, since, according to her, Michael wasn't a Platinum DoublePlus Star member and, frankly, she had much more profitable clients to attend to. Michael understood her point, but thought that the middle finger she flipped him on the way out was unnecessary.

As per the records she provided, the rent checks had been cashed at a convenience store in a particularly seedy part of town commonly known as "Squalor's Wallow," and they had been endorsed only with a crude X. His attempts to phone the store from the bank were routed to a garbled and angry voicemail greeting that ended with gunshots just before the beep. Michael left no message and decided he would not be following that thread in person.

Convinced that the money was gone and no other options remained, Michael headed back to the apartment. Desperate to avoid encountering a volley of Greek obscenities in the stairwell, he made his way up the building's fire escape. It was only an act of god which kept the rusted rungs from buckling under his weight, but after a slow climb, Michael was able to wipe the grime off his living room window and peer in to find Stephanie, her arms splayed across the back of the sofa and his laptop on her outstretched legs. Again, her bare feet rested on the coffee table. Michael rapped his knuckles against the glass. Stephanie looked up and, with a smile, waltzed over to let him in.

"You're home early," she said as Michael contorted his way through the window. "I've just been checking your email."

"My email? Wait . . . how do you even know my password?"

"Fantastic question." That was what Steph said when she wanted to avoid answering questions. "But hold on for a second. Because you wouldn't believe the people who want us to work for them."

"Work for them? What are you talking about?" Michael took a step back when the obvious realization oozed over his body like cold, unwelcome molasses. "No, not the detective thing."

"Yes. The detective thing," Stephanie's smile widened. "There were a few dozen emails in your spam folder. Everybody's asking after that ad, Mike."

"I told them to delete that!" He had sent a strongly worded email to the webmasters of the online classified site, but perhaps it had gotten deleted or, worse, ignored.

"I guess a bunch of people saw it before they took it down."

"No! This is not our ad and we're not going to investigate any damn mysteries!" If Michael had put his foot down any harder, it would have gone through the floor.

"So do you want me to tell our clients that we can't help them?"

Michael stiffened as the guilt burned through the back of his head, another ingrained response from his childhood. Always help others before helping yourself, his mom had said. This philosophy had never worked out for Michael in practice. In fact, it had only made his life more irritating. It was quite possibly the only reason he had saddled himself with Stephanie's inability to live a proper life. And now the very object of his generosity was using it to drag him into another scheme. He would have to thank his mother for giving Stephanie the right buttons to press.

Michael clenched his fist and tried to suppress the guilt with loud skepticism. "I can't believe there are people who actually want to hire a couple of detectives with no experience."

"Don't doubt the power of internet marketing," Stephanie said. "Also, the ad said we've been in business since 1989."

"We were born in 1989."

She shrugged, "So, technically, I guess. It's true."

"But we have no real skills!" Michael shook his head.

"Eh, I wouldn't worry about it. Can't be that hard. At the very least it'll be fun."

"Fun isn't the point. It's not that simple, Steph. We can't just waltz into people's lives and mess around with their problems! That could be dangerous. We could get arrested. Or killed. Or worse."

"Worse than killed?"

"Do you know what happens to detectives?" Michael asked. "The worst kind of things! I mean, probably. You don't see them around anymore, really."

"Even better. So there's literally no competition. And the market has zero barriers to entry." Michael couldn't be sure that Stephanie wasn't quoting phrases she'd picked up while absently watching CNBC.

"Do you even know what a private eye does, Steph?"

"No. Do you?" Stephanie fired back.

Michael had to admit that aside from the broad strokes he'd seen in TV and movies, he wasn't quite certain.

"See?" Stephanie said. "*Nobody* knows what they do! They won't know that we're just making it up on the fly. All we have to do is ask the right questions, look at the evidence and draw some conclusions. You're an analytical kinda guy, and I've got the charisma. I'm sure if we put our heads together we could do it and make enough cash to keep us from getting evicted. On top of that, these people need us. You should see some of these emails! They're practically begging for help. We'd be doing them a mitzvah."

Michael could appreciate that maybe she honestly did want to help people, especially in exchange for a little money. Still, he resented the fact that his own misplaced personal responsibility could be turned against him so easily. "No," he stood firm. "This is insanity."

"Just hear 'em out at least," Stephanie tilted her head, a puppy desperate to be thrown a bone. "That's all I ask. If you're still not moved by their plight, we'll shut it down."

"Okay. Fine," Michael cracked. "Let's hear it. Who're the people that are so desperate that they need our help?"

Stephanie whipped back to the computer and started scrolling through several email headers. "We've got a few of 'em. Missing Cat. Subpoena Service Request. Missing person. Ooh . . . someone wants us to check out a saucy affair. Mama like. Let's take that one."

Michael yanked the computer out of Stephanie's hands, placed it on his lap and continued to read. A memory tickled the back of his brain as he scrolled past a few other recent emails about missing people. "I think I heard something on the news about a doctor disappearing. You think these might be connected?"

"I dunno. It's easy to get lost. Remember when I went to that bar downtown and couldn't find my way home for six hours?

Michael glared across the couch. "You were drunk."

"Man, you better believe it," Stephanie stared away, wistful, before snapping back to the present. "Hey, maybe some of these people are drunk."

"They must be if they're asking *us* for help."

"Y'know . . ." Stephanie tilted her head, "maybe this has something to do with our disappearing rent."

"How so?"

"Missing people, missing rent," Stephanie turned her palms up, weighing the two options. "Right?"

"That doesn't make any—" Michael stopped his rebuttal as a name caught his eye and his heart caught in his throat. He was two beats shy of a full cardiac episode. "No. You've gotta be kidding me."

"What is it? Lemme see!" Stephanie yanked the laptop back over and her eyes went wide. "Well . . . that's interesting."

The subject 'Missing Person: Terri Bradshaw' was printed in bland, unassuming Arial, but burnt itself into Michael's retinas. A quick check revealed that the email had been sent at 5pm yesterday, from Terri's own account. The body of the email revealed nothing except the address of an apartment and instructions to watch the video file attached. The note was signed "Help, Terri Bradshaw."

"So . . . uh . . ." Stephanie cleared her throat. "You still against this whole detective thing?"

CHAPTER TEN

Missing Person of Interest

After gathering some supplies—a notebook and pen between them, which they ultimately would end up leaving in the car—the two potential gumshoes walked out to the Garbagemobile. Stephanie held the laptop—their font of information—aloft while Michael disengaged the brick parking system and leapt into the driver's seat to prevent the car from rolling away. Stephanie tossed the laptop through the passenger-side window and then crawled in behind it, urging Michael to get going when she was halfway through. As usual, the car refused to turn over, emitting squeals resembling a dying wildebeest. When it did give in, it handled with the precision of the very same wildebeest, with a pair of women's jeans dangling out the side window.

After Stephanie had pushed herself right-side up and re-fastened her pants, she opened the laptop and pulled up the email attachment that Terri had sent them. The first frame was Terri herself, her pale face framed by her cascading brown hair, but frozen in an off-center stare. Behind her hazel eyes lay something that Michael was all too familiar with: a general, persistent fear of absolutely everything. Unfortunately, the JPG-like compression of the video did her looks no favors.

"This is the laundry girl?" Steph turned to Michael. "Nice."

"Will you just push play already?"

Stephanie hit the space bar and Terri's face sprung to jagged, blocky life. As she coughed and cleared her throat, Michael struggled to maintain the balance between watching the road and Terri's message.

"Hi, Michael. Hi, Steph," Michael's brow furrowed as she mentioned Stephanie's name. "I hope this email finds you well. Thank you for taking the time to listen." Although her words were tight and professional, her tone was shaky and uncertain, as if someone had coached her, but not very well. "Please stick around the whole way through, because it's going to sound a little . . . surreal. I made this video so you could see exactly how serious I am," Terri took a breath, which reminded Michael that he hadn't been breathing, so he followed suit, "Well, here goes. I know for a fact that in the next hour, I'm going to go missing. I don't know where and I don't know why. And don't ask me how because it doesn't make much sense to me either. All I know is that I need someone to find out what happened to me, and it has to be you two."

"Why us, lady?" Stephanie looked down at the computer. "Why not the cops?"

"It's a video, Steph," Michael returned his attention to the road. "She's not going to answer you."

Terri ignored Michael's rebuke and insisted upon responding to Stephanie as the faint sound of thunder in the background audio garbled some of her words. "The cops won't be able to help me. That's why I came to you. It needs to be you," she forced a chuckle. "No case too tough, no case too crazy, right?"

"Nice. She knows our tag line!" Stephanie pointed at the screen. "That's some damn good marketing."

"If you're watching this now, it means I'm already gone. I can't offer you much in the way of clues, but I can direct you to my apartment: 226 Andrews Drive, Apartment 7H." The address checked out with the one in the body of the email. "Maybe you'll find something there that will lead you on your way. Hopefully I'll be seeing you soon." Terri moved her hand off-screen, but stopped. "Michael, sorry about missing our da—"

"Nah, we don't need to hear any of that," Stephanie clicked the laptop shut and looked up. "Okay. So she's definitely crazy, right? Crazy as balls."

"What?"

"Hundred percent coconuts. Boy, Mike, you sure know how to pick 'em."

"Terri was scared shitless, Steph! Didn't you hear her? And according to the news there's a serial kidnapper on the loose. If she's been taken . . ." Michael shook off the thought. "Listen, if you're going to insist that we be fake detectives, we can at least fake it correctly."

"Oh, now you're into it? I bet you just wanna salvage your chances of getting in her pants." Stephanie, unfortunately, had a point, although Michael wouldn't have put it that way and refused to acknowledge it. "Fine. Let's take a look at her apartment and see if there's something there. But right now, I'm gonna go with the idea that she's nuts. The simplest solution. Motorola's Razor."

"Occam's Razor," Michael corrected, then continued. "Whatever. Fine. Well, you're the one who always insisted on being the detective when we were kids, so what do you propose we do when we get there?"

"I don't know. Look for clues, I guess," Stephanie finally decided to buckle her seatbelt. "Maybe we can read her mail?"

"Isn't that illegal?"

"That depends on your definition of 'illegal.'"

"Not legal," Michael deadpanned.

"Oh," Stephanie said. "Then . . . maybe?"

Michael sighed. "This whole thing is probably illegal, Steph."

"So you think whoever put up that ad was trying to set us up for a fall or something?"

Michael had not thought of that. Maybe they were two cogs in some sort of vast conspiracy and had been forced into their role by someone—perhaps the kidnapper—who knew that the threat of eviction could spin them into an irrational panic. Then he realized that no conspiracy, no matter how vast, could have taken into account his and Stephanie's sheer incompetence at all things. "Probably not. Seems like there'd be easier ways to do that."

"Neato! Then we should be golden," Stephanie put her feet up on the dashboard. "This is gonna be fun. You think we should come up with some fake names?"

"Why would we do that?"

"So people don't know who we are."

"Nobody knows who we are, Steph!"

"Still, I've always wanted to come up with some cool aliases."

"You do that, then," Michael grumbled, resigned to his fate, and continued to grumble all the way to Terri's apartment. He spotted the building from the highway, the oversized glass windowpanes of each apartment reflected the brilliance of the late afternoon sun. Meanwhile, the exposed metal girders between each floor offered an implied semi-industrial aesthetic, despite being miles away from the nearest steel mill. The Garbagemobile rolled into a parking space across the street, sputtering to an uneasy halt.

Stephanie whistled as she swung out the car window. "Wow. Nice place."

Michael was ashamed to admit he was a little thankful that Terri had gone missing just so he could avoid the awkwardness of her ever witnessing the abomination that was his apartment. He feared the judgment would be too much to bear. He pushed past this thought and through the building's revolving door and into the wide lobby.

A doorman was there to greet them. He doffed his cap from behind the reception desk, "Hello! How may I help you?"

At this, Stephanie surged ahead, whispering back to Michael, "I'll take care of this," while winking a fair bit too much. She turned back to the doorman, and everything fell out of Michael's hands, "Hello.

My name is Jackie Steele," Stephanie said, clearly having put a lot of thought into a ridiculous alias. She continued, adopting the velvety, sultry voice a woman named Jackie Steele would possess. "And this is my associate . . ." Stephanie paused and looked at Michael. Her wide eyes implied that she had wasted all her time imagining the intricacies of Jackie Steele and hadn't come up with a suitable name for Michael. Michael crossed his arms, forcing her to grasp for straws to continue this chosen charade "Maurice . . . Sendak."

"The author of 'Where The Wild Things Are'?" The doorman raised an eyebrow.

Stephanie leaned back and whispered, "Mike, I think we've been made. Might wanna make a run for it. On my mark, 3 . . . 2 . . ."

Ignoring her countdown, Michael pushed her aside and approached the desk. "Yes, hi. My name is Michael Duckett. I'm here to see Terri Bradshaw."

"Oh, the detective? She mentioned you two would be dropping by today," the doorman slid him a pair of keys, which Michael cupped into his palm. "Go ahead. 7th floor. Apartment H. I hope everything's alright."

"Yeah, I'm sure it will be," Michael said out of the side of his mouth. "Thanks."

Michael hit the 7 in the elevator on the far side of the hallway. Steph managed to slide his way in before the doors clicked closed.

"Well, that worked out better than expected," she said.

"No thanks to you."

"So sue me. I've always wanted to use an alias," Stephanie shrugged. "I thought this was the time."

"It's never the time, Steph."

"Don't worry. I can come up with better ones." The elevator dinged a few more times before Stephanie spoke again. "Hey, Mike?"

"Yeah?"

"What kind of building has a doorman but no laundry room?"

Michael hadn't thought of that. He quickly scanned the buttons on the elevator to find a button that was indeed labeled "Laundry." Maybe Terri had been as awkward as Michael was and had gone to the laundromat just to hang out with him. All the more reason to try and get her back. Michael clenched his fists and bit his lip in elation, while another, deeper part of him fought to make sure his hopes didn't get too high.

The doors opened and deposited Michael and Stephanie into a roomy hallway with thick burgundy carpeting that absorbed their footsteps. A few feet to the left was apartment 7H. The key fit neatly into the lock and the door clicked open, although some part of Michael wished it hadn't. Terri's place was large and was kept dark and cool with the aid of thick drawn curtains and deep blue walls.

Stephanie took a long look around the apartment, not focusing on anything in particular. As per her usual M.O., she zeroed in on the couch and vaulted onto the rich leather. "Swanky. Girl's got taste! Except, clearly in men."

"Alright. Shut up," Michael's chest began to tense. Although Terri had expressly given them permission to come here, he could not help but feel like he was breaking and entering, with a pinch of stalking thrown in for good measure. It made him a little sick, but there was very little about the situation that didn't. "Let's look around real quick. I don't want us to be in here any longer than we have to."

Michael ran his hand across the wall as he traced the outline of the living room. There was much here to be admired: a fully-stocked bar, tasteful wall art, and a set of shelves lined with books that Michael wished he could lie about having read. A stack of mail lay neatly on the glass coffee table and, despite his earlier reservations, Michael filed through it. He discovered nothing of note, except that the Columbia House Record Club was still alive and well despite common sense. He sighed. Michael didn't know what he had expected when coming here.

Shaking off his worries, Michael blinked and looked around. Stephanie was no longer on the couch. "Steph?"

"Back here, Mike!" Stephanie's voice floated through the doorway towards the rear of the room. "The bedroom. Think I found something."

Michael jumped up and dashed over. As he passed through the doorway, he marveled at the large windows that dominated the western facing wall. He also marveled at the fact they had all been shattered and their twinkling remains were spread all across the hardwood floor and over a computer desk. "What the hell?"

Stephanie, however, had paid this no heed. Instead, she was standing on top of the bed, still in her sneakers, with her nose in the air.

"C'mon. At least take your shoes off," Michael pointed to her yellowing, untied Converses that could have sloughed off by themselves at any moment.

"Oh, *now* you want me to take my shoes off?"

"It's just common—"

"There's broken glass on the floor, Mike. I'm not taking my shoes off."

"But you're standing on—"

"Shhh!" Stephanie pushed a finger to her lips and then tapped the tip of her small nose. Her nostrils enlarged to a comical degree as she took in a large snort. "The air. It smells . . . weird."

"You need me to be quiet so you can smell?"

"It smells like . . ." Stephanie inhaled again deeply, trying to place the scent, "I dunno . . . like old magnets."

"Old magnets?" Michael repeated, without full comprehension.

"Yeah. Dusty ones. They'd be like from the fifties. The horseshoe kind you see in cartoons."

"That's rid—" Michael was about to retort out of impatience, but caught a quick, sharp whiff of ozone that differed from the subdued freshness of the living room. "Huh."

"Right?" Stephanie smirked. "Right?"

"Yeah. Smells different, I guess. I don't know where you get magnets from. That doesn't have anything to do with anything, though."

"If you have any better leads, I'd like to hear them."

"Yeah . . . about that . . ." Michael's eye was drawn toward Terri's computer desk. Beneath the monitor lay a stack of papers, covered by a thorough sprinkling of blue-green glass. "Actually, I think I might."

Michael brushed off the glass. Stuck dead center atop the pile was a yellow sticky note.

THIS IS FOR YOU.

"Looks like Terri left us some clues."

Michael flipped through the papers. Each was a newspaper clipping, or a printout of a clipping, referencing missing persons in the city over the last two decades. Michael perused through some of the names until he came upon one that he recognized.

"Coleman Supirn. That's the doctor that went missing."

"Then who're those other people?" Stephanie asked from the bed.

"I dunno. Haven't heard of them. Carrie McDermott? Tobias Wilkes? Arthur Finster? Kiara Hobson? When did these people—" Before Michael could dig any deeper, another paper at the bottom of the stack caught his eye. It was irritatingly familiar.

'MICHAEL DUCKETT AND STEPHANIE DYER— PRIVATE EYES FOR HIRE—NO CASE TOO TOUGH, NO CASE TOO CRAZY—REASONABLE RATES—ANY TIME DAY OR NIGHT.' The text shouted.

"Hey, it's our ad again," Stephanie had been reading over Michael's shoulder so quietly he nearly jumped.

Michael actually jumped when a loud pounding came from the living room. Someone was at the door. Michael, thrown into a tizzy, attempted to rearrange the stack of papers as best he could, in some sort of order with the sticky note on top. Maybe nobody would realize he'd messed with it.

"Shit. Shit. Shit," he panicked as he saw the ad printout still in his hand. Michael shoved the printout into his back pocket and dragged Stephanie into the living room.

"Terri!" The pounding resumed. "Terri, are you home?"

"Who the hell is that?" Stephanie whispered.

"I don't know! Just hide! Quick!" Michael ducked behind the thick blue curtains. Given the immense size of the apartment's windows, they were more than tall enough to conceal him. He swallowed his breath and pressed himself up against the glass, keeping every muscle tightly wound, including closing his eyes for some reason.

There was a click and clink as the apartment's locks released, followed by a rough, quick tread of footsteps across the burnished hardwood floor, before they came to a stop at what he assumed was the coffee table.

"Get out here," A man's voice demanded. "I can see your shoes poking out from under the curtain. And . . ." He didn't finish his sentence, but as Michael peered out from his hiding place, he found the man pointing at the couch, where Stephanie was sitting, holding a throw pillow in front of her face.

"Seriously?" Michael pushed up his glasses and rubbed his eyes with the heels of his palms.

"I'm sorry," Stephanie tossed the pillow aside. "You gave me two seconds to hide in an apartment I've never been in before and I panicked. Get off my back."

"Who the hell are you and what the hell are you doing here?" The man was maybe just a bit older than Michael and Stephanie. He had very little hair and that which was there was closely shorn, its streaks of silver glinting against his light skin. Hazel eyes similar to those that had gazed at Michael in the laundromat now stared out of a similar, but roundish face. It couldn't be anyone else. "Did you break into my sister's apartment?"

"Okay," Michael put his hands out in a vain attempt to control the situation. "I can explain."

"We're detectives!" Stephanie shouted from the couch.

"I'm sorry. What?" Jacob Bradshaw was not on board and Michael could not blame him.

"We're . . . uh . . . detectives," Michael did his best to believe what he was saying, but that was a completely unwinnable battle. "It's kind of a convoluted story, but the key is that—and I know it sounds weird—but your sister Terri is missing and she hired us to find her. It's okay, though. You and I work together, actually. At The Future Group?" Michael extended a hand in an attempt at a handshake.

Jacob paused and looked at Michael straight in the eyes. His mouth hung open in a state of surprise, confusion and concern. It was the concern of an older brother, the same concern Michael had once had for Stephanie, which had slowly withered away as she refused to take control of her life. Michael could feel Jacob and himself connecting on a quantum level bond between two brothers. After he finally took stock of the situation, Jacob exhaled a long breath and finally spoke, "Are you out of your goddamn minds?"

"He's taking it better than I expected," Stephanie said, continuing to observe from her post on the couch.

"It's hard to believe, I know. I was supposed to go on a date with her, but she didn't show up, but then she emailed us," Michael began to talk faster in order to clarify the relevant details, of which there were so many. He tried to slow down, but could not. "See, she probably saw this internet ad someone put out for us. We didn't put it up, but she even sent us a video!" Michael gestured to Stephanie. "Steph, pull up the video."

"Uh, dude. I left the laptop in the car."

"Crap," Michael said as Jacob's fist cracked against his cheekbone, knocking him off his feet and sprawling him on the carpet.

"Get out of here, you lunatics!" Jacob yelled.

Michael, still on the floor, used his fingers and palms to inch his way to the door. There was certainly no coming back from this. "Okay, okay! Sorry! We'll leave."

"If I ever see you again, I'm calling the cops! And so help me god if you have anything to do with my sister," he held open the door and watched Michael slink out into the hallway.

Stephanie followed suit, but lagged behind, sticking her hand out as he passed. "Hi, by the way, name's Stephanie Dyer. I know the circumstances are a bit weird, but I was wondering if you'd like to get a drink some time? I have a thing for bald men, I mean, bald ladies, too, but I feel like it just works better on men, y'know? Personal opinion."

"Get the hell out!"

*   *   *

Michael rubbed his stomach as he crouched into the Garbagemobile. "Ugh. That's it. I'm done with this. This was stupid to begin with."

Stephanie climbed in through the passenger's side window, this time a bit more deftly. "No, it's not. It's a good idea. We just got off to a rough start."

"Rough start? I would've loved to have a 'rough start!' This is a goddamn shitshow!" Michael hit the steering wheel with a force much less severe than Jacob's punch. Any harder and an airbag would have deployed. It was a good thing the Garbagemobile didn't have one. "Terri's brother thinks I'm insane! And we're no closer to finding out whatever happened to her! This doesn't make any sense!"

"Well, maybe we should look for more clues," Stephanie offered.

"Here," Michael reached into his back pocket and shoved the now crumpled paper printout at her. "You want a clue? Here's a clue. You look at it. Here's a hint: it's a garbage ad for two people who aren't detectives!"

Stephanie picked the paper out of its crushed ball form and turned it around in her hands. Michael, meanwhile, attempted to start the car, with limited success. After the second or third crank of the ignition, Stephanie said, "Hey Mike, you ever think to look at the other side of this? Looks like someone put a list on here."

Michael turned to face the unfurled paper that Stephanie held. Quite like the clear, bombastic ad for their questionable services, the words on the back yelled, but this time in the harsh jarring ink of a permanent marker. It was a simple list of twenty or so names, but Michael's eyes were drawn to four of them that weren't.

JACOB BRADSHAW

TERRI BRADSHAW

MICHAEL DUCKETT

STEPHANIE DYER

CHAPTER ELEVEN
No Case Too Tough

"What the hell is this?" Michael said as the Garbagemobile finally relented. In his surprise, he had put more force into the key that time. Maybe that was the trick. He'd have to check later. "Why are we on this list?"

"Fantastic question," Stephanie said. "I'm gonna guess it's for America's Top Twenty Hottest Failures."

"Thanks," Michael yanked the Garbagemobile into traffic as harshly as he wished someone would yank him out of this situation. "Who are the other people?"

"I dunno. Some guys, I guess," Stephanie smoothed the paper across her thigh. "Arthur Finster, Carrie McDermott, Matteo Carrera, Tobias Wilkes, Kia—"

"Wait. Hold on," Michael remembered some of those names. "It's a list of people who've gone missing! And now Terri's missing. Holy shit! What if this is the list of that serial kidnapper? I don't want to be kidnapped! I'm too young to be kidnapped!" Michael, against his best judgement, had begun to hyperventilate.

"Whoa, whoa, relax, Mike," Stephanie patted him on the shoulder. "First of all, technically, you're too old to be kidnapped. And second, we'll be fine. We can't go missing if we both know where each of us are."

Michael gave Stephanie a belabored grimace. What she said was true, but ridiculous. Par for the course, essentially. "Fine. I guess not everyone here is missing. We just saw Jacob and he's fine . . . except a little sore about the whole home invasion thing. And I don't remember seeing any mention of a Matteo Carrera."

"See? It's all good," Stephanie reached over him and clicked on the radio. "How about we just relax for a bit with some tuneskis?"

After a few seconds of garbled static, there emerged the fast-talking smarm of a career DJ giving it his all, as he was otherwise unemployable. "—inces of the Universe by Queen, on KHWK K-Hawk's all rock Rock Block. Don't get locked on the same old schlock! We'll keep you stocked with the Rock Block shock jocks squawkin' on The Hawk! We'll be back after an ad block from some guys who have some stock to hock. So don't touch that dial!"

Michael felt the command was directed at him, as the Garbagemobile was probably the only automobile on the road that still had radio dials. He was too afraid to touch them, anyway. If he did, the car's wheels would probably fall off.

"Are you in trouble? In way over your head?" The gruff voice of an older man was unfamiliar, but relatable enough to have understood Michael's current frazzled state of mind "Need help? Well, the solution is just a short phone call away."

"Hah. Maybe we should call these people," Michael scoffed after letting out his first easy breath in minutes. In hindsight, he should have waited two seconds longer.

"Call Duckett and Dyer: P.I.s for Hire!" The ad man continued. "They'll help you solve any problem that you might have. Cheating Spouse? Missing Person? Lost your keys? Think your dog is acting suspicious? Is someone stealing your shoes? Is your *dog* stealing your shoes? Well, don't worry, because Michael Duckett and Stephanie Dyer are on your side and on the job with reasonable prices. No case too tough. No case too crazy. Don't wait! Call today at 629-54232. They'll help anyone!"

Michael almost shoved his fist through the console in order to make it shut up. "What the hell was that?"

"Yeah. That's really weird," Stephanie pouted. "An online classified and now a radio ad? Whoever's promoting us really isn't trying to maximize our exposure in mainstream markets."

"No! Why is there a radio ad at all? Who's doing this to us? And whose phone number was that?"

"I dunno," Stephanie raised an eyebrow. "Wait . . . how many digits are in a phone number?"

Michael lack of an answer was cut short by a tremulous ringing. A muffled, yet proud tune. It took Michael a few seconds to place it, but when he did, he almost slammed on the brakes. The ringing persisted as he swerved into an empty spot next to a fire hydrant. It was a faint, MIDI version of theme tune from the Mighty Ducks.

"That's my ringtone," Michael said. That wasn't entirely true. It was the ringtone Stephanie had chosen for Michael's phone, and Michael had never figured out how to change it. That point was moot, however, as he had unceremoniously destroyed his phone in that tragic wake-up accident this morning. It was currently lying in pieces in front of their apartment building, as he had refused to clean it up out of spite.

"Hm," Stephanie popped open the glove compartment, wherein lay Michael's phone. Or, at least, one identical to Michael's. It was the same pathetic flip variety. It even had the same scratches and dings along the side. The song blared a little harder now, as loud as a tinny ringtone could. She thrust it toward Michael. "Well, uh, here you go."

Michael stared at it. It couldn't be his phone. But it looked like his phone, it acted like his phone, and it certainly played the Mighty Ducks like his phone. Michael flipped it open and eased it toward his ear. "Hell . . . o?"

"Hello," said the voice of a woman, quite older sounding. The kind of voice that would serve you Werther's Originals. A slight tremor indicated just how nervous—maybe scared—she was. "Is this Michael Duckett and Stephanie Dyer? The Private Investigators?"

"Um . . . I guess so?" Michael shrugged at Stephanie, who quietly urged him to turn on the speaker. Michael did so. "Who may I ask is calling?"

"Hi. My name is Elena Finster," the speaker added to the shake in her voice. "I heard your ad on the radio and I thought that maybe you could help me."

Finster. The name caused Michael's fingers to twitch. It was on the list. But not an Elena. An Arthur.

"Sure thing, Mrs. F!" Stephanie jumped in on the call. "Stephanie Dyer here, co-owner and CEO of the firm."

"CEO?" Michael mouthed.

"Always happy to help," Stephanie pushed his face away and continued. "Can you tell us exactly what your problem is?"

"It's my husband," Mrs. Finster's voice shook and almost choked. "He's missing."

"Mrs. Finster. Your husband. His name wouldn't be . . ." Michael paused, not wanting to say the name aloud, lest the mystery of the list gain any more validity. " . . .Arthur, would it?"

"Why, yes! It is." Damn the luck. "You must've read about the case in the papers . . . but you sound so young for that!"

"Young?" Michael mouthed to Stephanie.

Stephanie jumped back in, "Mrs. F, when did your husband go missing?"

There was a long silence before Mrs. Finster answered. "Fourteen years ago."

Michael covered the mouthpiece. "Fourteen years ago? What the hell? How are we supposed to do anything with that?"

Stephanie grabbed the phone back from him, ignoring his questions. "No worries, Mrs. F. We'll be right over to consult with you. Just give us your address and we'll be there shortly."

"What are you doing?" Michael said as Stephanie shut the phone. "We're not taking a case from a senile old woman. Even if her husband did go missing fourteen years ago, he's probably long dead by now and she's just confused."

"Mike, I think it's bigger than that. Remember what the radio ad said? 'They'll help anyone!'"

"The radio ad," Michael deadpanned. "The radio ad that some rando placed for us? The radio ad that in no way represents who or what we actually are?"

"Hey, if I were so dead-set on finding a hot missing girl that I wanted to plow," Michael frowned at the word "plow," "and there've been many of those—not missing ones, hot ones—I'd follow up every lead that could even slightly connect," Stephanie held up the paper. "Terri's on that list. Finster's on the list."

Michael stayed quiet.

"And, besides, I'm having a lot of fun," Stephanie smiled. "Plus, you got anything better to do this weekend? It's not like you have a date."

Michael sighed and turned the car back on. "You better be right about this."

"When have I ever been wrong about anything?" Stephanie asked.

Michael's grumbled answer was drowned out by the squeal of the Garbagemobile's tires as they pulled out into the street.

* * *

The Garbagemobile ground to a halt in front of a powder blue ranch style house a few miles outside the city limits. The little red flag on the aluminum mailbox confirmed that they had crossed the invisible border where hip and trendy storefronts devolved into the boring domestication of suburbia. The bold black stickers along the side that spelled FINSTER confirmed that they hadn't gotten lost on the way.

Stephanie angled her body out of the window and onto the curb, as Michael took the proper way around to the sidewalk.

"You ready for this?" Stephanie asked from the ground.

"Yes. Fine. Let's get it over with," Michael had the entire ride over to think about it, and still had a great deal of anxiety about the whole situation. Yet Stephanie had been surprisingly intent on following these threads, and it would probably be safer if Michael was there to chaperone. Besides, she had had a point: any tenuous link to Terri was a worthwhile lead to follow.

Stephanie jabbed her finger at the house's doorbell, never letting it finish a ding before starting another. After about seven of these, Michael grabbed her wrist to prevent another ring just seconds before an old woman appeared, her frame slight enough to fit in the crack between the house's inner door and screen door. "Yes, how can I help you?"

"Mrs. F?" Stephanie asked. "I'm Stephanie Dyer. You called us a few minutes ago? My associate Michael Duckett and I are here to be of service."

"Yes! Oh, yes," the woman's pale gray eyes lit up a translucent blue as she creaked open the screen door and ushered them in. "Come in. Please come in."

The door slammed shut behind them and Mrs. Finster led them through a small foyer, its walls covered in picture frames. One of them suggested "Live, Laugh, Love." Michael rolled his eyes, but after he passed three more frames bearing the same message, it started to feel more like a command. Pushing past the harsh demands, Michael found himself staring at all the frames, and the happy memories within. One showed the silhouette of a much younger Elena Finster walking along the beach, hand in hand with a taller, heftier figure. A quick glance across to another frame showed Mrs. Finster, much older, hugging her grown son, both their faces hiding the loss they had suffered years earlier. The last picture was of the happy couple on their porch a number of years ago, the stocky, heavy-set Arthur Finster with a head missing most of his red hair and his arm around his wife. Michael paused for a moment. Something about Arthur Finster struck him, but he could not be sure what . . . or why. He had little time to dwell on it before Stephanie dragged him onwards.

The living room was the same powder blue as the house exterior, and covered with pictures and pressings of flowers in elegant wooden frames that matched the glossy, cherry wood finish of the coffee table and the large, almost foreboding armoire that stood at the back wall keeping watch over the proceedings. Mrs. Finster gestured towards the couch and Michael and Stephanie obeyed, sitting on the faded floral patterns, their every motion amplified by the trumpeting of the plastic furniture covers beneath them. Michael shifted a bit more to assure everyone in the room that the noise was indeed due to the furniture and not his bowels.

"Can I get you anything? Tea? Cookies?" Mrs. Finster asked, then, confirming Michael's earlier supposition, added, "Werther's Originals?"

"No, thank you," Stephanie waved the offer away, and sunk her teeth into her detective character, a noticeable step up from "Jackie Steele." "We're here strictly in a professional capacity. You say your husband has been missing?"

" . . .For the past fourteen years?" Michael added.

"Yes . . . yes he has," Mrs. Finster tottered over to the armchair and sat down with another prolonged plastic squeak that she either ignored or could not hear. "He went to work one day and just never returned."

"Well, that's . . . certainly . . . strange," Unlike Stephanie, Michael was struggling to figure out his detective demeanor. But he maintained that he shouldn't have had to, since he wasn't a real detective! "Have you called the police?"

"Well, yes. I called them. They said that too much time had passed. At this point, my Arthur was gone. They told me to move on."

"Mrs. Finster," Stephanie leaned in. "When did you call the police? Fourteen years ago?"

"Well, I don't quite know. My memory hasn't been what it used to be recently. But . . . it's been so hard without Arthur," Mrs. Finster put a frail hand to her thin, wrinkled lips as tears began to well up in her already wet eyes. A burning surge of compassion and pity filled Michael's chest and washed through the gaps in his ribs. He wanted to help this woman. He really did, but he couldn't see what either he or Stephanie could actually do. In fact, based on their track records, they'd probably make the whole thing worse. "But then I heard your ad on the radio," Mrs. Finster continued. "I never thought about hiring a private investigator, but you said you'd help anyone. No case too tough, right?"

"Yes . . . that's . . . that's our slogan," Michael forced the words through a fake smile.

"I guess we can start at the beginning, right?" Stephanie looked to Michael. He could only give her a noncommittal shrug. "So your husband, Arthur, was it?" Mrs. Finster nodded. "Arthur disappeared after going to work. Where did he work?"

"Well, he was a—" Before Mrs. Finster could finish, the doorbell rang. Not in Stephanie's irritating staccato, but the measured single ring of a normal human being. "Now who could that be?"

"Are you expecting any visitors?" Stephanie's eyes tracked Mrs. Finster as she rose and toddled back into the foyer.

"No," she called back. "Excuse me. I should only be a second."

When Mrs. Finster was out of earshot, Stephanie turned to Michael, her voice dropping to a whisper, "Great. She's gone. Now help me find those Werther's Originals."

"Are you kidding me?" Michael hissed back. "You said you didn't want any of those."

"I didn't, but then I started to think about 'em and I can't get them outta my head. I've got a caramel craving," Stephanie reached across Michael's lap, her fingers grazing a glass candy dish on the side table. "You think there's any in here?"

Michael slapped Stephanie's hand away. "Would you focus, dammit? This was your idea! And besides, you don't even like Werther's Originals."

"That's true. They taste like feet."

Having covered that issue, Michael attuned his hearing to focus on the mysterious visitor who still held Mrs. Finster at the door. The man's deep, raspy voice exchanged words with Mrs. Finster's frail, wavery one, but the whole conversation was unintelligible. "Who do you think that is?"

"I dunno," Stephanie shrugged. "Probably some guy."

"Thanks," Michael said. "That helps not at all."

"Let's check it out then," Before Michael could object Stephanie was already up and in the foyer.

"Hey, wait up!" Michael followed, back past the countless photo frames and toward the front door, where Mrs. Finster was lost within the silhouette of a tall man against the daylight. As Michael approached, the man's skin remained dark, but his features resolved out of the shadow into an annoyed frown haloed with the graying stubble of an ill-shaved beard.

Michael reached the doorstep as Stephanie wrapped her arm around the old woman's shoulder as if she were a close relative eager to make it into her will. Steph turned to the man at the door. "Oh, hello."

The man tipped back his wide-brimmed hat with a grimace that projected the simple phrase "I don't have time for this" into the air around him. "Who the hell are you two?"

Michael opened his mouth, but couldn't manage a squeak.

"He's Michael Duckett and I'm Stephanie Dyer," Stephanie jerked her thumb at her chest with a wide smile that Michael wasn't sure was warranted. "We're P.I.s for hire. Oh. Nice. That rhymes. I need to write that down."

"P.I.s? I hate P.I.s," Now it really looked as if someone had taken a voluminous dump in this man's cereal. And judging by his expression, it had been chocolate cereal, so there would be a lot of difficulty in separating the two. To Michael's surprise and horror, the man flipped open a wallet which held a very shiny and very official police badge. "Always sticking their noses where they don't belong. Rex Calhoun. Detective. City Police. Get out of my way."

Stephanie stifled a laugh. "Your name is 'Rex Calhoun?' Get outta here with that!" She took a step back. "Are you from a 1930s gangster movie? Because that is bad ass."

Calhoun put his badge back into his coat and removed a notepad. Ignoring Stephanie, he turned back to Mrs. Finster, who was terribly confused by all of this. "Did you hire these two schmucks?"

"Why . . . uh . . . yes. I did," she stammered.

"Well, that's . . . unfortunate. Mind if I come in, Mrs. Finster?"

Mrs. Finster nodded and stepped aside. The detective—the real detective, complete with a real detective's badge and real detective's name—clomped his way through the door and, without any further politeness, made his way to the living room from whence Michael and Stephanie had come.

"Go home, kids," he grunted.

Michael leaned in towards Stephanie, "Okay. This is getting out of hand. Now there's a real police detective here? We could be in a lot of trouble! It's not a good idea to get messed up in this. Let's just leave now."

"Nonsense!" Stephanie smiled. "If anything, he can help us act like real detectives. He looks real hard-boiled. We need to be hard-boiled like that. All good detectives are hard-boiled. I read that somewhere."

"Where? The Denny's Breakfast Menu? Let's just cut our losses and leave!"

"What difference would it make? He knows our real names anyway. C'mon!" Stephanie dashed back toward the living room. "We've got nothing to lose!"

"I don't know if that's true!" Michael rasped, as he followed Stephanie into the living room. Calhoun and Mrs. Finster stood, discussing a photograph Calhoun had yanked from the hallway wall, leaving a noticeably lighter patch of paint.

He turned upon Stephanie's entrance, and his face performed a quick 180 from the good cop's bedside manner he had offered Mrs. Finster to the harsh scowl of a bad cop on the edge that had been pushed too far. "I thought I told you to get out of here!"

"Sir," Stephanie put her hands up in false authority. "Please. We'll be working with you today. Firstly, my colleague and I," she jerked a thumb back at Michael, who had only just caught up, "are new to the detective biz, per se, and we were wondering . . . how does one become 'hard-boiled?' I only ask because you seem to be quite hard-boiled yourself, sir. How would we, per se, get all up like that?"

"Stop saying 'per se!'" Michael turned to Calhoun. "Ignore her. Please."

"I was planning to ignore the two of you!" Calhoun gestured at Elena. "I'm here on important *official* business and I don't need you two getting in my way."

Stephanie cleared her throat. "Hold up. This dude's been missing for fourteen years and now you guys decide to investigate?"

"Listen, girl," Calhoun jabbed Stephanie's shoulder with the tip of his finger so hard that Michael could feel it. "Do I look like a guy who has a lot of patience? Get the hell out of here before I have you arrested!"

"No. How about *you* get out of here before I have *you* arrested?" Stephanie fired back.

"Excuse me . . ." Mrs. Finster's voice wavered in from the background.

Michael dug his fingers into Stephanie's shoulder and whispered in her ear. He could only just keep from yelling. "Are you insane?"

"Don't worry, Mike. I'm handling this. Just like we used to play when we were kids," Stephanie shook Michael's hand off and refused break her stare down with Calhoun. "We were retained as Private Investigators by our client Mrs. Finster and we aim to track down her husband. Isn't that right, Mrs. F?"

"Well . . ." Mrs. Finster began.

"Exactly," Stephanie finished. "You don't have to say another word, Mrs. F. Detective-client privilege." Michael was sure that wasn't a thing, but didn't want to dig them into a deeper hole by opening his mouth.

Calhoun's hands found their way into his belt loops, pushing aside his storm blue gabardine coat. His rough, hard-bitten exterior softened for an imperceptible second and Michael could almost see the crack of a grin beneath his silver stubble. Then it was gone, replaced by the hard stare of a man who was the living embodiment of "too old for this shit."

"Okay. That makes sense," his words were calm and measured, slipping out of his mouth in an orderly queue. "You're here for your client. Understood. Then I'll be on my way," he paused for a second, savoring his next phrase, "Once you show me your licenses."

Stephanie's eyes widened and darted back and forth. She leaned forward, as if expecting a clarification that Michael knew would never come. "I'm sorry. What?"

"Your licenses," Calhoun continued with relish. "If you two really are private investigators, surely you must have the required licenses. You do have them, don't you?"

Stephanie sucked a long breath through her teeth, then leaned backwards toward Michael. "Mike," she hissed. "I think I forgot our licenses at home."

"We don't *have* licenses," Michael said, through similarly gritted teeth. His nails dug into his palm so hard that they might have left gashes. "This is another one of the *myriad* reasons that this was a terrible idea!" Stephanie was steamrolling them directly into trouble, and he was frozen and powerless to stop it.

"Hm," Stephanie righted herself and turned back to Detective Calhoun, who had not moved a muscle. "So, Detective. What if—hypothetically—we didn't—hypothetically—have P.I. licenses?"

"Well, then that would be illegal!" There was a strong undercurrent of strange joy in Calhoun's voice. "Very. Illegal."

"Right," Stephanie nodded.

"I would have to arrest you," Calhoun nodded back, slowly. A grin crept across his face. It was unnatural, like seeing a goat smile.

"Hypothetically, of course," Stephanie said.

"Hypothetically," Calhoun confirmed, still nodding. "Of course."

CHAPTER TWELVE
Back Seat Confidential

Michael's wrists chafed against the cold steel handcuffs, but what hurt most was being thrown headfirst into the back of a police car. His skull connected against the opposite door handle and would be sporting a lump in short order. Stephanie followed suit, except her head connected with Michael's tailbone.

"Ow! Goddammit!" Michael had never been arrested before. It was the one thing he had hoped he could avoid during his life but, clearly, he had been very wrong.

"You two comfortable back there?" Calhoun yelled through the door before slamming it shut in advance of any answer. He had paraded them, handcuffed, a few blocks down through suburbia, as he had not found a closer parking spot.

Stephanie, her hands also cuffed behind her back, shuffled herself out of Michael's way and righted her body using only her feet. Michael didn't even want to look at her. The back of his head burned with anger at Stephanie and the top of his head burned with the still fresh pain of the door handle. He couldn't even imagine what his mother would say if word of his arrest made it down to Boca Raton. News traveled fast down there, he was told.

Calhoun walked around to the front of the car and angled his gaunt frame behind the steering wheel. A laptop mounted on a metal stand and gimbal extended over the passenger's seat. There was room there for a partner, but since Calhoun didn't seem the kind to make friends, Michael assumed it had been vacant for some time. Calhoun tried turning on the computer, but it clicked and gurgled in the way that computers shouldn't and did not respond. Not surprising, considering the laptop sported a few burn marks and other odd residual damage.

"You can't do this to us!" Despite Calhoun's reading of their Miranda rights, Stephanie was intent on providing him anything that could and would be used against them in a court of law. "We're detectives."

"What you *are* is interfering with a police investigation and operating as private investigators without the proper credentials," Calhoun craned his neck past his headrest and smiled at them. "And I'm going to make sure you're prosecuted to the full extent of the law."

"We were approached by our client—"

"Would you just shut up?" Michael barked at Stephanie and was met with a confused, hurt look.

"I don't care if you were approached by my ex-wife," Calhoun rebutted. "You're in a shitload of trouble," he reached for his radio, and after a brief crackle of static, spoke into it. "Brook. You there?"

The voice that came back was not the stoic one Michael had associated with the police, "Ugh. Calhoun. What the hell do you want now?"

"I've got two perps in the back here," he looked at the driver's licenses he had confiscated from them. "Michael Duckett and Stephanie . . . Aloysius Dyer. My computer's busted, so I need you to run a quick check for any priors. And make it snappy, too. I've got an elderly witness I'm questioning and I'd really like to get back to her before she dies. Over."

The voice on the other end garbled something that sounded like assent, but with a few extra curses tacked on for good measure.

"Detective," Michael opted to make one last, desperate plea for mercy, as he struggled to realign his glasses using only upward jerks of his head and neck, "We're incredibly sorry about all of this. We didn't know about the licenses. We were just trying to help out. You see, our rent went missing, and then this girl from the laundromat asked me on a date, which was weird for me, but then I went to this Italian restaurant and Stephanie dressed up like a waiter, but the girl stood me up, so we went to her apartment, and then there were ads. Like on the radio? For us. Do you understand what I'm saying?"

"Kid, nobody understands what you're saying!" Calhoun snarled.

Stephanie looked at Michael. "Maybe you should try that again, but this time take some breaks to breathe."

Michael's nose and face contorted into an almost hateful sneer. He was nearing his limit with Stephanie and was scared about what would happen if her antics were to push him any further. What could be further than actual jail time, Michael didn't know, but he did not want to find out. But beyond the fear and anger, Michael just felt tired. Stephanie had been his friend for so long, but keeping ahead of her ridiculous devil-may-care lifestyle and navigating her responsibilities for her had worn him down. He did not want to be responsible for her any longer. Especially when he couldn't really count on her for anything in return. It was just not fair. A mix of anger, guilt, and resentment sloshed around in his brainpan as Michael did his best to snap his face back into a less irritated look, but he was just forcing a flat smile.

"You never answered my question," Stephanie hadn't been paying attention to Michael's internal turmoil, as usual, and was eager to change the subject.

"I don't have to answer anybody's questions! Least of all, you. I'm the detective here!"

"Yeah, well, if you're such a great detective, why did you wait for fourteen years to investigate Mrs. Finster's missing husband?"

Calhoun leaned back over his headrest, "Why don't you mind your own goddamn business?"

"Because she's an old lady whose husband disappeared and you guys couldn't be bothered to care for over a decade!" Stephanie shouted with a strange undercurrent of caring behind her voice that Michael could not recall ever hearing before. "So why now?"

"It was a cold case. I only found the case file this week while sifting through some old records. And it's relevant to an ongoing investigation."

Michael paused his anger at Stephanie for a moment. "An ongoing investigation into missing people?"

"You know about this?"

"I know some Doctor named Coleman Supirn is missing and . . ." Michael paused with hope. "Terri Bradshaw?"

"What?" Calhoun asked. "The football guy?"

"No. Not the football—" Michael sighed. "Terri with an I. It's a woman. She's the girl from the date I told you about."

"Why, is she missing, too?"

"Yes!" Michael suppressed a groan. "I told you this."

"Was she struck by lightning?" Calhoun's face turned somewhat receptive.

"What? No! I don't know. Why would she be struck by lightning?"

"It'd be an excuse to get out of her date with you," Stephanie offered, before turning back to Calhoun. "But seriously, before we came to Mrs. Finster, we were hired to find Terri, too."

"Hired? By whom?"

"Uh . . ." Stephanie's eyes darted around the car. "I'd rather not say."

"Why not?" Calhoun growled. "Are you two hiding something else?"

"If we tell you," Stephanie winced, "you're gonna think we're crazy."

"We're already way past that point," Michael conceded. "Terri hired us to find herself."

Calhoun paused for a bit, inhaling and exhaling large amounts of air, before turning around, back to the steering wheel. "Okay. I'm done with you two screwing around with me. I have had it up to here!"

Michael couldn't see exactly where Calhoun was pointing but, if context clues would serve, it was probably a bit above his head.

"It's true, Rex!" Stephanie said, suddenly on a first name basis with the man. "Terri hired us on as detectives. She sent—"

"But you're *not detectives*!" Calhoun yelled. "That's why you're in the back of the car, and I'm in the front. Now if you don't shut up, I'm going to drive you down to the station right now so they can book—"

Calhoun's tirade was interrupted by another burst of static from the police radio. The voice of Brook—the cop that Calhoun had called earlier—garbled its way through the speaker, "Uh . . . Rex. What'd you say you're holding these two on?"

"They're operating as P.I.s without proper licenses," Rex snarled into the radio.

"Well, uh . . ." Brook paused. "According to records here, their licenses are current since last month."

"What?" Calhoun and Michael yelled, almost in unison.

"You better not be friggin' messing with me, Brook!" Calhoun continued. "This really isn't the time."

"I'm not screwing with you, Rex. They're real P.I.s. Proper docs and everything. I'm looking at them right now," Brook's harsh, staticy voice said. "You might wanna let them go."

"Yeah, Rex," Stephanie's smile was as big as a half moon. She was entirely too satisfied with this. "You might wanna let us go."

Soon, they were outside the car and Calhoun was unlocking their cuffs, grumbling. "I don't believe this."

"Yeah, me neither," Michael mumbled. He rubbed his wrists. He had only been in the cuffs for a few minutes but, still, they felt sore.

"Well?" Stephanie crossed her freed arms and glared at Calhoun.

Calhoun glared back, with greater intensity. "Well, what?"

"Where's our apology?"

"The only apology you're going to get is my boot in your ass."

"Well, that doesn't sound like an apology from any culture I've ever heard of," Stephanie tilted her head. "But I'll take it."

"I do *not* care," Calhoun's palm met his face. "I can't waste any more time with you assholes. Just get the hell out of here."

"C'mon, Steph," Michael's surprise and frustration had boiled over and made his fatigued bone-weariness clear to the world. Terri may be in trouble, but they weren't getting anywhere except into trouble themselves. He grabbed Stephanie by the loose shoulder of her jacket and tugged, desperate to leave. "Let's go."

"Nuh-uh," Stephanie shook her head. "We still have a client who's requested our services."

"Steph, no—"

"You wanna talk to the old lady? Fine!" Calhoun's irritation had boiled over and he was yelling, despite the fact that he was only a few inches away from their faces. "But you're coming with me!"

Calhoun led the two—Stephanie basking in her victory and Michael just as miserably reluctant as ever—back up the street to Mrs. Finster's house, with the powder blue paint job that complemented the dark navy wooden window shutters and the bright white door that hung ajar.

"Wait," Calhoun stopped at the foot of the walkway, extending his arm across Michael's chest like a protective mother. "Did you two leave the door open?"

"We were in cuffs, remember?" Michael muttered.

"Stay here," Calhoun drew his gun from his coat and stalked up the front stairs. After a good thirty seconds with his back against the wall, he pivoted into the doorway and out of sight.

"Well, that seems ominous," Stephanie said.

Michael let out a sigh that had been building in him for a while. "Steph, please. Let's just go. This whole thing is getting to be more trouble than it's worth. Terri hates me. She probably made this whole thing up to avoid dating me. I'm just that undateable. It really is the simplest solution. And whatever this Finster thing is almost got us arrested. It's time to call it quits. I'm getting really tired of—"

"No way, Mike. I'm staying right here," Stephanie stamped her foot on the ground, as if that amplified her statement. "Besides, aren't you the least bit curious about what's going on? The ads? That list? All the missing people? We might have no choice! And most importantly, we promised Mrs. Finster we'd help her out, and damn it if I'm not going to honor that promise. And shame on you for thinking otherwise. She trusted us and I don't intend to betray that trust. I refuse to let that sweet old lady down!"

Before Michael had time to digest Stephanie's little speech, Calhoun's frustrated yell pierced through the quiet suburban air. "Goddammit!"

Michael and Stephanie rushed inside.

CHAPTER THIRTEEN

No Case Too Crazy

The living room was in ruins. The coffee table was upturned and the rug beneath scrunched and bunched in various unnatural positions. The couch caught the worst of it, with its beautiful, if faded, floral patterns cut to ribbons. Their plastic covers had done little to protect them. And by the far wall, the fallen armoire, the sentry of the room, lay across the floor. Its solid wood construction remained undamaged, but that could not be said about the decorative plates and knickknacks it contained. Their pieces were strewn and scattered around the body of Mrs. Elena Finster.

"What . . . what happened?" Michael stared in shock from the archway between the hallway and the living room.

"Your guess is as good as mine, Dyer," Calhoun grumbled with a detached coolness Michael couldn't comprehend.

"I'm Duckett," Michael corrected. "She's Dyer."

"I don't care." That much was clear.

Somehow, Stephanie had managed to sneak past the two of them and knelt on the floor beside Mrs. Finster's lifeless body and amongst the shards of fancy china that littered the ground. "I am so sorry, Mrs. Finster. We failed you! We're not worthy! We beg your forgiveness! Please forgive—Wait. My bad. She's still breathing," Stephanie turned back to Calhoun. "She's just out cold."

Calhoun scrunched up his face. "Would you get the hell away from there? This is an active crime scene!"

"Sorry! Sorry! Sorry!" Stephanie tiptoed back to rejoin Michael and Calhoun at a safe distance. She cleared her throat and straightened her ratty jacket as if it had lapels. "So . . . uh . . . who do you think did this?"

"I don't know," Calhoun removed his fedora and gripped it so tightly it nearly crumpled in on itself, then jabbed it in Stephanie's direction. "What I do know is (a) that this whole thing is a bigger fiasco than I thought. And (b) you two better get the hell out of here, otherwise I'll definitely charge you with interfering with an investigation. I've already radioed for back-up and an ambulance. So cut your losses and make yourselves scarce."

"But it looks like we've got another case on our hands!" Steph attempted.

"You have *nothing*. Your client is the victim of a vicious assault and you no longer have no reason to be here. Just cut your losses and keep out of it," Calhoun replaced his hat on his head. "And thank your goddamn lucky stars I'm not taking you downtown."

"C'mon, Steph," Michael grabbed her shoulder and tugged once again, to no avail.

"But what if I knew who did it?" Stephanie blurted out for reasons Michael couldn't comprehend.

"Kid, seriously," Calhoun was getting tired, and, apparently, when he got tired he became kind. "Leave it to the professionals. You don't have a clue. Don't make me throw you out of here."

"Yeah," Michael agreed. "Let's just go. I'd rather not be tossed out onto the sidewalk. It looks like it hurts."

"But aren't you the least bit curious? Mrs. Finster's assault looks really suspicious. She was in a house all by herself! Who could've got in and out without leaving a trace?"

"Well, I mean, there're plenty of traces . . ." Michael gestured to the wanton destruction that had splayed itself across the living room.

"The details of this entire situation have been cherry-picked and orchestrated so magnificently as to be undecipherable. Except the perpetrators didn't count on one thing," Stephanie narrowed her eyes. "Me."

"Yes, I took a step backwards and looked at the bigger picture. Someone wanted to silence the old woman. Someone . . . or some thing."

"Steph, please stop," Michael pleaded.

Steph continued, even louder. "A sheet has been pulled over our eyes. Not just any sheet, but a woven blanket of deception. But, in the end, there is only one solution. And it is obvious," Steph paused to emphasize the drama of this asinine play she had created for herself. "A ghost did it."

There was only one appropriate response to that, and Michael gave it. "What."

*　　*　　*

The drive home was quiet. As Michael predicted, the impact of the concrete sidewalk had bruised most of his hips and backside, as well as any remaining sense of trust and camaraderie that had existed in this one-sided friendship. All in all, there was a rich tapestry of bruises, numerous and deep.

It was only when the sun started to go down, causing the sky to erupt in a brilliant red and purple, that Michael himself erupted, "You stupid idiot. A ghost? Why would—rrgh!"

"Listen, if you knew the things I knew, that wouldn't sound so crazy."

"And what do you know, Stephanie? Because from where I'm standing, it's *nothing*," Michael strained through gritted teeth, as his grip on the wheel tightened, "We almost got arrested and a woman is dead and you thought it was ghosts?"

"Just one," she corrected. "Let's not go bananas here."

"Jesus, what kind of backwards bizarro planet do you live on, Stephanie?" Michael crouched a little behind the steering wheel as a fleet of police cars passed them on the other side of the highway, sirens blazing. He knew where they were heading. Once the flashing red and blues no longer showed up in the mirror, Michael continued. "I mean, what the hell were you thinking? And on top of that, Terri is still missing and we're going to get evicted! This has been a gigantic waste of everyone's time."

Stephanie shrugged. "Hey, at least I got us out of there."

"That means absolutely nothing, Steph! It means jack shit!" A shorter silence passed before Michael let out a sigh so long, he might have died of hypoxia. "Y'know what? I've had it. We're done. Once we get back, you're getting those ads deleted. I don't care how curious you are about the situation. We're going to leave these disappearances to the real cops. If Terri really is missing, she'll be in better hands. And we're done here."

"Yeah. Okay. No more detecting . . ." Stephanie nodded and threw up her hands. There was a bit of sadness in her capitulation. "You were right, it was a bad idea to begin with."

"That's not what I mean," Michael gripped the wheel tighter and turned to Stephanie, "We are done. You and I. As soon as we get back, I'm packing up my stuff and I'm going to find a new apartment I can afford. By myself."

"Wait," Stephanie blinked, struggling to process this. "What are you talking about?"

"I'm sick of dealing with you, Stephanie!" Michael's knuckles turned white as he clutched the steering wheel and finally, after years and years of polite repression, he let his emotional floodgates fly open. "I've had to cover for you time and time again because you think you can just coast through life and not care about anything . . . at all! That's not how it works, Steph! That's not how it works and it's high time you learned that. I can't deal with you anymore. Paying for your rent. For your food. Keeping your ex-girlfriends and ex-boyfriends from finding you, and now navigating a murder that you seem way too interested in despite the fact we really could get arrested! Getting sucked into your black hole of a life is not what I had planned for my mid-to-late twenties! And I've had it. I've really had it."

"But . . . Mike . . ."

Things continued to pour out. "You live in some sort of ridiculous fantasy world where private detectives and ghosts exist, and you expect everyone else around you to accommodate you. You need to grow up, and fast! For the absolute longest time, I've done my best to support you and be a good friend. I always get suckered or guilted into it, even though you never learn. But today has made me realize that it's not worth it. It's never been. You're an embarrassment, Stephanie. A complete embarrassment and I am so out. I'm just so . . . tired."

Once he had finished, Michael felt like a huge weight had been taken off his chest. Like he could breathe again. But the long silence that followed threatened to suffocate him.

"Okay." was the only thing Stephanie said before going uncharacteristically quiet for the rest of the ride.

Eventually, the Garbagemobile ground to a halt across the street from their apartment. Michael inserted the tire brick with grim stoicism and the two of them walked up through the building, with Stephanie trailing at least one flight of stairs behind Michael in order to avoid his air of grim disapproval. The dim moonlight filtered through the musty, caged hallway windows, casting shadows across the linoleum floor, which was caked with god knows what. They both would miss this place, although Michael was unsure as to exactly why. Though their official eviction was a week away, it felt like the last time they would be here. Michael was surprised by how reserved Stephanie was. He expected her to beg for forgiveness, but she didn't. Not that she would have gotten it. It was far too little and far too late.

Michael went straight into his room and shut his door without a word. Sitting on the edge of his bed, he put his head in his hands and sighed. The cold evening air whistled through the brickhole. He did feel a little bad about how he had treated Stephanie. But he was justified, wasn't he? After years of basically acting as the parent to a twenty-something womanchild, wasn't he entitled to finally put his foot down? It was a legitimate grievance. His mom and dad—well, mom, mostly—had enforced strict boundaries on him when he was a kid. Maybe too strict, but at least he turned out to be a functional adult for the most part. Had Stephanie's aunt and uncle never laid down the law? Steph never talked about them—nor her parents—and when they did come up in conversation, she blew it off as if they didn't matter and cracked a joke about something else. Just like she treated everything else in her life.

A small whooshing noise brought Michael out of his head and back into the world. Michael glanced across the room and saw a large open book lying on the floor. Even from his position on the bed, Michael could see the tell-tale selection of black and white group photos that telegraphed "yearbook."

Michael walked over, lamenting the fact that he lived in an apartment where the space between the door sill and the threshold was wide enough to slide a yearbook through. Bent at the waist, he gazed down at the open pages: a snapshot of his and Stephanie's time through middle school. It was blatant emotional manipulation, but Michael bit anyway. There were pictures of the French Club, the JV

Basketball Team and the Chess Club. Neither Michael nor Stephanie had belonged to any of those organizations, but on Steph's dare, they had both managed to sneak into their yearbook photos. Michael almost found himself smiling. He remembered the Coach, their PE teacher at the time, being furious when he saw it at the end of the year. Then again, Coach Finster was always angry at the two of them. It didn't help that his son was a good-for-nothing bully.

Oh, no. God damn it. Michael thought as the obvious dawned on him. That's why he was so familiar. Arthur Finster had been their elementary school gym teacher. Neither of them ever looked back after graduating, so if he did indeed go missing, they wouldn't have known. Michael picked up the yearbook. It tilted in his grip due to something heavy weighing down the back cover. He flipped to it—the faculty listings—with Mr. Finster's bald headshot smiling at him with a small, yet annoying, chip on one of his front teeth. What had been sandwiched between the pages was a familiar picture frame. "Live. Laugh. Love" it commanded, just as it had on Elena Finster's wall from which Stephanie had certainly pilfered it. A sticky note with the words **GUESS WHO** obscured a man's stocky build in a photo. Removing the note revealed Arthur Finster's chubby face, balding red head, and chipped tooth. All the bells in Michael's head finally rang.

This wasn't just emotional blackmail. Stephanie was trying to drag him back into the private eye thing again. This was getting out of hand, and Michael still wanted no part of it. Strange as it sounded, he wanted to wait out the rest of the weekend and return to his normal, boring grind at The Future Group on Monday. If the universe wanted this bullshit solved, it would have to do it without his help.

"Nice try, Steph," Michael yelled as he snapped the book closed. "We're not doing this. I'm not forgiving you, and I'm not going to follow this weird breadcrumb trail you keep insisting on putting together."

When no reply came back, Michael picked up the yearbook and moved to the door. He had to, yet again, confront Stephanie, since she still hadn't got it through her thick, obstinate skull. Now, more than ever, as far as Michael was concerned, the last straw had been placed.

But it really hadn't.

"Holy hell!" was the appropriate response to seeing an anonymous woman standing two inches away from one's face upon opening a door. It was the appropriate response for a lot of things that were happening today, and, given his experience, Michael delivered the line exceptionally well. Michael stumbled back, clutching his chest and dropping the yearbook in the process. The picture frame tumbled to the ground, its glass splintering.

"Oh, god. It's you," Michael said once he caught his breath. "How the hell did you get in here?"

"I told you I'd come to you." Her icy blue eyes glared at him beneath loose, frizzy locks dyed so blonde that their visible brown roots popped. She crossed her arms. "We haven't discussed my case yet."

Stephanie's door creaked open and she stuck her head out, shooting repeated glances between Michael and the young woman. "Mike, do you know this lady?"

"Yes. Unfortunately. This is uh . . . um . . ." Michael rubbed the back of his neck as he realized that he didn't know the woman's name. "This is a crazy lady who won't stop stalking me."

Stephanie whispered, despite the fact that all three parties were standing mere inches from one another. "I dunno why you always say you have trouble with women," her eyes scanned the woman's body, in spite of the fact that it was hidden beneath a trench coat. "Mama like."

"Dorabell Underwood." The woman finally put a name to her crazed face.

"Cute," Stephanie nodded. "Did your parents misspell 'adorable' or 'doorbell?'"

Dorabell gave that comment the glare it deserved.

"Silent type, huh? Very nice. Wanna buy me a drink sometime?"

Dorabell gave up on Stephanie and turned her attention directly to Michael, "I'm here to talk to you about my fiancé. I think he's having an affair. I need you to investigate him."

A grin began to make its way across Stephanie's face, but Michael cut it off at the pass. "Yeah. The problem with that is that we're *not detectives!* He switched into his manic mode. It was not much of a transition from his usual anxious mode, just louder. "And how the hell did you get into our damn apartment?"

"Well, I rang your buzzer a few minutes ago, but no one answered," Dorabell said. No one would have answered, as the apartment buzzer was broken, along with pretty much everything else in this shithole. Dorabell continued, "Then I saw that your window was open, so I decided to climb in."

Michael was less than thrilled. "You can't just climb into people's apartments in the middle of the night! Who does that? Maybe that's why your fiancé is cheating on you!"

"Hey," Dorabell said. "I think you've got some issues."

"I've got some iss—" Michael ran his hands through his loose mop of hair. "Rrgh! Listen, Dorabell, or whatever your name is. I've had kind of a long week. My date stood me up, then she went missing, then we went to see an old woman who got murdered, and now I've come home to a crazy person who's broken into my apartment! Which won't even be my apartment anymore because this moron here doesn't know how to live a real life. Of course I have some issues."

"Yeah, I don't care about any of that," Dorabell waved Michael's litany of irritations away. "I'm hiring you to investigate my fiancé. So leave your personal problems out of it. Now are you gonna listen or not?"

Stephanie remained silent, but the look in her eyes was pleading for a yes. Michael still did not know why she was so gung-ho about all this detective business. She had never been gung-ho about anything except being lazy.

"No. I'm not going down this rabbit hole," Michael shook his head. "Not again. I'm done. I'm going to bed."

"Look, guy," Dorabell pivoted around Michael so fast that she may have been magic. She stood between him and his room and poked her manicured finger in his chest. "I don't care about whatever lover's quarrel you two are having. But I'm not leaving this apartment until you agree to help me. I'm hiring you whether you like it or not."

Michael stood still for a minute, her intimidating glare focused up through their five-inch height differential. He rolled his eyes. "Fine."

"By the way, your P.I. licenses were in your mail," Dorabell held up two envelopes. The seal of the city's Department of Security and Investigative Services, a golden eagle using binoculars, was emblazoned on the corner. "I don't want to tell you how to do your jobs, but you might want to keep these safe."

"You went through our mail?" Michael yanked the envelopes out of her hand. He tore open the first envelope to find a certificate from the Board of Licensure with Stephanie's name on it. He assumed the other one contained his.

"Whoa!" Stephanie grabbed the certificate from him. "Neat. How'd that happen?"

"How should I know?" Michael's voice hit an annoyed pitch. "I didn't take a test. Hell, I don't know if there is a test!"

Michael stopped his whining as Dorabell cleared her throat. "Thank you. As I was saying, my fiancé has been leaving the apartment at odd hours during the past month."

"Alright, fine," Michael said. "Does he just get out of bed and leave? If he's having an affair, I would think he'd be sneakier than that."

"Well, no. He leaves with me. I work the night shift at the hospital," Dorabell, finally providing an explanation for her dress, opened her long coat to reveal her mint green scrubs.

"He leaves . . . with you?" Stephanie asked. "What excuse does he give?"

"He says it's late night lab work at the university. He has to check on some models he 'left running.'"

"And you don't trust him," Michael finished her thought.

"No," Dorabell was surprisingly firm, she pushed a few curls out of her eyes, "But I love him and I want you to prove me wrong."

"Not to play couple's therapist here," Stephanie flipped her wrist. "But if there's this kind of unsubstantiated distrust this early, I don't think marriage is the right direction for you two."

"Unsubstantiated?" Dorabell dug through her pocket and slammed something down on the coffee table. "I found this in his jacket. How's this for unsubstantiated?"

Her hand slid back to reveal a matchbook. The cover design was awful, purple text on a bright yellow background. It read: 'Des Creté Motel. One Inconvenient Location. 7113 Spruce-Pine Lane.'

"Alright. Fine. I guess that's evidence," Michael admitted. "Why would he be carrying this? Does he smoke?"

"No, but I do," Dorabell yanked a pack of cigarettes from her purse. "He might have picked it up for me subconsciously. At any rate, he mentioned his 'models' again tonight, so I'm betting he's going back there. I need you guys to follow him. And I hope you don't find him with the literal kind of models."

"Couldn't you just stalk him yourself?" Michael asked. "You seem to be pretty good at it."

"I would, but I've got another shift tonight. The morgue's not going to watch itself."

"You work the graveyard shift at the morgue?" Stephanie took a step back.

"Yeah," said Dorabell. "Is that a problem?"

"Actually, maybe you can help me with a theory of mine." Stephanie lowered her voice. "Ever see any of the bodies . . . come alive at night?"

"Are you serious." The look on Dorabell's face indicated that this was not a question, but more of a statement.

"Do they do the Monster Mash?" Stephanie continued, anyway.

"You," Dorabell pointed to Stephanie, "shut up." She turned again to Michael, "You. Do this for me and I'll get out of your hair. I can pay you as much as five hundred dollars."

Michael sighed. He just wanted to go to bed, but with Dorabell's attitude, he knew that wasn't going to be an option. He would have to budge yet again. But this. This would be the last time. "Yeah. Great. We'll get back to you."

"Good. I'll text you a picture of him and my address, if you need it," Dorabell walked into the living room, realigning her handbag over her bony shoulder. Michael followed, with Stephanie hanging behind. Dorabell walked over to the still open window and slung her leg over the sill and onto the fire escape.

"Y'know, we have a door," Michael said.

"Whatever."

"Hey," Stephanie called over Michael's shoulder, directly by his ear. "We're kinda new to the whole detective thing, so, it'd really help us out if you told us what your guy's name is."

"Matteo," Dorabell replied before disappearing into the night, "Matteo Carrera."

"Shit," Michael said, as Stephanie let out an extended "ooh."

CHAPTER FOURTEEN
An Affair to Forget

Michael and Stephanie made their way up to the edge of town, past the Finsters' slice of suburbia where some semblance of a forest began. Nestled carefully amongst the deciduous greenery alongside a road much less traveled was their point of interest. Despite its fancy name, the Des Creté Motel was a traditionally trashy complex that sat in its own little bubble: a poorly lit realm of discarded trash, hazardous waste, and rusted vehicles. The air was musky and the shadows told no tales. For people who moved in such illicit circles, it was the perfect place for sexy liaisons and the kind of place Michael's mother had always told him to avoid.

Michael maneuvered the Garbagemobile to the far corner of the parking lot and it screeched to a halt. Michael and Stephanie emerged from the car and settled in the darkness amongst the bushes that surrounded the parking lot, providing them with more than adequate cover.

"So tell me I'm not alone in this: do you think those bodies at the morgue really do the Monster Mash?" said Stephanie, pushing aside a thicket of dark leaves. "I've been told it was a graveyard smash."

"Are you still talking about that?" Michael poked a set of binoculars through the undergrowth, "This is your problem, Stephanie. You can't take a damn thing seriously. Either you don't care or you're just making jokes. You can't just be a functioning, responsible adult."

"I can be responsible!" Stephanie scoffed and pressed her hand to her chest in a sign of offense. "Remember that time I invested our money in an IRA?"

"You invested our money in *the* IRA!"

"Man, whatever. You know what *your* problem is? You take things way too seriously! You always get paralyzed by anxiety, Mike. It's kind of annoying. You need—"

"If you're going to say that I need you," Michael snapped, "you can shove it. Nothing's going to change my mind. I'm already mentally packing my stuff."

"I was just going to say that you need to chill the hell out. Nothing matters nearly as much as you think it does. Life can just be confusing sometimes, y'know? So relax."

"Maybe I'll finally get to relax out once you're out of my life. There'll be no one to drag me into stupid—ttssh!" Michael raised his hand. "Someone's coming!"

Through the binoculars, Michael made out a figure walking down the far end of the motel. Its occasional forays into the sodium glow of the parking lot's lamps revealed a young man, about Michael's and Stephanie's age, with coffee brown skin and almost silken black hair that fell over his oversized glasses. Based on a picture Dorabell had texted Michael, this was almost certainly her fiancé, Matteo Carrera. At least, he resembled the low-res picture, but was slightly less blurry in real life.

"It's him," Michael confirmed. "But why was his name on the list of missing people?"

"Great question. Don't know. Now lemme see!" Stephanie grabbed the binoculars, snapping them in half at the hinge. Perhaps using binoculars from a children's fast food meal was not the best choice for this assignment, but they were the only ones they could procure on such short notice.

Michael glared at her, but Stephanie paid him no mind, squinting through her half of the newly-formed monoculars. Michael took the other half. Matteo Carrera did a brief check of the surroundings, as all suspicious people do, before engaging in a two-minute struggle with his motel room door. He bashed it open with his shoulder and slinked inside.

"He's going into room 110," Michael caught a glimpse of the numbers on the door, painted in what looked like whiteout.

"Oooh," Stephanie's fingers danced in the air. "Looks like someone's gonna get saucy."

"Alright," Michael tossed his half of the binoculars over his shoulder and began to walk back to the car. "We're done here."

"What?" Stephanie spun around, "Aren't we going to find out who he's doin' it with?"

"Of course not! We found out he's having an affair. That's it. Dorabell will pay us regardless."

"Well, it wouldn't hurt to find out," Stephanie shrugged. "We could even get a bonus. Plus, we might get to see Dorabell and the side chick duke it out. I'd pay good money for action like that."

"Y'know what? You stick around and look. As for me, I'm done. I don't—" A thunderous crack interrupted Michael and he dropped to the ground, in order to avoid potential bullets. But no further gun noises came, only a loud rumbling that devolved into a faint tremor. "What the hell was that?"

Stephanie remained crouched and steady. She put the monocular to her eye and stared back out at the motel, "Uh . . . Mike, do motel rooms usually glow?"

"What are you talking about?"

"Like . . . bright blue," Stephanie whispered. "Because this guy's room is doing that."

Michael turned around. He didn't need a monocular to see that the door and windows of Room 110 were ablaze with a strange blue glow that couldn't be natural. "What . . . the hell?"

"This is shady as shit," Stephanie said. "Dude's up to something."

"Yeah . . . uh . . ." Michael had to agree. He couldn't stop staring at the light. "I think you're right."

"Go check it out. I'll be right back," Stephanie jumped up. "This is so cool that I gotta go to the bathroom!"

As she darted away, Michael crouched down and, with his arms hanging over his knees, scuttled himself through the bushes and over to Room 110. He attempted to peer over the edge of the window, but the thick red curtains obfuscated any view of the events transpiring within. He could only see two vague dark blurs ensconced in a sea of blue light blurs. The light, though dim, still managed to hurt his eyes, so Michael ducked back down and leaned against the sheetrock motel wall.

What was going on in there? What did Matteo Carrera have to do with anything? Whatever was going on, it was either completely bonkers or Stephanie had finally driven Michael past the point of insanity and this was a symptom of a complete mental break. Given the strain of the past day, the second option seemed incredibly likely.

"Heyo!" Michael almost jumped as Stephanie rejoined him beneath the window. "You figure out what this is all about?"

"No," Michael whispered back. "I can't see a damn thing. Did you find the bathroom?"

"Nope. Just went in some bushes," Stephanie said, tossing away a multi-tool she had been carrying. "On my way back I slashed Matteo's rear tire so he can't get away if we have to chase him. And now my Swiss army knife is busted, so you're welcome for that sacrifice."

"You had a Swiss army knife?"

"You know me. I'm always prepared."

"I do know you and you're never prepared," Michael scoffed as he came to a realization. "Wait. How did you know which car was his?"

"Well, I wasn't sure, so I did it to all the cars in the parking lot. Just to cover our bases."

Michael breathed in and covered his face, anticipating the answer to his next question. "Did you also slash *our* rear tire?"

The eerie glow danced across Stephanie's face as she bit her lower lip. "There wasn't a lot of time to think. So . . . uh . . . I'll have to check."

Michael sighed.

"Anyway, now that we can't leave," Stephanie dusted off her hands and rose off her haunches. "Let's go in and see what this glowing business is all about!"

"I dunno . . . we don't know what he's doing in there," Michael whispered up at her. "This could be dangerous. We need to hang back and think of a pl—"

"Too late!" It was indeed too late, Stephanie had already backed up ten feet and took a running start at the door. At the last minute she jumped into the air and delivered a flying kick to the door's hollow, plastic broadside and with a loud bang she fell into the room.

Michael peered in after her. Above Stephanie's body, which was splayed at an odd angle across the door that lay dented and broken on dingy motel carpet, stood Matteo Carrera with his eyes open so wide that they almost filled the giant lenses of his glasses. Matteo's loose flannel shirt ruffled in the rough breeze caused by the giant, swirling, blue vortex that bathed the entire wood-paneled room in its hypnotically pulsing glow. Michael couldn't comprehend what it was or where it had come from. But one thing was for sure: it was precisely the type of vortex you would not expect to find on the lower floors of a backwoods sex motel.

"Oh. Whoops. This isn't our room!" Stephanie grinned up from the floor. "We'll have to call the front desk about the door. And about this giant blue hole in your wall. Is your bathroom leaking?"

Beside Matteo, who remained shocked and speechless, stood a woman who looked remarkably familiar. As Michael's eyes adjusted to the brightness of the room, he realized that it was Dorabell Underwood. But she looked altogether different. Instead of her hospital scrubs, she was dressed down in jeans and a conservative, knitted cream sweater. Her frizzy blonde hair from earlier in the night had been wrangled and bunched into a tight, professional ponytail. What caught Michael's attention, though were her eyes, still a striking ice blue, but the fierceness that had stared him down earlier was absent.

Dorabell rolled her eyes and sighed, before doing a quick about-face and stepping into the portal behind her. It absorbed her with a loud glorp, as if someone had upturned a jar of mayonnaise and let the contents drop out onto a kitchen floor.

Matteo turned and reached out to his disappearing fiancée, "No! Wait! It's not what it looks like."

"To be honest," Stephanie picked herself up off the floor, "I'm not exactly sure what this looks like. Mike, you got any ideas?"

Michael could only stare agog.

"Okay, Mike's outta commission," he faintly heard Stephanie say as she turned back to Matteo. "You're Matteo Carrera, right?"

"Uh . . . yeah," Matteo pushed his glasses up his nose and stood with his hands on his hips, attempting to look indignant, despite having been found at a clear disadvantage, "Who . . . who're you?"

"I'm Stephanie Dyer," Stephanie jerked her thumb over her shoulder. "This over here is my associate, Michael Duckett. We're private investigators."

"You don't look like detectives."

"Well, we're new at this. Didn't have time to get the right hats. Anyway, you mind telling us what's going on with all . . ." Stephanie waved her hand limply in the direction of the terrifying portal that had devoured the wall between the bed and the bathroom. " . . . all this noise?"

"Oh, this?" Matteo attempted a weak smile, and glanced back at the whirlpool of intense swirling, roiling energy. "This is . . . uh . . . nothing. Nothing at all. These old motel lights . . . must be malfunctioning."

"Bullshit," Stephanie pressed on, determined. "What's going on here? Your fiancée hired us to track you and now it looks like you're in cahoots? What was she doing here?" Then added, "Oh, and you wouldn't be responsible to all those missing people, would you?"

"And why did your girlfriend jump into that goddamn vortex?" Michael finally found his words.

"Yes. The vortex is also a concern," Stephanie concurred. She pulled out her cell phone from her pocket and flipped it open. "Give us some answers, Carrera, or we call the cops!"

"I'm not doing anything illegal!"

"Okay," Michael said. "Then we'll call your fiancée!"

"Oh, god. No!" Matteo waved his hands and began backing up, desperate to avoid that fate. "Please no. I promise I'll tell you everything. Just give me . . . one . . . minute!" With a quick turn and leap, Matteo Carrera escaped, glorped up into the wild blue yonder.

"Well, we should've seen that coming," Stephanie turned to Michael. "We should go after him."

"Stephanie, no! I don't know what this is, but it is not cool!" Is what Michael would have said, had the portal not started to judder, shake and discharge arcs of electricity which scorched the motel room floor. The stench of burnt, urine soaked carpet filling his lungs. Michael could only utter a quiet yelp as Stephanie did not wait for an answer, grabbed his hand and once again yanked him into something he did not understand and toward a fate he didn't want anything to do with.

CHAPTER FIFTEEN

Next 'Verse

Michael woke up in bed. Or, more accurately, on a bed. Blinking twice, he sat up and took stock of his surroundings. Judging from the poor interior design which, based on the presence of wood paneling, dated back to the 1970s, and the dank musty smell, which may have dated back to the 1870s, he was still in the Des Creté motel.

"Steph?" Michael whispered, using his voice to probe the room. He fixed his glasses which sat askew across his face. "Steph, are you there?"

A woman's hand emerged from the narrow crevice between the bed and the wall and slammed itself down on the comforter, letting up a plume of dust. Michael nearly screamed until a muffled "Yo!" followed.

"Would you get up?" Michael sighed as he swung his legs over the opposite side of the bed. He smacked his lips together, trying to rid his mouth of a dry chalky taste that had somehow found its way in there, coating his tongue. Failing that, Michael walked across the room and drew open the curtains. The purple-orange glow of a late summer evening filtered through the motel's window grime. How long had he been asleep? Had it been almost 24 hours?

Stephanie flopped backwards across the bed. "My mouth tastes like rocks, though."

"Yeah, mine too."

"So what happened? Did *anything* happen?"

"Steph, I don't know and I don't care!" Michael turned around. "The whole thing was nuts. Thank god we're still alive! Let's just cut our losses and go home."

"Alright, Mike. We lost him," Stephanie nodded with solemn regret and joined him at the door. "You were right again. We shouldn't have stuck our noses where they didn't belong."

Michael opened the door and let the remnants of the day stream in before walking out into the parking lot. An errant breeze stirred some fallen leaves, and the street lights' low buzz jittered a bit before continuing uninterrupted.

"Stephanie," Michael sucked in a deep breath and bit his lip.

"Yes, Mike?"

"Where's our car?" Indeed, the Garbagemobile was not where they had left it. In fact, the lot was completely empty aside from the stray leaves and some oil stains. At least, Michael hoped they were oil stains. "Where are all the cars?"

Stephanie shrugged.

"Son of a bitch."

*   *   *

It took Michael and Stephanie nearly an hour of walking before they spotted a lone cab searching the edge of suburbia for a fare like a grandparent canvassing a toy store for a "Nintendo Playstation." Soon, they were on their way back to civilization, Stephanie gazing out the window, and Michael digging around in his pockets for the strange cell phone, but having nothing to show for it. "Are you kidding me? I'm missing my phone now, too?"

"I thought you said it couldn't be your phone," said Stephanie, making eye contact with the outside world with her chin resting in her palm.

"That's not the point. It's the principle of the thing," Michael stopped his phone hunt. He remembered leaving it in the car, which was now conveniently also missing. "Whatever. Screw it. Do you mind telling me what happened?"

"I dunno, dude," Stephanie's tone was flat and matter-of-fact. "We jumped into a glowing portal thing that spat us out where we came from. What else do you want me to say?"

"*We* didn't jump anywhere. You dragged me into it without even thinking or considering what I wanted to do," Michael said, as the cab driver shut his scratched-up plexiglass divider, correctly anticipating a fight.

"Because otherwise you were just going to freeze in place like you always do."

"If I did, then at least I'd still have a car," Michael pinched his nose where his glasses had made indents over the night. "I don't understand. You keep on dragging us head first into this nonsense. And egging me on with that yearbook? That was low, even for you. Why do you want to follow this through? Why now? You've always been content being mediocre and lazy. You've never cared about anything before!"

Stephanie finally turned to face Michael, her voice just shy of yelling, "And why don't you? You're not the least bit curious! I thought you'd at least care about Terri going missing, but the moment things got too scary for you, you gave up. At least I kept trying. You're the one who doesn't care about anything. And what yearbook?"

Michael was taken aback by the sudden fervor, an oddity in the otherwise lax emotional spectrum of Stephanie Dyer. Soon, he found his words. "Don't play dumb and don't turn this shit on me. Today has been far too long and far too ridiculous. I'm a simple guy, Stephanie. I don't want to die or get arrested. Both of which we've narrowly avoided today, mind you. All I want to do is get up, go to work, come home, go to bed and enjoy my life."

"You call that 'enjoying your life'?"

Michael ignored that. "I'm not built for this, and my mental state would be better off without it. But you insist on dying on this hill and I don't know why!"

"Yeah?" Stephanie crossed her arms and looked away. "Well maybe you don't know everything about me."

The second ride in the space of 24 hours passed in tense, uncomfortable silence. After taking an unwanted, more scenic route, the cab stopped in front of their apartment, which somehow looked even more dilapidated than they had left it. Stephanie got out and walked away, leaving Michael to deal with the fare. Michael threw whatever bills he had in his wallet through the window of the cab, and stormed after her into the building.

"Where the hell are you going?" By the time Michael called out to her, Stephanie had already cleared the hallway and was bounding up the stairs two at a time.

"If you're gonna continue to be up your own ass, I'm gonna solve this thing myself," her voice echoed down the stairwell and began to fade out.

Michael sighed and started the trek up after her. Five flights later, he was heaving out his lungs. Leaning on his knees, he pushed open the door that Stephanie had left ajar. If there had been any more air in him, the sight of a completely empty apartment would have knocked it out.

"What?" He gasped. "Where's all our stuff?"

The apartment didn't respond, but a stiff autumn breeze blew through the open window and across the barren, patchy carpet. Michael's only reply came in the form of a loud, repeated banging from what was, or perhaps had been, Stephanie's room. He walked down the hall, taking his time to inspecting the walls as if hoping that the framed pictures of him, his family and Stephanie would suddenly reappear. He spotted Stephanie through her doorframe, raising a large monkey wrench over her head and slamming it into the baseboard with a resounding crack.

"Got it," she tossed the wrench aside and yanked the wood plank out of the wall. She rolled up one sleeve of her loose jacket and reached blindly into the hole.

"What are you looking for?" Michael asked. "There's nothing here. Mr. Doppelopolous must've moved all our crap out while we were gone."

"Well, if that's true. Ain't no way he found this." Stephanie's thoughtful grimace turned into a grin of victory as she extricated what she had apparently been looking for: a non-descript white sack containing an oblong, bulky object. The object weighed heavy in her hands as she wiped off the accumulated dust bunnies with her sleeve.

"What is that?" Michael asked.

"Don't worry about it. I need it," she snapped and pushed past Michael on her way back out, cradling her mysterious sack in her arms. "I've got better places to be."

"Where are you going?"

"I told you! I'm going to solve this thing," Stephanie said as she walked out the front door, leaving Michael standing in the emptiness. A moment passed before her head popped back in, "If you want to come, you can. But, for the record, I don't care anymore."

*   *   *

"You know, it'd help if you told me where exactly we're headed," Michael yelled after Stephanie. He was trailing her by about half a block, but not out of choice, she was storming headfirst toward wherever she was going. At least she seemed to have a plan, for once.

"You haven't noticed have you?" She didn't turn back.

"Noticed what?"

"Never mind. I don't want to spoil the surprise. We're going to find Matteo and Doorbell. Those two lovebirds have a lot of explaining to do."

"How do you know where they are?"

"She texted you their address. I remembered it. Try to keep up." Michael could feel Stephanie smiling. "Not so great being the Robin to a Professional Batman, is it?" Having been the only responsible person in their friendship, Michael hated to admit that it was a little uncomfortable being left in the dust of a self-described "Professional Batman". Only after mulling this over for a few moments did he realize exactly what Stephanie had found in their apartment.

*   *   *

"This is stupid," Michael repeated for the third time, his arms crossed.

Stephanie, also for the third time, paid him no heed and instead focused on aiming the grappling hook gun she had removed from her secret white sack. She aimed the shooty end up towards the apartment that belonged to Dorabell and her fiancé.

"Stephanie, this is stupid." The fourth time. Michael remembered her off-hand comment about buying a grappling hook, but he never bothered to ask why she hid it behind a wall, nor how she could afford a grappling hook but never make the rent. But those concerns were secondary at the moment. Right now, Michael had to manage this impromptu break-and-enter. "How do you even know that's the right apartment window?"

Stephanie lowered the gun and sighed. "Doorbell's info said they lived in 4C. That's the fourth floor and it's the third apartment from the right. 4C."

"Oh, yeah? What if it's alphabetized the opposite way?"

"Then we'll burn that bridge when we come to it," Stephanie pushed her hair out of her eye line and recommenced her deliberate aiming procedures.

"Have you ever even shot a gun before?"

"Maybe. No. Does it matter?"

"Kinda, yeah!"

"Shut up. I'm trying to concentrate."

Michael sighed, taking off his glasses in exasperation. A few minutes of quiet focus later, Stephanie pulled the trigger. With a silenced puff, the three-pronged hook sailed through the air, its rope fluttering behind it. Surprisingly, her aim was true and the hook did indeed make it to apartment 4C, but, instead of latching onto the bannister of the fire escape, it made contact with the window and shattered it. Stephanie winced. She pushed a secondary button on the side of the gun, which retracted the hook, but instead of snagging the hook onto anything relevant, it merely pulled itself four stories back down, landing on the sidewalk with a loud clatter. The two of them steeled themselves, expecting to be yelled at, but nothing came. Perhaps the couple wasn't home.

"Okay," Stephanie reeled in the remainder of the rope and aimed again. "Next time I'll get it."

"And if you do get it? What then?"

"I'll just hoist myself up," Stephanie did not divert her gaze from her target.

"You can't possibly believe that you have the core strength necessary to scale your way up the side of this building."

"I did like five push-ups earlier today, dude. I'm good. Like, man push-ups, too."

"Give me that!" Michael yanked the grappling hook gun out of Stephanie's grip. He re-aimed it a great deal lower and pulled the trigger. This time the hook hit its mark: the lower rung of the fire escape ladder ten feet away. With a quick tug, Michael pulled it down to ground level. "There. How about that?"

"Yeah, alright. That might work," Stephanie said, then added, "Thanks."

"No problem," Michael grumbled as they clanged their way up four flights of fire escape. The two of them gingerly picked away any remaining shards of broken glass left in the window frame and hoisted themselves in.

Stephanie let out an impressed whistle as she surveyed the apartment. "Huh. Not bad. Much nicer than ours was."

Michael grimaced. Everyone else was able to afford an apartment where the walls weren't made of lead and rats. Matteo and Dorabell's was similar in layout to Michael and Stephanie's apartment, but at least twice as large. A beautiful sofa with leather the color of artisanally crafted coffee ruined by 2% milk stood against the wall, flanked by a large fish tank aglow with specialized lighting. How they could afford this on the salaries of a morgue attendant and a graduate student was beyond comprehension.

As Michael walked past the coffee table, the mail and newspapers atop it neatly arranged beneath a bevy of remote controls, Stephanie turned her attention to the fish tank. She tapped on the glass, and the fish inside scattered like a frightened rainbow. "Hey, look! Fish!"

"Stop touching things! This isn't our stuff," Michael snapped as he turned on the lights. "Now what do we do?"

"I dunno. It doesn't look like they're here. I guess we wait?"

"This is the stupidest thing we've ever done," Michael said, then added, "this week."

"Hey, I dunno about you, but I want to get to the bottom of this. And these two are up to some sort of hanky-panky, so we're going to grill 'em," Stephanie jabbed her finger into Michael's chest before turning around. "So do you think we're allowed to feed their fish?"

"I don't know, Steph! I don't know what the proper courtesies are when committing a crime!" Michael's face met his palm and he took a seat on the leather sofa, cradling his head in his hands. "I don't know what's going on here. But you—" He was silenced as the deadbolt lock of the apartment door swung open to reveal Matteo Carrera. Behind him was Dorabell herself, in her knitted cream sweater with her hair tied back into a tamed ponytail. She looked exactly as Michael and Stephanie had seen her the night before, just prior to her disappearance into the strange blue portal.

"Holy Hell!" was the correct response to seeing a random man and his gun-toting female friend standing in the middle of your apartment at three in the morning and Matteo Carrera delivered it beautifully. Unlike Dorabell, Matteo had changed his clothes since last night. No longer was he wearing his loose flannel shirt, but was sporting a more traditional button-down, not unlike the light blue officewear that made up Michael's usual wardrobe, and a set of much more mature looking dark rimmed glasses, also strangely like Michael's. "What're you doing in our apartment?" He demanded.

"We were about to ask you two the same question," Stephanie ambled over to the couple, waving her grappling hook around. "Actually . . . maybe not the same question, I guess. Still. Some sort of question. Y'know what? Scratch that. Same question," Stephanie's voice slid back to accusatory. "What are you doing in this apartment?"

"This is our apartment!" Matteo bristled. "How the hell did you get in?"

"Well, I happen to be the proud owner of a grappling hook," Stephanie patted the side of the gun, which promptly discharged its hook and line into the backlit aquarium, shattering it. Amidst the rising tide of algae-tinged water, broken glass, and soon to be dead fish, she turned back to Matteo and blinked. "It was like that when we got here."

"That's it," Matteo yelled, his voice breaking with traces of a light Spanish accent. "I'm calling the—" Before he could finished, Matteo gasped and clammed up. His blind horror and rage subsided into a more calm bewilderment, as if he could finally see Michael and Stephanie for the first time. "Oh. Wait. It's you two. Oh no."

"Okay, man," Stephanie pressed on. "Something real fishy is going on here. And I'm not talking about the ones on the floor. Technically, that's my bad," Stephanie lowered her gun. "Your crazy fiancée over here hired us to expose your affair. Which, based on what we saw, wasn't much of an affair at all! Maybe you guys just want people to burst in on you having sex in front of a giant mysterious vortex. I don't know how you get your rocks off, but tricking us is just not cool. Also, what the hell is up with that vortex? We're here for answers!" Although it was a stream of almost unconnected thoughts and interjections, Michael agreed with most of it.

"I know." The words came out of Matteo's mouth in a flat tone, as if they had been pre-planned.

"Well, then answer me this: why—" Stephanie started, but was cut-off by Michael's sudden interjection.

"Wait . . . what do you mean 'you know'?"

Dorabell sighed. Michael, who had wished she had never spoken to him in the first place, was ironically eager for her input. She looked to her husband. "Matteo, I think it's time."

Michael rolled his eyes. Why did everyone have to be so goddamn cryptic? "Alright. Somebody tell me what's going on or I'm going to explode."

"Okay," Matteo said, pointing to the couch. "You might want to sit down for this one."

Against his better judgement, Michael obeyed, gripping the edges of the armrests with little regard for the condition of the leather. Stephanie plopped down beside him, her grappling hook finding a cozy place in her lap.

Matteo and Dorabell swung to the opposite side of the room, parking their butts on the precarious edge of the television stand. This allowed for a large gulf of space between them and the couch, filled only by the coffee table and a large turquoise rug of indeterminate age. Michael could have sworn they were intentionally staying as far away from him and Stephanie as possible. Although Michael couldn't possibly hold that against them.

"Michael, Stephanie," Matteo brought his tented hands up in front of his thick rimmed black glasses. "You don't belong here."

"Oh for god's sake! Just tell them," Dorabell, despite her more buttoned-down appearance, still retained some of her trademarked attitude. "This isn't your universe."

The empty space in the living room, with the coffee table and the rug, filled with the crushing sense of impending doom, which handily displaced out all the air. An unbelievable amount of pressure built up in Michael's lungs and the back of his head before it was abruptly shattered by Stephanie's next proclamation.

"I know."

CHAPTER SIXTEEN

Same As The First

Michael's head whipped around, "What do *you* mean 'you know'?"

Stephanie had leaned back on the couch, slouching into her most comfortable position and was not at all phased by the impossible science fiction premise that had just been handed to them. "Man, Mike. Don't you watch TV? This is some 'Sliders' shit. I knew it when I saw Doorbell dressed up like a respectable human being. She sure as shit wasn't the same crazy morgue lady that barged into our apartment," Stephanie turned to face Dorabell, whose sneer was weapons-grade. "No offense."

"You knew and you didn't tell me?" Michael's brow furrowed.

"Well, I didn't 'know' know," Stephanie backtracked. "I had an inkling. How do you think I figured out where the grappling hook was? If this universe's Stephanie's anything like me, I assumed she'd have stashed it away in the same place. And I was right. Doctor Who over here just confirmed it."

"I can't believe you kept me in the dark!"

"Well, I knew that you'd freeze up. Or flip out and get all pissy, which you're doing now, by the way, so thanks for proving my point."

"Uh, guys," Matteo cleared his throat. "I think you're glossing over the real issue here."

"In a minute!" Michael raised his hand. "I let you be in charge for an hour and already—"

"Hey, idiots! Shut up!" Dorabell's voice could have shattered glass. She turned to Matteo, "Go on, honey."

"Thanks. Maybe you guys would like to know what exactly is going on?"

"Yes. Okay. That'd be helpful," Michael deadpanned.

"So first things first, I don't think we've been properly introduced. I'm Dr. Matteo Carrera. And you may know my wife, Dr. Dorabell Carrera."

"Okay, wait. Doctors?" Michael cocked his head. "I thought you were a grad student. And you," Michael pointed to Dorabell, "were nuts."

Dorabell rolled her eyes and Matteo continued, "Yeah, we'll get to that. But you're right. I was a grad student . . . in theoretical physics."

"Oh, here we go," Stephanie said.

"As best as I can tell, the Matteo from your universe was the same. His research area must have been space-time manipulation and he was testing an experimental form of universe-bridging technology."

"To meet me," Dorabell concluded.

"You?" Michael asked. "Why would he want to meet you?"

"Well," Matteo looked away and struggled through his words, "If I was to . . . um, hazard a guess. I'd say he was trying . . . to uh . . . get her to participate in . . . a ménage a trois with your universe's Dorabell?"

The grappling hook gun clanked to the floor as Stephanie fell off the sofa laughing. "Holy shit, man. Are you kidding me? He wanted a threeway so bad he needed to rip space and time apart?"

"Hey, don't judge him. Maybe he wanted a chance to try out his fantasy and test his research at the same time!" Matteo snapped.

"You did this, too, didn't you?" Michael asked, point blank.

"Um . . . uh . . ." Matteo stuttered. "I may or may not have done something similar . . ." He sucked a long breath in through his teeth, "About three years ago."

"Whoa whoa whoa," Stephanie picked herself up off the floor and climb back onto the couch, "So you built an interdimensional space bridge device to get some threeway action, too?" Stephanie bit her knuckle. "Oh, man. This is too good. You know about this, Doorbell?"

"Yes. I was recently made aware," Dorabell forced her words through gritted teeth. "Bringing it back up again isn't really helping."

"Yeah, sorry to have to remind you that your husband is a hyperdimensional pervert," Stephanie said.

"Hey," Matteo sprang to his own defense. "I wanted a threeway, but I didn't want to be with any other woman because I love my wife. I happen to think that's kind of sweet."

Stephanie arched an eyebrow. "You had three years to justify this to yourself and THAT'S what you came up with?"

"So that's the difference in this universe?" Michael was eager to get back to the main thrust of the matter. "It's just three years in the future?"

"No. Not really. Space and time are inseparable, and the fabric of the multi-verse is in constant flux. Think of a big ball of multi-layered goop, where each layer is a different universe. Each layer stays separate, but behaves in its own way. So when you travel between different universes, it's hard to determine where and when you'll end up on the other side. You just happened to land in this universe three years in your relative future. The whole thing is basically a crapshoot, but the dice have infinite sides. The universe is chaos and nothing really matters."

"See?" Stephanie pointed at Matteo, but looked accusingly at Michael. "That's what I always say!"

"That's incredibly alarming," countered Michael. "So what *is* the difference in this universe?"

"Our Beyoncé is white," Dorabell said.

"Ugh," Stephanie wrinkled her nose. "Is that legal?"

"Wait, so if your universe's Michael and your universe's Stephanie chased you through a portal three years ago . . . you must've jumped into your own alternate universe and we all eventually made it back."

"Yeah, that's right," Matteo confirmed.

"So you must know what happens!" A wave of relief cashed over Michael's shoulders. "You can tell us exactly how you all got back."

"Well . . . no. I don't really remember anything about what happened after I jumped through the universal barrier."

The wave of relief turned into a tsunami of acid. "Crap."

"But hold up," Stephanie said. "Once you got back, you must have seen your Stephanie and Michael, right? Didn't they tell you what happened?"

"Well, yeah, but I didn't want to poke the bear and risk creating a multidimensional collapse. That, and they were just really busy."

"Busy?" asked Michael. "Busy with what?"

"Running their detective agency," Matteo said.

"But we're *not* detectives!" Michael bellowed. "How many goddamn times do I have to keep saying that?"

"Could've fooled me. You guys were—" Dorabell stopped short as Matteo squeezed her shoulder. "Well, I guess I shouldn't tell you. Apparently we're not supposed to directly influence the path of your reality . . . or something."

"Right. Sure. Whatever," Michael waved his hand. "How about we work on getting us back home? Can we just do that? I'm really ready to wash my hands of all of this. Maybe the other difference between our two worlds is that we're not going to become shitty detectives."

"That's entirely possible," Matteo agreed. "But I think I can help you out. The one thing your counterparts *did* tell me was that it was my space-time tech that helped you return home. So I mothballed it and saved it for just such an occasion. We'll just have to go back to my lab to retrieve it. Should be simple. It's Sunday. Nobody will be around."

"Okay," Michael said. "Now we're getting somewhere."

"Right. Makes sense," Stephanie concurred. "Just one question."

"Shoot," Matteo said.

"So . . . is Jay-Z still black here?"

"Yeah. He is."

"Well, I guess that's fine, then."

CHAPTER SEVENTEEN
A Little Bit Louder

"Okay, you're going to have to run all this by me again, because I totally wasn't listening back there," Stephanie grabbed the back of the passenger's seat from the rear. Matteo's head snapped around, giving her a nervous glance. Beads of sweat were just on the way out of his pores.

"Could you, uh, just sit back down?"

"Sure thing, chief," Stephanie slammed her body into the back seat, sending Michael rebounding a bit beside her.

Michael continued to stare out the window. The world outside wasn't very dissimilar from the universe he was used to – they weren't *that* far in the future – but he noticed a few slight differences he hadn't picked up on earlier. Billboards for products he didn't know existed. Campaign posters with the wrong year on them and featuring incredibly surprising candidates. And, most disturbingly of all, his place of work, The Future Group tower, was absent from the skyline. In its place was just a hole filled with darkening, puffy clouds. At that, however, a wave of strange relief washed over him. Though it could have just been that the Future Group did not exist in this universe, Michael secretly hoped their boring, irritating asses had been shut down. Either way, good riddance to bad rubbish, he supposed.

Stephanie leaned forward, her tousled hair bouncing, "So, Matteo, you're saying we can time travel?"

"Well, yes and no, in a sense." Matteo's eyes returned to the road. "Have you ever heard of the grandfather paradox?"

"Is that the one where you go back in time and have a freaky threeway with your grandparents?" Stephanie raised a coy eyebrow.

"No," Matteo deadpanned. "It's the one where you go back in time and kill your grandfather before he can father your . . . uh . . . father, thus preventing your existence, and your ability to time travel. It's a bunch of circular logic that cancels out, making it impossible.

"But, it was theorized that if, instead of time traveling back in your universe, you could take advantage of the existence of a multi-verse. With enough energy, you could breach the barriers of your universe and slide sideways across to a very similar parallel universe and backwards in time to kill your alternate grandfather. Then you can see how the world would progress without you. And you wouldn't have to disappear."

"And you built this technology and used it for sex stuff."

Matteo refused to respond to that.

Stephanie digressed, "Anyway, so if that's true, once we travel to a parallel universe . . ."

"Like we've already done," Michael interjected.

"Yes, like that. Once we travel to a parallel universe, couldn't we just use that universe as our base and travel over to our universe, but backwards in time? So we could effectively travel to the past?"

Matteo was silent for a while, looking away and doing complex differential calculus in his head. "Actually . . . I don't see why not. That . . . makes a lot of sense. You'd just have to be in an alternate universe that is temporally ahead of your own."

" . . .like we've already done," Michael interjected again, this time with a wisp of hope in his voice. "It's our future here, essentially."

"Cool! So we should be able to get back home real easy, then!" Stephanie smiled at Michael. "No muss, no fuss."

"Thank god," Michael muttered as Matteo hung a sharp left into the campus of City Technical University. Much like the City Tech Michael had attended in his universe, this version was located downtown and was a hodgepodge of outdated class buildings and dorms strewn about in an unregulated and incomprehensible fashion that implied that they had allowed freshman urban planning students to lay it out, which, in fact, they had.

Matteo slid his car smoothly back into his faculty parking space which was nestled beneath the monolithic brutalist monster that Michael recognized as the Aaron M. Glass Physics building. During his college days, he had made careful pains to avoid the imposing modularity and gloomy concrete façade that cast a grim pallor over anyone who ventured within its orbit. Luckily, he was a psychology major and had dodged most of the core Physics requirements. But it was only fitting that fate brought him back here, now in the most damning of circumstances. Maybe if he'd taken the courses they'd suggested, Michael mused, he wouldn't have been in this situation, or at least he'd have been able to understand it more clearly.

The girl who had never set foot on a college campus in her life whistled. "Nice. You work here? Looks like it was built out of Legos. But . . . like the off-brand depressing kind from ebay."

"Right, yes. C'mon," Matteo walked around the front of the car and sidled up against the wall, again keeping his distance from Michael and Stephanie. "This way," he led the three of them around the corner and through the smudged glass double doors beneath the chiseled name of Aaron M. Glass, a billionaire benefactor that had nothing to do with the school, but wanted to see his name embossed somewhere. A slight drizzle began to patter against the sidewalk behind them.

"Looks like we got inside just in time," Matteo yanked himself up the stairway bannister, taking the steps two at a time. "I'm up on floor three."

Michael and Stephanie looked at each other and followed Matteo up the concrete staircase that was somehow grayer than the building, despite being made of the same material. The third floor landing opened up into a stone hallway with a bit more color, but that color was that of a sallow corpse, with the occasional black trim. The wooden double doors that led into each lab were thick slabs of weathered wood that hadn't been replaced since the seventies. Matteo creaked one open and beckoned them inside. Stephanie entered and Michael followed.

Michael didn't know what he had expected, perhaps a pristine white room with shiny glass equipment and perhaps a supervillain trapped behind a clear lucite wall shouting "I'll get out someday, then you'll pay!" Something fitting the milieu of someone with the ability to traverse multiple dimensions. But alas, it was the meager space of a grad student turned un-tenured professor, nothing more than a cubicle with a computer and a few pictures of his scary wife. It reminded Michael a bit of his cube at the Future Group. But the Future Group had the luxury of vast office space. Matteo would have been crammed in here with three other professors, or, if he was unlucky, grad students. In any case, there wasn't any place to put an interdimensional space-time ripper, Michael imagined that such a thing would take up the floor of an entire building. There was barely any room on Matteo's desk to fit a coffee mug. Nor were there any windows, which was disturbing for other health and safety reasons.

"Okay, Matteo. Where's your science machine? Let's get this over and done with," Michael grunted.

"It's right here," Matteo lifted open the door of a metal bin that hung over the top of his cubicle. Inside were a bunch of papers, books, snacks and a half empty Mountain Dew that looked older than Mountain Dew had any right to be. Matteo craned his arm up and over the tomes of 'Quantum Eraser Theory and You', 'Relativistic Hypertime', and a book simply titled 'Irony' by Claire Colbrook, and extricated a small metal lockbox roughly the size of a tissue box labeled "Student Debt Records."

"I had to label it something people would want to avoid on first glance," Matteo admitted. "That was this first thing that came to mind."

He lay the box down on his desk and unclasped the latch that held it shut. Michael and Stephanie were both relegated to peering over his shoulders to catch a first glimpse of the fabled device that they had heard so much about over the past two hours.

Matteo stopped glanced back at them, "Would you uh . . . mind backing up a little?"

"Oh, uh, sorry," Michael coughed and stepped back, dragging Stephanie by the collar of her jacket.

Matteo spun around, the lockbox now open and presented to them, housed in specially shaped foam padding, two rings and a digital timekeeping base unit. The room was silent except for the buzzing of the fluorescent lights overhead.

"That's it?" Michael scowled. "It looks like you took a stopwatch and glued some extra stuff on it."

Matteo slammed the box closed and yanked it away. "You make your own dimension hopping device on a grad school budget and see how it looks."

While Michael was unimpressed, Stephanie was much more taken with the device. Her eyes had widened and an almost scary grin had taken up residence on her face. "So this thing can take us through different universes and back and forth through time?"

"Yeah. I'll show you how to use—" Matteo started, but Stephanie jumped back into the fray.

"So we could arrive back in our own universe at a time before we left?" Stephanie started nodding, ostensibly to herself.

"Yeah. If that assertion you made earlier is correct. Sure. I'd have to run some calculations to be certain, though. It's been a while since I worked on this."

"You go ahead and make those calculations, dude. This is so cool I have to go to the bathroom!" Stephanie pivoted on her heel and dashed out through the cubes, but not before giving Michael a warm double pat on the shoulder.

Michael let out a breath. "Okay, while she's gone, you can tell me all the important stuff. So how does this thing work?"

Matteo dug the stopwatch-looking thing out of its foam nest. "So this is the base unit. It's what allows us to rip through the space-time fabric of one dimension and pass to the next. It works by manipulating information density."

"Information density?" Michael arched an eyebrow, unaware of the deluge that awaited someone after questioning an academic about their research topic.

"Well, the universe – universes, I should say – is just a complicated way of storing information. But instead of bits and bytes, the universe decided to make it altogether more complicated."

"The universe tends to do that."

"Right. The universe stores its information in atoms and matter and . . . life, as well as all the interactions of those things. But there's always a natural limit of how much information you can store in a particular area. If you exceed that limit, no matter what medium you store it in, a hard drive or human being, it will consume itself."

Michael's face scrunched up in a vain attempt to parse the information. "Could you repeat that, but in English?"

"No. Of course I can't. I'm a Ph.d and this is incredibly esoteric physics. This is the simplest English I can use. It's not my fault you don't have a technical degree. Just trust the scientist, will you?"

"Geeze. Alright. Fine."

Matteo shook his head and continued. "Each universe in the multi-verse has its own natural information storage limit. Your universe has a very similar limit to ours, with a digit shift in a lower decimal place, which causes the differences."

"White Beyoncé."

"Right. This base unit assesses that difference and navigates based on the target density limit, creating a contained singularity dense enough to rip through space-time and the interdimensional void to get you from universe to universe."

Michael understood the word 'singularity' having seen a few episodes of the Magic School Bus at an early age. "You're kidding me. You're traveling across dimensions using black holes?"

"Yeah. Plus I made the whole thing light up blue. Took me a whole weekend to figure out how to do that. I think it looks cool," Matteo was quite pleased with himself.

"Right," Michael waved his hand over to the box, where the two silver rings still remained. "So what about those?"

"Oh, yeah. These are super important. Take one. Put it on."

Michael picked the ring off the desk and turned it around in the palm of his hand. It was a heavy silver thing, with dark indicator lines etched into it as well as a triad of inset divots. It looked as if it belonged at an archaeological site rather than a physics lab. Regardless, Michael did as he was told and slipped it on his ring finger. Immediately, a static shock crawled across his skin. For a brief instant, Michael's innards tingled and prickled, as if his arm had fallen asleep and the rest of his body thought it was a good idea to follow suit. As quickly as the sensation started, it stopped again, giving Michael an entirely different kind of shock and caused a sharp intake of breath.

"Cool. Right?" Matteo laid a warm hand on Michael's shoulder, the first instance of physical contact between them since they had met hours earlier. His other hand held the remaining ring aloft.

"Uh . . . yeah. I guess. What are they?"

"These are dampening units. They prevent a lot of . . . side effects from occurring."

Michael pursed his lips. "What kind of 'side effects'?"

"Let's just call it catastrophic data loss," Matteo turned back to the lock box and shut it. "Why do you think I've been keeping my distance from you guys this whole time?" Matteo sighed and refused to turn around, choosing instead to speak at the box. "Data from different universes isn't exactly compatible. They might store data similarly – an identical planet, or periodic table, or humanoid creature – but when similar data structures from different universes come together, there's an unstable link between universes, creating a sort of data singularity that could violently erase one of the entities from existence throughout the entire multi-verse," Matteo coughed, "I think."

"You think?" Michael narrowed his eyes.

Matteo finally turned, "I've never tested it out. Too dangerous."

"Then how do you know this?"

Matteo paused. "You told me. Well, my you. This universe's you. Three years ago. When you came back."

"And what else did I tell you?"

"That you would punch my face off of my head."

"How about something more specific to the situation at hand?"

"I can't say."

"And why can't you say?"

"Disparate dissemination of overlapping information could cause unintended . . ."

" . . . side effects," Michael finished the thought. "Yeah, yeah."

"And those effects could be exponentially compounded if you met or traded information with alternate universe versions of yourselves," Matteo stated with grim resolve.

" . . .but you're the guy who wanted to have a threeway with two of his wives."

"Would you *please* stop bringing that up?" Matteo moved to Michael and grabbed his ringed hand. He was no longer afraid now that Michael had been appropriately "dampened." "Just take a look at this," Matteo gingerly twisted the frontmost part of the ring, which clicked slowly around Michael's finger while the other two-thirds of the ring stayed in place. A font of bright red light erupted from the three divots, projecting a holographic display onto the wall of the cubicle in front of them. It was filled with pertinent information that read like gibberish to Michael.

USER_HOME:\\10E63.99873445219

USER_TIME:\\20130913190387235

```
CURR_UNIV:\\10E63.99873445218
CURR_TIME:\\20160821133746852
INPT_DEST:\\ _
```

The underscore cursor blinked, inviting input.

"We can input your universe and time into the base unit, and you guys will be on your way," Matteo smiled.

"Perfect. This whole thing is . . . it's way too much. I just want to go home and deal with normalcy. Which was already a goddamn hassle."

"I know what you mean," Matteo picked up the base unit once again. "Now let's just—"

The clatter of the door slamming into the office's heater announced Stephanie's entrance. "Do you know how hard it is to find a bathroom in the place? Geeze!" Her head snapped toward the cubicle wall and the projected display. "Whoa. What's with the laser light show? Is that the space-time machine?"

"Yeah. We've almost got it set up," Michael said. "We're gonna go back home."

"Aw, yes! Hell yeah!" Stephanie pumped her fist in the air before dashing over to Matteo and enveloping their last tangible hope of survival in a big bear hug. "We owe you big time! I don't know what would've happened—"

With a bright spark and a deafening crack of thunder, the body of Matteo Carrera ripped itself apart. Chunks of flesh and bone rocketed throughout the office. Blood, bile, and other fluids splattered across the walls and Stephanie's body. In addition to the effluents, Stephanie's face was also covered with a wide-eyed look of blank terror. Her arms were still locked in a hugging position around scraps of meat that tentatively hung from the pieces of a smoldering ribcage. Silence reigned for a long while.

"What.

"The.

Fuck!" Michael screamed. He had been spared the brunt of the disgusting liquid human discharge, but was by no means less distressed.

Stephanie was still frozen, the thick hair atop her head soaked and matted with blood and bodily fluids. Once the ribcage fell to the floor, the only movement was the trembling of her jaw, "Oh God. What happened? I . . . I . . . only wanted to thank him."

"Yeah! And now he's dead! What the hell did you do?"

Stephanie spun around to face Michael's confused rage, "I . . . I don't know. I didn't do anything. I didn't think—"

"Where's the thing? Where is the thing?" Michael, driven by the knot of fear in his stomach rather than the blood and guts slathered across the floor, fell to his knees and searched the discrete remains of Matteo Carrera in order to find the space-time base unit. Luckily, its antenna, made of firm black rubber repurposed from an early 2000s era flip phone, stuck proudly out from behind a large chunk of what appeared to be liver. Unfortunately, a large dagger of bone fragment stuck, equally proudly, out of the small LCD screen of the device, rendering it sparking and thus quite useless, even if Michael had been able to figure out how to work it.

"Dammit. Dammit! *Dammit!*" Michael jumped to his feet started to bounce up and down and shake out his hands. It was the dance he sometimes did when his anxieties began to overwhelm him. It was also the dance he did when his bladder began to overwhelm him. So right now, it looked like he needed to pee really bad, which may have also been the case. "We were seconds away from sorting this whole thing out! Now we're really screwed! Goddammit, Stephanie!"

Stephanie remained silent, but she could do little else except stumble back as the space that Matteo Carrera had just inhabited began to warp and bend. Light's straightforward pathways twisted in upon themselves and the middle of the room transformed into a fifth-grader's attempt to use every photoshop filter at once, just because they looked cool. On the contrary, the utter disregard the office was showing for the rules of space and time made Michael sick to his stomach. And rightly so, as this was not something any human was meant to see. Stephanie, rather, stared on in wonder as the fabric of space and time tore open and bathed the entire room, bloody entrails and all, in an eerie cerulean glow. She stared into the abyss and Michael could swear he saw it stare back into her.

"Maybe we're not screwed after all," she spoke into the portal. "Maybe there's a bright side . . ."

"Bright side? *Bright side?*" Michael stopped his retching and began to step toward his roommate, but stopped as he realized there was a literal gulf in the universe between them. Instead he opted to yell over the portal's crackling and sizzling. "*Reality is beginning to unravel!* All because we had to stick our heads into a place where they clearly *did not* belong. All of this . . . the rent . . . the detective stuff . .

. the missing people . . . we're all going to die because of this! Because of you!"

"I . . . don't think so, Michael," Stephanie's words were oddly calm. After what felt like an eternity - and it might have been an eternity, since the concept of time seemed to be flying out the window - Stephanie turned to Michael. "Life can be confusing sometimes. But . . . I think we need to embrace the confusion."

A bolt of lightning shot out of the hole, causing the tear to widen further and forcing the entire room to descend into utter chaos. The overhead locker door that the bolt had stuck now sported a scorch mark, and flew open, allowing the books and papers inside to fly out and begin circling the vortex alongside drops of Matteo's blood and chunks of his organs. All of them spun toward the portal, draining out of reality like leftover peas in an unstoppered sink. The lighter papers were sucked in with little fanfare, but the larger books orbited the vortex for a short time before being stretched into infinity and spaghettiing out of existence. 'Relativistic Hypertime' was the second to last to go, the last, of course, being 'Irony' by Claire Colbrook.

Next, the loud shriek of a heavy desk carving a rent in the stone floor filled the room, as the cubicles began their advance. Michael, however, was distracted, as he felt his center of gravity rise to an uncomfortable level. His feet were lifted off the floor and his stomach began to drag the rest of him toward the unyielding blue horror. "What the hell is happening?"

Stephanie, too, had begun to experience the same thing, but she looked content with it. Michael, on the other hand was literally bending over backwards, attempting to grab onto anything in the office that could slow his approach. "I don't know . . . but I don't think we have another choice."

Michael stared at his oldest friend floating across the way, his eyes dead blank with an unfortunate realization. "Is this it?"

Stephanie looked back at him, her face warped to comical proportions by the lensing of the space-time anomaly, but this allowed Michael to see, for the first time, true worry in her eyes, which up until now had been too minuscule to notice. "If it is . . . I'm . . . I'm sorry Michael. I just want to say—"

The air was sucked out of the office, along with Stephanie's words. Her body soon followed, stretching out into the blue infinity before snapping out of view. Michael, physically and metaphysically unable to protest or resist, followed in an interminable instant.

Once the two were ensconced in the slipspace between universes, the portal winked out of existence, but not before the remaining papers, books and desks in the room – as well as most of the traces of Matteo Carrera – were vacuumed out. Air suddenly rushed into the office, creating a sonic boom that would have shattered every window, had the room possessed any. And with an extreme delay, a pair of embarrassing glorping noises rang through the air, as well as a quick, short zip.

CHAPTER EIGHTEEN

And A Whole Lot Worse

"Ow! Are you *serious?*" With a brusque shove, Michael pushed his way out of a bush full of thorns, which only served to get more thorns stuck in his skin. "Why do I always land in the bushes with prickers? It happened now . . . it happened at math camp—"

"It happened that one time with the cops," Stephanie chimed in.

"You pushed me into that one!" Michael stopped and looked around. His brain began to catch up to the situation. He had passed out just after entering the vortex and could only remember the roiling blue energies dancing before his eyes and a vague, dull ache in the back of his head and the same bland chalky feeling in his mouth. "Hold on . . . we're . . . alive. We're alive!" Michael touched and felt up his whole body as only people who've just recently found out they were alive do. "How are we alive?"

"Maybe God loves us."

"No, that can't be it," Michael took tentative steps forward, unsure if his care was at all necessary. His jubilation shifted to curiosity as he wiped condensation off his glasses and took a look around. "Where are we?"

"More like—"

"If you say 'more like *when* are we?' I'm going to punch you," Michael snapped. "So where are we?"

"Forest, it looks like." Stephanie's assertion was on point. But it was an altogether stranger type of forest than one would expect. The trees about them were spaced few and far between, yet the canopy was thick and full, letting only the occasional beam of light deposit its photons on the moist, wet dirt. The trees' wide berth, though odd, was not unreasonable, given that their deep red trunks were each as wide as a skyscraper.

Stephanie pushed herself up off a bed of packed leaves and dirt, which had made for an altogether softer landing on her part. She was still covered in Matteo's blood and pieces of his flesh, although it appeared to be drying. Her hair was clumped and matted across her face in streaks of red until she slicked it back.

"These trees are enormous," Michael winced as he pulled at some particularly nasty thorns, which had lodged themselves in his flesh with great zeal for their natural purpose. "What the hell is this place?"

"Mike," Stephanie sniffed at the cold, damp air, "Mike."

"What is it?" Michael turned back to her.

"You smell that?" She said. "Old magnets."

"Again with the magnets?"

"Yeah . . . just like we smelled back at Terri's apartment," Stephanie raised her hands toward her face and took another snort. "But it's in my hands now, too. Here, smell." She advanced on Michael.

"What? No! I'm not smelling your hands. You're still covered in Matteo juices!" Michael backed away as Stephanie's blood-encrusted digits wriggled dangerously close to his face, "Get away from me!"

Stephanie chased Michael around the trunk of the nearest tree and Michael retreated as if she were holding dog doo on a stick. This lasted for quite a bit longer than one would expect – they made it around about half of the tree. By that time, Michael realized that he had nothing to be afraid of, as he and Stephanie were from the same universe and her touch would not be as explosively fatal to him as it had poor Matteo. Maybe. He hoped. Besides, he was wearing the ring.

The ring.

Michael skidded to a stop and Stephanie overshot him by a good ten feet before turning back around. By the time she returned to him, Michael had rotated open the ring, releasing the light projection onto the ground. It projected clean, resolute red text into the forest's odd smelling dirt.

```
USER_HOME:\\10E63.99873445219
USER_TIME:\\20130913190387235
CURR_UNIV:\\10E63.99870213216
CURR_TIME:\\11380509133746852
```

```
INPT_DEST:\\ _
```

The underscore cursor blinked, mocking Michael to input a destination, despite knowing full well that he could not. Stupid piece of junk.

"What the hell is that?" Stephanie asked over his shoulder. She had taken an enormous dewdrop off a large fallen leaf and wiped most of the blood and viscera off the visible parts of her body, but was still pretty disgusting.

"This ring . . . Stephanie," Michael said through gritted teeth. "Is what prevents people from *exploding* when they're touched by someone from a different universe."

"Oh . . . uh . . . cool," Stephanie offered a weak grin. "You got another one of those, maybe?"

"I *did* . . ." Michael did not finish the thought, nor did he have to.

"Right. So . . . uh . . . what does it say?"

"I have no goddamn clue. But the numbers don't match, so we're not back home. And there's no way for us to get back home without a device that lets us input our destination."

"So do you have that device?"

"I *did* . . . " This time, angrier.

"Right. So what now?"

"I don't know," Michael slumped against the tree trunk, wishing that he could worry about the stuff he was worried about just a day ago. His crappy job, their missing rent money, his date with Terri. Any or all of those would be a welcome reprieve from whatever fantastical rigmarole he was currently trapped in. "We're alive, but we're just as screwed as we ever were."

"Well, they say when god closes a door. He opens a window and throws you out of it. Or something. I never really paid attention in church," Stephanie sat down on what appeared to be a mushroom thirty times its normal size. "Never really went, either."

Michael ignored her and resorted to silently cleaning off the loose bits of Matteo that were stuck to his glasses and wiping them against the giant tree trunk. He had just removed what looked strikingly like a sliver of optic nerve when an unearthly shriek broke through the damp air. It was an ear-splitting screech of a bird of prey that transitioned into the deep baritone of a fairly large highland cow. The ground vibrated.

"What . . . was that?" Michael whispered.

"It wasn't me," Stephanie said.

"I know that!"

"Sounded like Bigfoot," Stephanie added. "Could've been Bigfoot."

"It's not Bigfoot!"

The sound reiterated itself. It was louder and almost more unrecognizable the second time and was accompanied by a low rumble that permeated the soil. Loose clumps of dirt began to bounce along the ground as the rumble morphed into a percussive thumping.

"Oh, my god. What's happening now?" Michael thrust his arms out to maintain balance, but still found himself stumbling.

"Uh, Mike . . ." Stephanie stared off into the distance, eyeing the shadowy swaths of land between the giant redwood trunks. "What's that?"

Michael spun around and looked where Stephanie pointed, the barest tip of her finger emerging from the blood-splattered cuffs of her once-green jacket. An ominous black mass, roughly the size of a typical city bus, barreled toward them between the trunks. It was still a ways away, but moving fast, unlike a typical city bus. As it passed each successive trunk, Michael caught glimpses of its form as it sped through the occasional beam of light. Enormous front teeth and blood red eyes inset in a muscular, yet blobby fur covered body did not inspire confidence. Neither did the large sprays of dirt it kicked up in its wake using its powerful back legs.

"Whatever it is, it's not good! C'mon!" Michael grabbed Stephanie's shoulder and wheeled her around, forcing her to join the hasty retreat he was already beating. He had no real plan, of course, but running was better than nothing and cowardice, his default plan, had never failed him before.

They dashed through the forest, around the gargantuan trees and over felled branches, which were about the size of normal tree trunks in their universe. But, as Michael and Stephanie had never bothered to properly exercise after gym classes ceased to be mandatory, the giant creature continued to close the distance between them at an alarming rate. The ground quaked beneath Michael's feet with such an intensity that he could barely keep his knees from buckling. Although he was terrified to peer back at what he was certain was impending doom, Michael did so to make sure he hadn't lost

Stephanie. She was still with him, though just as worse for the wear as he was. Out of the corner of his eye, he spied the black ball of fury – a football field's length between them – suddenly pivot and dash off to the right, taking the groundquakes with it.

Michael slid to a stop and stretched out his arm to have Stephanie do the same. He doubled over on his knees, attempting to expel the deep burning that had invaded his chest.

Stephanie let out a deep breath and staggered towards the nearest trunk, holding herself up against it with her arms. "Whoo! That was fun, right? There's my workout for the year. What do you think that was?"

"I . . . have . . . no idea!" Michael gasped, recalling painful memories of his childhood asthma inhaler. He doubted his doctor's proclamation that he had outgrown it. "Whatever universe we're in," he continued as his lung function returned, "it isn't as normal as the last one."

"Well, good," Stephanie said. "That last one was boring. When I think alternate universes, I wanna see some crazy shit. Like . . . I dunno . . . Cyborg Samurai or something. Wouldn't that be neat? This big black monster thing is pretty cool, too, though, I guess."

Michael had neither the words nor the wherewithal to respond, nor did he have to. The thunderous crack of a fallen branch echoed as the shade of the forest around them deepened by the addition of a looming shadow the size of, of course, a city bus.

The ears of the colossal jet black rabbit flattened against its back as it leaned over the fallen log it had sat upon and sniffed daintily at the top of Michael's head. Occasional flits of its tongue just served to muss up his hair further.

Stephanie aww'ed aloud. "Oh, this is adorable. I love this universe. Everything's big here. Including the rabbits!"

As Michael nudged the rabbit's face away, a suit of knights' armor clanked to the ground, having released itself from the saddle and stirrups perched on the rabbit's back. The armor was bruised, dented and had certainly seen better, more silvery days. Whoever was inside attempted to maintain their balance before slipping on the edge of the log and tumbling to the ground. They drew a short dirk from their scabbard and thrust it up in Michael and Stephanie's direction.

"Who are you? Why do you trespass in the forests of the Evannoch?" the knight's voice and labored breaths reverberated against the helmet, producing a distortion not unlike a less intimidating Darth Vader. "And why are you covered in lifeblood?"

"Listen, dude," Stephanie said. "We're just as confused as you are. Now, if you just put that thing away, we'll be happy to help you with whatever you and your giant rabbit want. I would do anything for that cutie."

This placated the knight, and the dirk went back into its scabbard. The knight extended a gauntlet and Stephanie gave it a friendly shake.

"No," he groaned. "Help me up!"

Stephanie motioned to Michael and the two of them hoisted the knight upright, which was an effort that warranted much grunting and snarling. Michael was glad Terri wasn't here to see how little upper body strength he possessed.

"Many thanks," the knight said as he retreated back to the safety of his mount, which had started to gnaw leaves of a nearby branch. "I will trust you two for the time being, until we reach Steppenhold. But we must away forthwith. For this is not a safe place for humans. Evannoch rule these woods."

"What the hell is an 'Evannoch'?" Michael asked.

The shriek from earlier broke the forest's silence, answering Michael's question and confirming the knight's point. It had not been the rabbit, as Michael and Stephanie had thought earlier. In fact, the rabbit's head shot up in panic, ears at the ready, but to its credit, it did not bolt.

"Come. It's on the move," the knight hoisted himself onto his rabbit, and beckoned to Michael and Stephanie to join. Michael was all too quick to accept the knight's offer, as another shriek shattered the air, this time accompanied by the violent sounds of rampant destruction rapidly approaching. The knight yanked Stephanie up onto the saddle behind him. Eager not to mess up the rabbit's fur with her blood soaked everything, Stephanie perched up on the saddle and looped her arms around his armored waist. Michael grabbed handfuls of the rabbit's smooth, soft hair and thrust himself up over the saddle, behind Stephanie. The rabbit huffed, but it was used to this sort of treatment.

"Onwards!" Shouted the knight as he kicked at the rabbit's side. "We must make haste!"

"Whoa!" Michael bit his bottom lip as the rabbit took off without a moment's notice, jerking him backwards off the precarious sliver of saddle he was seated on and onto the rabbit's slick, soft back. His glasses flew off into the woods, never to be seen again.

Seconds later an object came thundering through the trees where they had just been, taking out huge chunks of bark and wood from the tree trunks and leaving a gouged out wound in their place, before flinging itself like a pinball to the next trunk and towards them in an erratic, but directed chase. Michael and Stephanie glanced back as the thing's shriek transformed into a bone-rattling roar. Michael, despite his blurred vision, saw the monster's gaping, human-like mouth chomp in desperate hunger. He also saw that the mouth was surrounded by two all beef patties, lettuce, cheese, pickles, onions tomatoes and a sesame seed bun. Special sauce foamed around its lips.

"Is that a freakin' *hamburger*?" Michael yelled over the rush of the wind, as the rabbit continued to just evade the monster's mouth.

"We call them the Evannoch," the knight's voice was drowned out by the din, but Michael got the gist of it. "They are savage hunters and the scourge of this land. This lone hunter killed and ate seven of my bannermen during the last fortnight."

"I don't care what you call them! It's a hamburger!"

"Okay, yeah," Stephanie said, her words flowing back with the wind. "This is a pretty cool universe."

"Take this!" The knight passed back a flintlock rifle that he had removed from a saddlebag. The rogue burger continued its chase, pushed across the forest floor by two spindly arms of extraordinary strength that kicked up clouds of dirt and debris in its wake.

Michael looked blankly at the gun he had been handed. The rifle sported tasteful gold filigree about the butt and barrel. "What do you want me to do with this?"

"Shoot it, you idiot!" Both the knight and Stephanie said.

"Okay," Michael grabbed the gun with his right hand, his left still clinging for dear life around the knight's metal waist. He struggled and fumbled to find a comfortable position. "I don't . . . I don't know what the hell to do here!"

"It's a point and click interface, Mike!" Stephanie yelled.

"What if I miss?" Michael believed that was a 100% certainty.

"You'd better not," the knight called back. "If you do, we are done for."

"I can't aim for shit if we're bouncing around like this! And without my glasses, things are kinda blurry!"

"We've only got a mile until the clearing!" The knight was right. Michael could see the forest begin to break ahead of them and open up into a blinding white light. He couldn't see what lay beyond, but it had to be better than what lay behind.

"Aim true, sir! Aim true!" The knight urged.

"I don't know what that means!" Michael yelled into the dented steel helmet, a burning pressure beginning to crush his lungs. "I can't do this! We're going to die!"

"Hey!" Stephanie bellowed over the din. "Listen to me, Mike. You got this. I know you've got no glasses, and you've never shot a real gun before in your life, and you're freaking out as usual, but you can do this. I know you can do this. Remember the grappling hook gun? It's like that. A point and click interface." She placed a warm hand on his shoulder. "Just breathe and relax. You're better than you think you are."

Michael looked back at her to see that she was serious. The hamburger was mere feet away from the rabbit's tail, chomping maddeningly and pushing roaring grunts through what he assumed was its nose. Another second and they would be devoured in the most ironic way possible.

Michael closed his eyes and steeled himself. Stephanie was right, it was now or never. His mind went surprisingly blank as he pushed past his anxiety. The pressure on his chest subsided and Michael released his arms from around the knight, digging his heels deep into the rabbit's side, and aiming over Stephanie's head. He used all the strength in his finger to pull down the trigger, letting loose a thunderous crack. The hamburger released an angry yowl and peeled off, retreating into the depths of forest whence it came.

"I did it," Michael smiled at Stephanie. "I did it!"

The burger monster's squeals of pain were drowned out by the loud crash of brush and twigs as the knight's rabbit leapt through the last heavy wall of forest greenery and onto a cobblestoned roadway bathed in fresh, warm daylight. The knight pulled back on the rabbit's reins and it skidded to a halt across the sandy stones.

"Whoo!" Stephanie cheered as she jumped off the rabbit's back. Michael followed her down. "That was badass. Good shot, man. I knew you had it in you." She gave him a light punch which caused the flintlock rifle to fall from his hands, which had been frozen in claws around it. The gun clattered to the floor.

"Take care with that!" The knight slammed onto the cobblestones with a clank, his dirty, damaged armor gleaming as well as it could in the direct sun.

"Sorry. Here." Michael's stomach gurgled in unease as he picked up gun with his fingertips and gingerly handed it to the knight.

"Thank you," the knight said acidly as he took the gun out of Michael's hands, wiped it down with a rag, and slotted it in a leather loop in the rabbit saddle. "But I suppose I do owe you my life. I am eternally grateful."

Michael unease was replaced with a small surge of pride that welled up in his chest and reddened his cheeks. He'd never really been thanked like that. Even if it was in some far off alternate dimension beyond his understanding, it felt . . . good. For a moment, he even forgot that he and Stephanie had been banished from their home dimension through incomprehensible science and may never return home. For a moment.

"Hey, hey, hey," Stephanie met him halfway and patted him on the back. "You did it, Mike! I knew you had it in you."

"Thanks, Steph. I wouldn't have been able to do it without you."

"Yeah, of course," Stephanie nodded. "Now let's figure out where we are."

"Well, we're literally in a universe where *hamburgers* eat *people* and I am not okay with it," Michael was back to distress mode again and bounced on his heels. "How're you not freaking out?"

"Alright, alright. Calm down. Maybe this guy can help," Stephanie spun around and swept over to the knight, who had returned to fumbling around in his saddlebag. "Hey, Knight Rider! As you can imagine, my friend and I have a couple of quick questions for you."

"Certainly. Let me just . . . take care of something," Michael walked up as the knight shed his right gauntlet to reveal not the rough, sinewy hand of a man, but a daintier, slighter hand. "There. That's better." He – no, she – reached back into the pockets of the leather saddle and pulled out a large carrot, feeding it to her mount with care. After giving the rabbit a quick, welcome scratch, the knight turned back to Michael and Stephanie. "Yes. What would you like to know?"

"Uh . . ." Michael eyed her hand. "Who exactly are you?"

The bare hand reached up to remove the armored helmet, revealing a pale white face with a set of hazel eyes that froze Michael with their gaze. Hazel went with everything, even medieval armor.

"Sir Terri of Steppenhold," she said, her voice finally free and clear of all echo.

Michael said nothing.

Stephanie said, "Hahaha, nice!"

"Terri?" Michael squeaked once his train of thought began to creep out of the station.

"Yes?" She asked, an eyebrow raised up into her helmet.

"Oh, this is perfect. This is great," Stephanie threw her hands up in the air. "See, Mike? We've found someone from our world. That's gotta mean something right? Like we're on the right track?"

"I . . . I guess . . ."

"Excuse me," Sir Terri raised a finger. "What do you mean 'your world'?"

"It's . . . uh . . . it's complicated," Michael rubbed the back of his neck. "We can explain it on the way to wherever you're going."

"I am going to Steppenhold. Surely you must be familiar."

"Well, yeah. We all know Steppenhold," Stephanie rolled her eyes. "But just pretend we don't for a second."

"The seat of power of the Glass Dynasty." A strong undercurrent of wonder and loyalty filled Terri's voice, already tempered with the regal pronunciation of medieval times. "It is home of the King: a powerful wizard with limitless power to whom I am forever loyal. Glory to King—"

"Yeah, yeah, I don't care," Stephanie waved away the words. "But did you say he was a wizard?"

"Yes. A powerful—"

"Perfect. We might need one of those," Stephanie turned back. "See, Mike? Chaos delivers. Now, ma'am. Before we depart, I must give you my sincere thanks," Stephanie clasped Terri's hand in hers, before giving her a gentle kiss. Sir Terri, being from a medieval shithole, did not reel away from Steph's filthy, disgusting state. In fact, Michael could even see Terri's cheeks blush, as did his own, but for an entirely different reason.

"Stephanie!" He yelled.

She turned to face him, "Hey, just 'cause I got to lay one on your girl and you didn't, doesn't mean - oh . . . right. The explosion thing."

Sir Terri's suit of armor began to clatter against itself. Soon enough, like Matteo Carrera, Terri's body exploded, sending not only blood and guts, but shards of metal and bolts careening through the air. Michael had grabbed Stephanie and dragged both of them to the ground, narrowly avoiding a jagged plate of steel that whizzed by their faces. Shaking it off, Michael looked up to see a roiling, vibrating hole in the medieval countryside, hanging as unnaturally as an aboveground pool in midair. He felt its inevitable pull, both mentally and physically, as his and Stephanie's bodies were dragged forth, bouncing across the cobblestones.

Everything went blue and the musty smell of old magnets filled the air.

CHAPTER NINETEEN
Beating Around The Bush

"You good here?" Rex Calhoun gave the EMTs a gruff nod, as they loaded the unconscious Elena Finster into the back of their ambulance. Calhoun groaned as a couple of black and whites pulled up to the curb. He knew who was in them and did not want to deal with them right now. The entire thing had been a total shitshow, once those two idiot P.I.s had entered the picture, and now Calhoun was left holding the bag, which only contained more shit.

The doors to the cop cars slammed shut, almost in unison as Lieutenant Lin and a few uniforms piled out. Lin was young, but he was fierce and had blasted through his stint as a beat cop in less than a year, moving up the ladder to a ranked desk job with the precision and grace of a guided missile powered by paperwork. Calhoun never cared much for rank, he only cared about the job. Lin, on the other hand, only cared about what would make him look bad and delay -

not prevent, never prevent – his inevitable promotion to Captain. Calhoun knew he'd be in for it now.

"What the hell is going on here, detective?" Lieutenant Lin threw his hand in the air as if he had the ability to call lightning down from the heavens. Luckily, he didn't. If he did, the case would have been closed and an awkward arrest would have to be made. "Brook tells me you shoved him off of your narcotics task force, which is now investigating old women?"

"And he's calling me at odd hours to do his internet searches," Brook, in meek, sniveling form, peered out from behind Lin's shoulder.

"Shut up, Brook," Lin turned back to Calhoun, his eyes blazing. "Can you explain to me why I've been called down to the ass end of the suburbs to find one of my Detectives lording over an assault case in a district we have no jurisdiction in?"

"And ask him why he had to call me at midnight."

"Brook, if you don't shut your face, I'm going to pin this whole old woman assault on you," Lin snapped. "Don't think I can't."

"Sir," Calhoun said, "Elena Finster was a lead I was chasing down in conjunction with Tobias Wilkes and the Trick Ponies."

"You think this elderly lady is peddling drugs in Squalor's Wallow."

"Finster's husband and Wilkes disappeared under the same circumstances, along with the doctor that Detective Hobson in the 35th was chasing." Calhoun avoided mentioning the disappearances of Hobson herself and Carrie, lest he garner any further dressing down.

"And what circumstances would those be?" Lin crossed his arms. Brook shot Calhoun a smirk from behind him.

"Sudden. Mysterious." Lightning-based with a sticky note-based perpetrator present.

"And suppose I follow you on this magical mystery tour you're going on?" Lin rolled his eyes. "Why did you leave one of your leads, a geriatric one at that, alone, when you wanted to ask her questions?"

"Well, sir, there were these two little idiots," Calhoun's blood boiled just thinking about them. His fingers tensed and his face began to flush. "Unlicensed P.I.s that were snooping around. I had to arrest them."

"Brook tells me they had their licenses."

"I only found out about that after the fact."

"Y'know what? I've heard enough," Lin furrowed his brow and pointed away. "Calhoun, get your ass back to the station. Brook and I will clean things up here. And when we get back, we'll call in Captain Braddock to see what he thinks about your narcotics task force and its consistent lack of results."

Calhoun almost spoke up, but Lin's glare shut him down. He grumbled to himself and walked back toward his car, flipping Brook off when he was sure Lin wasn't looking. He slung himself into the bucket seat of his aging Crown Vic and let his hands hang over the wheel at ten and two.

He was just about to feel sorry for himself when his car radio crackled to life.

"10-57 called in. 226 Andrews Drive, Apartment 7H. Any available car please assist."

Calhoun snapped up his radio and chirped back, "2177. Calhoun here. I'm on my way back in that direction. I'll swing back and check it out."

Technically, he would have to go out of his way to pass by Andrews Drive, but for a 10-57 – a reported missing person – he'd make the extra effort.

CHAPTER TWENTY
Close, But No Cigar

"Ow, dammit! Again? Really?" Michael stumbled out of the bushes onto the sidewalk, removing literal thorns from his side. Birds chirped in the distance, either ignoring or mocking his pain.

Across the street, Stephanie waved to him from an alley. An alley he recognized, "Hey Mike, I think we're back in normal times. We're only a couple of blocks away from home!" She looked both ways before running across the empty street, and sidled between the line of parked cars that separated them. Stephanie had avoided being doused in more blood and guts, thanks to medieval Terri's suit of armor, but she was still pretty disgusting. "Check your ring thingy."

Michael rotated the ring on his finger and the projected display sprang out once again. The red light was difficult to see in the bright daylight, so Michael moved it onto the deep green bush from which he had just emerged. He squinted to make sense of the number, scattered by the bush's prickly leaves.

```
USER_HOME:\\10E63.99873445219
USER_TIME:\\20130813190387235
CURR_UNIV:\\10E63.99873445211
CURR_TIME:\\20130604284015846
INPT_DEST:\\ _
```

"Well, we're not home . . . but we're in a very similar universe . . . and a month in the past," Michael wasn't quite sure of his reading, but he wasn't quite sure of anything anymore, so his guesswork would have to suffice.

"The past! Yes!" Stephanie pumped her fist in the air. "So we can travel to the past. That's awesome."

"Why are you so excited?"

Stephanie shrugged off the question, "It's just cool is all."

"How about we focus on how to get ourselves home, and not how cool everything is?" Michael chided. "I think our best bet is to find this universe's Matteo Carrera. And keep your hands to yourself this time!"

"Fine. Whatever. How's about we just go up into our apartment? We could probably use alternate you's computer to email Doorbell so she can put us in touch with Matteo."

"That's . . . a reasonable suggestion," Michael blinked in surprise. "But what if the alternate you or alternate me is up there? Matteo said that could be disastrous."

"What's the date?"

Michael looked back down at the display. "June 4th. I was out of town visiting my mom. Maybe this Michael is, too."

"And that was when they had the Monster Movie Marathon down at the Cine-odeon. Alternate me wouldn't be anywhere near this place."

"Let's hope so," Michael shut off the ring and the light projection vanished.

Michael and Stephanie walked around the familiar corner of Iris Street, and trudged up the steep hill towards what could or could not be considered their apartment. The legality of the whole situation was beyond him. Would he really be guilty of breaking into his own apartment, even if this was a slightly different version of himself? But what if, in this universe, everybody was half-dinosaur? Would that be a different enough Michael for it to still be illegal? These were questions no one needed to ask themselves.

The relative similarity of this universe to their own proved valuable, as Michael's keys to their apartment in their home universe were still a perfect fit in this one. The front door swung open to reveal the same narrow hallway, but this one was well illuminated by several bright wall sconces with tasteful metal filigree. The floors also looked like that had been swept and mopped on a regular basis.

"Well, that's new," Stephanie said.

She was the first to proceed down the hallway and up the stairs at the end. Michael followed, taking in the noticeable differences. No longer did mint green asbestos-laden paint flake from the walls. Instead, they were neatly painted a less eye-straining shade of neutral off-white that held fast. The stairs were well finished in a chestnut brown and did not creak. Nor could one hear a drip from a single bit of exposed piping, as there were none.

"Damn. This is the kind of apartment I'd've liked to live in. What'd these guys do right?" Michael muttered as he ascended the final flight of stairs. He stared at the polished wooden door that led to their apartment, admiring the tasteful golden peephole cover that glinted in the hall light. Stephanie nudged him forward and he shoved his key into the lock, turning slowly to allow the tumblers in the lock to release as quietly as possible. If this universe's Stephanie *was* in there, he'd rather avoid catching her attention altogether. The lock released without an errant click, smooth as if lathered in butter, and Michael pushed the door open a crack to peer in. Stephanie maneuvered beneath him to have a look, too.

There didn't appear to be anyone on the couch, so it was a safe bet alternate Stephanie wasn't around, so Michael pushed open the door and the two of them took in a sight of splendor . . . and jealousy. As beautifully re-modelled as the halls and stairway of the building had been, their apartment was even more unrecognizable. The far wall now featured more windows, allowing natural light to stream in, throwing the rest of the improvements into sharp relief. The walls had been painted a pleasant robin's egg blue, and were home to a variety of framed pictures and posters. Across from the 65 inch LED TV sat the massive couch.

"Yoink!" Stephanie took a running start towards the couch, aching to be absorbed within its rich black leather, like a star being sucked into a black hole. But before she could seal the deal, Michael caught her by the collar.

"Are you kidding me? You're covered in human remains! Take a damn shower."

"Aw, man. You're no fun," Stephanie hung her head and slunk off toward the bathroom. A few minutes later, she called out, "Hey! The toilet water in here is blue. This place is classy as shit!"

Michael ignored her and surveyed the rest of the room. On the far wall, in front of one of the windows that were no longer caked with the grease and grime of the city, sat a glass desk which was home to a pristine desktop computer.

"Hm. That's new," Michael walked over and turned it on. The fan whirred and the computer booted up to a login screen. It was Michael's name in the user field and the screen beckoned him for a password. He grimaced for a moment, before realizing that, given the similarities so far, this universe's Michael probably used the same password for everything as he did. He knew that wasn't a good idea, for security purposes and all that, but he was just too lazy to do otherwise. At least his password was a good combination of letters, numbers *and* a special character. No one could fault him for that.

'17SPT99!'

He opened up the browser and typed 'Dorabell Underwood' into the URL bar, to initiate a search. Curiously, the first thing that popped up was a link to his personal email. Raising an eyebrow, he clicked it, and it took him directly to his spam folder and an email from Dorabell within.

FROM: Underwood.Dorabell@dogpile.com

TO: MDuckett3@dogpile.com

SUB: Private Investigator Needed – Urgent!

Hello Michael,

I'm in urgent need of your help. I'm going to marry my fiancé in a few months and I suspect he's cheating on me. I saw your ad and I think you'd be able to help. Please contact me.

Dorabell Underwood

372-14765

"So, you find anything?" Stephanie waltzed back into the room, wrapped in a thick white towel, her hair still dripping.

"That was fast. Did you even use soap?"

"Don't ask questions you don't want to know the answer to," Stephanie leaned over his shoulder, glancing at the computer screen.

"Well, whatever. We have Dorabell's phone number. Looks like there's a few differences in this universe. Phone numbers have an extra digit, and everybody uses Dogpile for email and web searches."

"Hahah. Dogpile?" Stephanie snorted. "You're kidding me."

"Yeah. That's pretty ridiculous," Michael grimaced as cool drops of water splashed onto his wrist. "Could you maybe dry off and stop dripping onto the computer?"

"Good idea. I'm gonna raid this Stephanie's closet. Maybe she's got some cool shit I can swipe."

"And while you're at it, see if there's a phone around her we can use.

"There's one right here," As she walked off, Stephanie grabbed a small flip-phone that had been lying, camouflaged next to the bunch of remotes on the coffee table. "Catch!" She threw it over her shoulder to Michael, who caught it in cupped hands close to his chest.

"Careful!" Michael cried, but Stephanie was gone, leaving only footprint shaped puddles on the hardwood floor. He opened his hands and looked down at the phone she had tossed him. It was his. The same black and silver flip phone he had destroyed in their own universe, right down to the telltale scratches and scuff marks. It wasn't his original phone, but he had held this one before . . . and remembered leaving it in the Garbagemobile. He squinted at it. "Wait a minute . . ."

That's when it rang. Michael almost dropped it in surprise. The ringtone was, again, the MIDI version of the Mighty Ducks theme song. He sat, enraptured in quiet awe.

"What are you doing?" Stephanie called out from her alternative room. "Answer it!"

Michael clicked it open and carefully lifted it to his ear. "Hell . . .o?"

"Mike, is that you?" A familiar voice that Michael couldn't place but could place him squawked at him out of the phone.

"Uh . . . yeah. It's me" Michael, unsure how to proceed, went for the first thing that came to mind. "New phone. Who dis?"

Technically, it was true.

"Hey, man. It's Jacob. Are you at your apartment?" Jacob Bradshaw, Terri's brother, who had angrily kicked them out of her apartment, seemed to be on much better terms with them in this universe.

"Uh . . . yes. Hi Jacob. I'm here," Michael answered. "How're . . . you?"

"Great. Real great. Listen, I know it's Sunday, but I got some work stuff to run by you for FG." Michael assumed he meant "Future Group." "Do you mind if I swing by?"

"Sure?" Michael wasn't sure.

"Cool. I'll be there in a few. Ciao!"

Michael closed the phone and turned back to Stephanie, who had just returned, wearing a near exact simulacrum of her previous outfit, just less encrusted with Matteo chunks. "That was Terri's brother. He's coming over here to ask me a favor."

"Hm. So we have an in with the family Bradshaw in this universe."

"Maybe. But right now, I'm hoping we're outta here before he comes to collect," Michael tossed the phone to Stephanie and swiveled back to the computer. "Let's call up Dorabell. The number here is 372-14765. Put it on speaker."

Stephanie dialed away and set the phone down on the coffee table. After a few rings, a harsh echo of Dorabell's voice forced its way out of the tinny speakers. "Hello? This is Dorabell Underwood."

"Dorabell!" Michael almost yelled. "We need your help. Can you put us on with Matteo?"

"Who is this?" Dorabell asked. "Is this some sort of joke?"

Stephanie leaned in, her chin hovering over the phone, "Its Stephanie Dyer and Michael Duckett. The detectives? You emailed us about your fiancé and we'd like to talk to him," she said, then added, with a wink, "Sorry for the delay. We know you have your choice in detective agencies, and thank you for choosing Duckett and Dyer."

Michael was about to roll his eyes but Dorabell's voice cut him off in an angry yell so loud, it caused the phone to vibrate. "You two? I've been waiting on your response for a month and you call me *now* when it's too late?"

"What do you mean 'too late'?" Michael asked.

"Matteo's gone missing!" Dorabell choked on what sounded like a sob. "Hell, he's probably run off with some big titted floozy! And I can't do anything about it!"

"Oh, no," Stephanie cooed. "You shouldn't blame yourself . . . or your tits."

"I don't!" She spat back. "I blame you! You'll be hearing from my lawyer. And the cops! You idiots can go to hell! You hear me? Go to hell!" And with that, the phone went mercifully silent.

Stephanie turned to Michael, "So how do you think that went?"

Michael raised an eyebrow, "Matteo is missing now? Why is Matteo missing? He wasn't missing in our dimension. Or the other one."

"Well, not until I blew him up," Stephanie donned a smirk, but as quickly as it appeared, it vanished. "Wait a minute. The list. The list of missing people. Do we still have it?"

"I gave it to you."

Stephanie got up and went back into her alternate universe room. She returned carrying her bloody jacket that had distressingly begun to crust over. Using the tips of her fingers she reached inside the side pocket and pulled out a folded paper that had been dyed red and was in danger of falling apart.

"Okay. That's pretty disgusting," Michael said as Stephanie tossed the jacket onto the leather couch with a plop. He was glad it wasn't technically theirs.

Stephanie unfolded the paper as best she could in order to avoid further damage, although any more might have actually constituted an improvement. She squinted at the names, rattling them off one after the other. "Matteo, Terri, Jacob, some lady named Carrie McDermott, then a few that kinda run together. Y'know, on account of the blood. And the last couple are: Kiara Hobson, Tobias Wilkes, then Mr. Finster and that Doctor: Coleman Supirn. Hm."

"Oh, no," Michael's face fell. "What're you thinking?"

"Okay. Stay with me here," Stephanie put out her hands. "Well, we don't know how to use Matteo's dimension hopping machine, right?"

"Right," Michael confirmed.

"But . . . we kinda have been anyway . . . because, to put it bluntly: everything I touch turns to shit. Since I don't have one of Matteo's rings, my . . . dimensional aura . . . or something clashes with everyone else's and every time I touch someone, I create some sort of anomaly in time and space that jumps us to another universe. This is a list of people we have to find and explode before we can go home."

"Huh. That . . . actually makes sense," Michael was impressed. Maybe Stephanie had some critical thinking skills after all.

"Really? Because I was just pulling most of that out of my ass. It's like Quantum Leap, but if Scott Bakula had a concussion."

"This is really weird, though," Michael winced. He didn't really feel comfortable with exploding people with extreme impunity. "I . . . uh . . . don't know if we should do this."

"Mike, it's the only option we have. Matteo's missing in this universe. Probably in all universes since I blew him up! I'm not going to get another one of those rings, and I'm going to eventually have to touch someone anyway. Might as well be in order," Stephanie folded up the paper and put it inside her jacket, in a pocket that nestled against her chest.

"So you're telling me that, given that he's on the list, our best bet at moving forward is to kill Terri's brother?"

Both Michael's and Stephanie's heads swiveled around as a knock on their apartment door answered Michael's question.

A voice they only vaguely recognized echoed from behind the thick, lustrous wood. "Hey, Mike! It's Jacob. You in?"

"Oh, boy," Stephanie rubbed her palms together. "This is going to be fun."

"Just . . . just hold on. Don't kill him," Michael crept to the door and unlatched it, revealing the close shorn hair and prim pressed figure of Jacob Bradshaw. Unlike the last time he had seen Jacob, he was smiling.

"Hey, Mike. How's it going?"

"Uh . . . not bad. Not bad. Yourself?" Michael remained, bracing his arms in frame of the doorway.

"Yeah, I'm alright. Just needed to drop by to ask you something," Jacob leaned to one side and peered over Michael's shoulder. Michael leaned with him to block his view, and then again when Jacob leaned to the other side. He leaned back, uncertain. "Uh . . . can I come in?"

"Oh! Uh, yeah. Sure," Michael, with great reluctance, stepped aside and welcomed Jacob into what was only his home in an existential sense.

"Hey Steph," Jacob chuckled as he spotted Stephanie standing off to the side. "You still living with this guy? I thought my sister would've kicked you to the curb once they started dating."

"Hahah. Yeah. I guess," Stephanie grinned, and extended her hand for a shake. "Nice to see you again, Jake. Put 'er there."

Michael, valiantly trying to avoid the myriad thoughts that flooded his mind upon learning Terri and he were dating in this universe, grabbed Jacob's shoulder and maneuvered him away from a vengeful Stephanie and towards the couch. "So what brings you by . . . buddy?"

Jacob entered and sat down on the couch without an invitation. If he had noticed Stephanie's disgusting jacket on the other end of the couch, he gave no indication. Just to be safe, Michael positioned himself between Jacob and the jacket. "I need to talk to you about work."

"Work?" Michael hadn't thought about work in what felt like ages. To be fair, he had bigger fish to fry at the moment. That and he hated thinking about work.

"Yeah, some of the other guys and I have been talking about your performance."

"What? What are you talking about?"

"Yeah, we feel like you're not giving The Future Group your all. And it's kinda making us look bad. Especially since we've got a big release coming up."

This was the first Michael had heard about a release of any kind. Still, he found himself not caring at all, and more irritated than anything. "And that's why you came here. On a Sunday."

"Since you're dating my sister and all, the other guys at work – Ravi especially – thought I should be the one to have a personal heart-to-heart with you."

"You're here to berate me," Michael squinted. "About work."

"Oh, Mike. I wouldn't say 'berate. '" Jacob pressed his hand to his chest, in mock offense, and it was a simple pivot from there to condescension. "We're like family, you and me. Practically brothers-in-law!" He made an attempt to throw his arm around Michael's shoulder, but when Michael leaned away, he dropped it, and continued unabated. "But, more importantly, thanks to The Future Group, we're part of the same 'work family', y'know? But you've never really been pulling your weight. I'm sure you know that. And I'm just here because we want to help you. For the good of the 'family.' We wouldn't want you to get kicked out of the family. Right?"

"Right," Michael muttered.

"So I'll see you tomorrow bright eyed and bushy tailed?"

"You will," Michael forced a smile.

"Great," Jacob smiled back, then, as all Future Group employees seemed to be mandated to do, added: "Thanks, in advance."

Michael's bile rose in his chest. He turned to Stephanie, who had stood by silently letting her smile grow into a terrifyingly enthusiastic rictus, and nodded. Jacob nodded back, as if it was meant for him. Satisfied, he pushed himself up off the couch.

"Well, great. I'm glad we had this talk. Thanks, Mike," Jacob smiled again, a vapid shit-eating grin, and began to walk out.

"Well, Jacob, as always, it's great to see ya!" Stephanie rushed over to the apartment door, and opened it for him, still all smiles. As Jacob passed her, Stephanie grabbed him by the cheeks and gave him a long, cartoonish kiss and a harsh shove over the doorjamb. She slammed the door shut behind him and braced it with her back."Hahah! That's *two* Bradshaws I've got on you, Mike. Now let's see if we can find their mom next time!"

A slow rumble, followed by what sounded like the popping of an enormous pimple, reverberated through the bones of the building.

As the universe once again began to crumble around him, Michael couldn't help but feel a little bad for ruining the first beautiful apartment building he'd ever theoretically lived in.

CHAPTER TWENTY-ONE

Thunderstruck

Calhoun's Crown Vic screeched to a halt outside 226 Andrews Drive: a mid-level apartment tower that looked like the love-child of a fancy hotel and the skeleton of an aircraft carrier. Calhoun, personally, would've preferred to live in the full aircraft carrier, but he was aware that his tastes didn't jive with what was popular. He also was aware that whatever was popular was shit.

Calhoun flashed his badge, avoiding any unnecessary eye-contact with the doorman and made his way up the elevator to floor 7.

Apartment 7H itself was nice. It had a classic style. Dark blue walls, thick gray curtains and a rich leather sofa that reminded Calhoun of his own, albeit without the cigarette burns. He saw this all over the shoulder of an angry bald man who blocked his way through the door, his arms crossed over his untucked shirt. Couldn't have been older than 30.

"Detective Rex Calhoun. City Police," Calhoun flashed his badge and the man's expression softened, and he allowed him in. "Jacob, is it? I understand you reported someone missing."

"Yes," the man confirmed, as he closed the door. "Terri Bradshaw."

Calhoun stopped in his tracks as the name set alarm bells off in his head. He remembered one of the two idiot P.I.s mentioning her. The male idiot. He had said his girlfriend was missing. This was that same girlfriend. Maybe they had been on to something. "What does she look like?"

"Well, kind of like me. She's my sister. More hair, though. Dark brown, with hazel eyes."

"When did you notice she was missing?"

"I was supposed to get lunch with her today, but she never showed up. I stopped by after work to check on her and she was gone."

"Right," Calhoun jotted all of this down in a small notebook and tapped his pencil to his bottom lip. "Any . . . unusual circumstances surrounding her disappearance?"

"Well, when I got back I had to kick a man and a woman out of the apartment who claimed they were P.I.s investigating Terri's disappearance. They said Terri hired them herself. I was more than a little upset, and I may have hit one of them when I kicked them out."

"Eh. I'd say you were well within your rights," Calhoun shrugged. He didn't need to ask for their names, but he did any way.

"Duckett and Dyer, they said."

Of course it was them. Calhoun's lip twisted. "You think maybe they might be responsible?"

"No. They didn't look like they'd be able to tie a pair of shoes between them." That was as accurate a description as Calhoun had ever heard. "And one of them works at the Future Group with me. No way a Future Group employee would hurt one of their own. We're like family."

"Uh . . . huh." Calhoun had heard of these Future Group types. A real bunch of corporate cultish weirdos. "You said you punched one of them."

"I wasn't thinking straight. Actually, I might owe them one. They were the only reason I considered the possibility that Terri might be missing. That and the state of her bedroom."

"Mind if I take a look?" Calhoun gestured to the back of the apartment. Jacob nodded his quiet assent and led him toward the bedroom.

Unlike the well-kept living room, the bedroom was a disaster area. It was subject to a brisk draft, as the large windows which covered most of the westerly wall had been shattered, leaving pieces of glass all across the floor and the computer desk, like glistening sand. The bed itself was also quite messy. Not unmade, as it appeared no one had slept in it, but the sheets were tousled and stained with dark, dirty shoeprints. Calhoun's first glance estimated them to be from some sort of canvas shoe, but a pair that was nearly worn out.

"Any idea who broke in through the windows?" Calhoun's hand swept across the room as he began to scan the area.

"Could've been those P.I.s, I suppose," Jacob shrugged.

"Doubtful. We're seven stories up." As much as he wanted to pin the blame on those bozos, it was simply improbable. "No way a couple of random idiots get up this high and break through plate glass. Not without some serious equip—"

Calhoun's gaze stopped at the computer table. The shattered bits of glass covered all of it, safe for one area occupied by a bunch of papers. No glass sat atop the paper stack, but a familiar yellow sticky note did.

THIS IS FOR YOU.

This note, like all the others, taunted him. Within a second, Calhoun tore a leather glove from his inner pocket and wrenched it on, grabbing the note and spinning toward Jacob. He waved the note in his face. "What the hell is this? Do you know who wrote this?"

"What? The note?"

"Did the P.I.s leave this?" Calhoun barked. "Duckett and Dyer?"

"No . . . no! Not that I know of."

"Then who wrote this?" Calhoun was yelling now and nearly gnashing his teeth.

"I don't know!"

"Is this your sister's handwriting?" He couldn't leave any possibility unexplored. If this Terri Bradshaw had alerted Duckett and Dyer that she was going to be taken, it was entirely within the realm of plausibility that she was in cahoots with the Sticky Note Specter, if not the Specter herself. She would be the reason Wilkes slipped through his fingers. The reason Carrie was gone. "Is it Terri's handwriting?"

"No. It's not! I . . . I don't think so."

"Then why was it on her desk?" Calhoun was so involved in his questioning that he did not notice the room begin to grow dark as clouds began to gather outside. He realized he was starting to go over the edge, but after the last few days he'd had, he wasn't going to stop himself. "You better not be jerking me around. People are missing. Including two cops. If I find out that either you or your sister were involved, things are going to get really bad, really fast."

"I didn't know that. I didn't know about any of that!" Jacob cried as the wind whistling through the broken windows picked up speed into a desperate howl. "I didn't do—"

Calhoun attempted to grab Jacob by the lapels in a brand of aggressive interrogation, but before he could do so, the world turned white and blue, and he once again experienced a sensation he had not been dying to repeat. His eardrums nearly burst with the force of the thunder. Luckily, Calhoun closed his eyes just in time to prevent being completely blinded, although he could see the blood vessels in his eyelids with remarkable fidelity. However, he had been lunging toward Jacob at the time the lightning struck, and Jacob was no longer there, so Calhoun's momentum carried him forward through the bedroom. Still momentarily stunned and without the full use of his vision, he stumbled cross the broken glass and fell into the computer table with a sharp crack. Calhoun howled in pain, even though he couldn't hear it.

He grunted as he fell to the floor and felt around for the nearest wall. Upon finding it, Calhoun hoisted himself back to his feet and leaned on it to support himself. The wall, however, happened to have other ideas as it ended in a hole that used to be a window. A hole that a blind, deaf, and injured Rex Calhoun fell out of.

Calhoun couldn't see the seven story drop, but felt the force of gravity in his stomach and the rush of wind around him. He also felt the arms that encircled his waist and did their best to grab onto him. On the way down, Calhoun managed to blink some spots out of his eyes, replacing them with a quick glimpse of a pair of welder's goggles. A pang of recognition and, as usual, anger fired off in his brain, as he and the Sticky Note Specter continued to plummet to the ground.

CHAPTER TWENTY-TWO
Touched By An Angle

This time Michael was not thrown into a bush full of thorns, but all this universe jumping was taking a toll on him. The transition from world to world was a little like taking your head for a ride in a running washing machine, and then setting that washing machine on fire. Thus, after popping back into existence gods-knows-where, Michael promptly emptied the contents of his stomach onto the ground.

Once his doubled-over heaves dried up, he noticed the juices that had come out of him were oozing across the floor in a manner he wasn't used to. As he waited for the acrid aftertaste to disappear, he watched his lunch take sharp turns around the raised edges of the ground which featured strange gem-like facets. A second wave of nausea rose and fell in Michael's disturbed gullet as he realized it wasn't just the floor but the entirety of this reality that had adopted a crystalline structure.

Tessellations of orange clouds and violet-red sky extended overhead until it met the jagged, patterned horizon. Around him lone trees dotted the topaz desert wastelands, their foliage a smattering of fractals that infinitely repeated in on themselves. Michael checked his hands and body, somewhat relieved to find that he still consisted of soft, fleshy curves. More than he'd like, but that was a self-image issue. Turning his attention back to the world around him, Michael's head began to spin. It was as if a kaleidoscope was yelling at him to get out. That he didn't belong. And he had to agree.

He heard a quick zip and turned around to the closest tree. Avoiding the sight of its dizzying leaves, Michael found Stephanie sauntering over to him.

"Hey, Mike," she cleared her throat. "Sorry. I had to take a whiz. This place is pretty wacky, though. My pee looked like stained glass."

"Steph, I really don't want to be here right now," Michael was glad to hear his voice hadn't transmogrified into some mathematically symmetrical waveform. "Who's next on the list so we can blow them up and get out of here?"

Stephanie removed the bloody list from her jacket, "It says Carrie McDermott. But after that . . . all the names run together and turn . . . uh . . . red. So we might have a tough time."

"Crap," Michael's anxiety began to take control, but he forced it back down. "Well, at least we don't have to worry about that until we find this Carrie person."

Michael had never heard a gun cock before in real life, but the next sound he heard was what he had imagined it to be. His anxiety buoyed back up and inflamed his brain.

"Now why'd y'all be lookin' for me?" An angry southern drawl, high pitched enough to veer into the comical, accompanied the gun click. Michael's hands shot into the air. Shaking, he turned around to face a cubist nightmare: a woman whose features were so distorted and fractalized, she appeared to be talking out of her inner ear. Her skin, a blotchy mess of inhuman colors, shifted and changed shades based on the corner of her body that was closest to the waning light and a shock of red hair jagged down over her shoulder. Squinting, Michael could make out the distorted shapes of a cowboy hat and associated Wild West style clothing that jutted out from her head and torso in unnerving points.

Behind her, stood a gang of similarly dressed individuals of various geometric shapes, some on the cracked ground, and others atop equally cracked, distressing beasts that appeared to be horses. All of them were brandishing pistols.

"Oh, Jesus," was all Michael could say.

"Gee, Carrie," One of the others – a man with a wide moustache that splintered like broken glass – cackled. "Seems like some varmints stumbled onto our claim."

"Seems they did, Horace. What'n you say I oughta do with 'em?"

"String 'em up on the nearest cactus!" Another one suggested, causing the entire group to erupt in laughter.

"Uh, um . . . excuse me," Michael raised a finger. "Are you . . . Carrie McDermott?"

"That I am," she spat from another hole in her head. "My associates and I've been out in these here wastelands for days trawlin' for gold. No one else comes 'round here," she literally cracked a smile. "You're lucky we found y'two."

"Yes, yes. We're all very lucky," Stephanie reached for the sharp edges of Carrie's shoulders.

Michael grabbed Stephanie by the wrist, in order to stay Carrie's execution. Besides, who knew where the various jagged points of her body would fly once she blew up. Someone could get their eye put out. And with Michael's luck, it would be him.

"Carrie," Michael cleared his throat, "would you mind if me and my associate shared a bit of a sidebar? Just for a moment."

"I dunno about no 'sidebar.'" She turned her nose up at the last word, seemingly unfamiliar with the concept, and giving it its due disdain.

"Don't worry. We'll just be over there for a second." Using Stephanie's wrist, Michael motioned toward another tree further away. "You can shoot us later. Besides, it's not like there's anywhere for us to hide, right?"

"Carrie, you ain't gonna just let them go, are ye'?" The one named Horace asked, through a mouth of what looked like broken teeth.

"Shut yer mouth, Horace. They ain't goin' nowhere. Besides, if they try anything, ain't nothin' stoppin' us from doin' a little 'sidebar' of our own," Carrie smiled at Michael. Now it was abundantly clear that she had no idea what a 'sidebar' was. She waved them away. "G'wan then."

"Much appreciated," Michael forced a smile back and dragged Stephanie away toward the other fractal tree.

"Nice smooth talkin', Mike," Stephanie whispered once they were a reasonable distance away. "But that jigsaw lookin' chick had a gun! And she's on our list. Why'd you stop me from touching her?"

"Well, first of all, I don't feel very comfortable with the level of power you've been granted. Exploding people shouldn't be fun! It's a means to an end."

"But it is pretty fun, though," Stephanie chuckled.

"Would you stop? Just stop. Carrie is the last legible name on our list for a while. What are we supposed to do in the next universe, when we don't know who to explode? I say we stay here, try our luck with Carrie McCowboy and her Pixelated Posse, and try to figure something out before we go flying blind like you usually do. We need a structured plan here."

"Fair point, Mike. But have you thought of this?" Stephanie poked his chest. "Maybe it doesn't matter who we explode. I can just touch the first person or thing we come across, and we'll eventually get back home. Nothing we do will really matter."

Michael blinked at Stephanie's nihilistic, scattershot suggestion. "What the hell are you talking about?"

"Think about it." Her finger moved from the area on Michael's chest where pecs would be on a non-skeletal man, and to her temple, where it began to tap. "Whoever wrote that list knew the order we'd encounter all these people. Matteo, Sir Terri of McDonaldland, Jacob, now our last jump landed use directly in front of this Picasso wet-dream Carrie McDermott. There's no way that's a coincidence. I figure the universe'll automatically guide us to the next name on the list and we'll eventually get to the last guy," she pulled out the list, which was already fraying, and glanced down at it. "Coleman Supirn. And by that time, we'll be home."

"That sounds too easy."

"Maybe, but the way I see it, there's someone out there looking out for us. And they're powerful enough to know our moves before we do. So we'd be stupid not to trust them."

Her logic made a bit of perverse sense, but Michael would never admit it aloud, "And you think whoever wrote the list is trying to lead us home through a string of missing persons from our universe?" Michael paused as a macabre realization dawned on him. "Every person you've exploded turns up missing. Even Matteo was missing in that fancy apartment universe. Are . . . are we erasing people from existence throughout the multi-verse?"

"Eh, maybe," Stephanie shrugged. "But if we don't, we're going to be stuck in someplace like this for eternity." As she gestured at the highly symmetrical, but visually jarring environment around them, a crystalline bird with a dodecadehronal head alit on a tree branch, sending a few fractal leaves falling to the floor, accompanied by a solid teardrop of poop that shattered on contact with the ground.

"Okay, fine. You might have a point," Michael squinted in uncertainty. Besides, the blocky, tessellated aesthetic of this universe unnerved him and was beginning to upset his delicate constitution. "We'll try it your way. But you better be right about this."

"Trust me, it'll be fine. When has it not been, right?" Stephanie smiled with no hint of irony, then whipped around and cupped her hands over her mouth. "Carrie! C'mon over here. We've got something to show you!"

A short while hence, reality splintered into mathematically pleasing shards of blue and white.

CHAPTER TWENTY-THREE

Skies On Fire

Calhoun came to with a massive headache, lying in a pile of trash. If this wasn't the best metaphor for his life, he didn't know how to improve upon it. Pushing himself up and off the mass of black, oozing plastic bags, he struggled to gain purchase with his feet and eventually managed to stand upright in the middle of the dumpster. Calhoun hoisted himself up and out of his foul smelling prison and directly into a puddle of garbage water. Cursing to himself, he craned his neck upwards to find the last wisps of smoke curling up and away from Terri Bradshaw's 7th floor window. It was all he needed to see to know that Jacob Bradshaw was gone.

Along with his eyesight, his hearing had also somewhat returned, as if he had been building up a tolerance to direct lightning strikes. A rustle from the end of the alley caught his attention and Calhoun wheeled around to see the black coat and scarf of the Sticky Note

Specter filling the alleyway with a windswept silhouette. The waning light of day glinted off the goggles he wore over a thick black balaclava and what looked like a sawed-off gray shotgun hung by his waist. Immediately, Calhoun's own gun was up and out, trained on the silhouette's center of mass. He certainly wouldn't be making the same mistake twice.

"Freeze! Police!" Calhoun shouted as he had done several times before. To prevent this becoming a stale catchphrase, this time he added the old chestnut of "Drop your weapon!"

Of course, Calhoun's loud advice was less convincing than he had hoped and the Specter darted out of the alleyway and into the street.

"Goddammit," Calhoun lowered his gun and dashed after him. At least, this time they were in broad – albeit cloudy – daylight, so there would be far fewer shadows to lose him in. It also helped that Andrews Drive wasn't a particularly busy street. It did have its fair share of foot traffic, due mainly to a nearby bus stop that brought the upscale young locals downtown. A few of those very same upscale young locals erupted in gasps as the Sticky Note Specter sped by, and Calhoun shortly thereafter. As they rounded the corner into a slightly less populated side street, Calhoun had had enough and fired off a warning shot into the air. The Specter ducked, stumbled and skidded to a halt and dropping his gun in the process. Calhoun stopped his pursuit, keeping his gun raised.

"Thank you," Calhoun forced the words through gritted teeth. "Now that I have your attention, turn around, get down on the goddamn ground, and put your hands behind your head where I can see them."

The Specter spun around.

"Slowly!" Calhoun barked. "You move too fast, I pop you in the goddamn head."

The Specter obliged, and gradually kneeled. Drawn by the noise, a few curious passersby milled into the street around the stand-off, eager to catch a glimpse of something interesting happening in their neighborhood. Quite unlike the typical reaction in Squalor's Wallow, Calhoun mused, where a gunshot was treated as a proper warning and sent people scuttling for the hills. At least the Andrews Drive contingent were smart enough to keep their distance.

Calhoun turned his attention back to the Specter, whose long black coat pooled around his knees. "You're under arrest for the suspected kidnapping of, well, a damn lot of people." As Calhoun inched toward him, he realized that the Specter wasn't as tall as he had thought he was. A lot smaller, and less muscular than Calhoun assumed he would be. Calhoun kicked the shotgun that the Specter had dropped far out of his reach and continued. "And the assault of Elena Finster. Let's throw that one in there, too, just in case."

Satisfied, Calhoun holstered his gun and grabbed the handcuffs on his belt, eager to slap them on the mysterious stranger that had dogged him for the past few days. He launched into what had become a mantra for him after all these years, "You have the right to remain silent. Anything you say can and will be used against you in a court of law. You have the right to have an attorney. If you cannot afford one, one will be appointed to you by the court. With these rights in mind, are you still willing to talk with me about the charges against you?"

Using his Miranda rights, the Specter opted wisely to say nothing. Instead, he used his head to nod up and to Calhoun's left, apparently indicating his right hand.

"Yeah, no," Calhoun said as he wheeled around him and began to attach the cuffs. After securing them, he came away with another sticky note in his hand that the Specter had gently placed there. "What're you trying to pull?"

YOU'RE MAKING A MISTAKE. The note said. **I'M NOT THE BAD GUY HERE.**

"Not from where I'm standing." Calhoun didn't know how this guy had prepared these notes ahead of time, but he wasn't really in the mindset to care. By this point, a fair amount of people had gathered to watch the proceedings. What had also gathered was an onslaught of menacing clouds that blotted out the sun an otherwise beautiful day. Thunder rumbled in the distance.

The Specter nodded, down this time, toward his other cuffed hand. Calhoun extricated a second note. Somehow he had written these in advance, and Calhoun found that irritating.

I'M JUST TRYING TO HELP. THINGS ARE GOING TO GET WORSE BEFORE THEY GET BETTER.

"Is that a threat?" Calhoun growled, grabbing the Specter by the collar and spinning him around so they could meet eye-to-goggle. He drew his gun again and ripped off the goggles that had taunted him for so long. Beneath lay a set of eyes whose emotions he couldn't place, bright, with a dark undercurrent framed by surprisingly delicate eyebrows. Impossible to read without the full context of a face.

The Specter's eyes darted down and moved around in an awkward fashion, coupled with a bobbling of his head. After a few seconds, Calhoun realized he was signaling to the other side of the note.

"Why can't you just use your words, you son of a bitch?"

JUST LET ME OUT OF THESE CUFFS AND I'LL TELL YOU EVERYTHING.

"Yeah, alright. Nice try," Calhoun grimaced. "Not gonna happen, pal. Now tell me what you did with all those people you took. And what's with all the lightning?"

Another awkward head bobble. The back of the first note.

I HAVE AN ANSWER FOR THAT, BUT YOU'RE NOT GOING TO LIKE IT.

Calhoun snarled and brought his gun up to the Specter's temple, clutching at the top of his balaclava. "Where is everyone? Where is Carrie McDermott?"

The Specter, out of his trademark notes, just shook his head wildly. Calhoun had had enough and began to yank off the mask. As the black knitted fabric began to slip off, a bolt of lightning struck the throng of people that had gathered. Andrews Drive was bathed in a blinding blue and white light for the second time today. Calhoun instinctively threw up his hands to shield his eyes. He hadn't been directly hit this time, but he didn't want to take any chances.

As the spots swimming before his eyes dissipated, Calhoun whipped his head around. A woman in the middle of the crowd of onlookers had been incinerated, and the people who surrounded her had been scattered by the impact, some thrown across the sidewalk and into the street like rag dolls. Nothing of the woman remained, as if she had vanished into thin air. Once the crowd came to and realized what had happened, chaos ensued. They scattered and fled haphazardly into the streets, surging past Calhoun, who struggled to remain upright. Once he managed to get his bearings, Calhoun found that the Specter had taken advantage of the commotion, and disappeared.

It was then that the Specter's prophecy came true, and things got much worse when the second lightning bolt struck, erasing a thin bald man from existence. Then a third hit a nearby building, sending a shower of sparks flying and setting fire to the structure. Calhoun joined the surging tide of human fear and pushed his way back onto the main road of Andrews Drive.

A fourth bolt impacted the front of an oncoming bus which, now missing a driver, decided to veer sharply right, lose control and tip over on to its side, skidding and sparking its way across the asphalt toward Calhoun. Calhoun froze, staring at the wall of metal rushing toward him, the designation B1318 emblazoned across the roof as a literal harbinger of his death. Just before the bus hit, the Specter, hands still cuffed behind his back and blinded by an off-kilter balaclava, barreled into Calhoun from the side and shoved him to the ground. The bus skidded past them before friction slowed it down and stopped it just in front of a streetlight.

Calhoun let out a sigh of relief. He was safe. Momentarily. The wind began to pick up and howled through the city streets as more lightning flew down from the heavens, igniting the sky with the blue hot fires of hell, until the air was thick with the harsh stench of ozone. Calhoun sat, sprawled on his butt, in the street as the pandemonium swirled around him, while the Specter had toppled over on his front and was struggling to right himself with his bound hands.

"What the hell is going on?" Calhoun yelled, his voice barely carrying over the din. "What are you doing?"

The Specter finally managed to stand up. Though his fierce eyes were now covered by his half-off mask, the bottom of his face, though slight, possessed two thin, hard lips that couldn't have been more serious. Calhoun could only imagine those fierce eyes staring him down as the wind blew out the Specter's coat, causing a wave of sticky notes to emerge from the pockets within. They swirled around the Specter in a yellow tornado, giving him such a terrifying, ethereal quality that Calhoun found himself crawling backwards. A gust of air pushed one of the flying notes back toward Calhoun.

DON'T WORRY. IT'LL BE FINE. THEY'RE REAL CLOSE TO CLOSING THE LOOP.

"Loop? What loop?" Calhoun couldn't make heads or tails of this nonsense. "What the hell are you talking about? 'They'? Who are 'they'?"

A second note flew towards him, this one with a note that riled up his already raging blood.

DUCKETT AND DYER.

"Those two morons? Jesus Christ. Are you shitting me? I knew it. I knew this was their fault. I'm gonna make sure they rot in jail."

YOU MIGHT JUST WANNA KEEP AN EYE ON THEM.

"An eye on 'em?" Calhoun rocketed to his feet, anger his fuel, and towered over the Specter. Both of their long coats billowed in the wind, as if two wizards were settling a dispute. "I'm gonna kill 'em!"

JUST BE PATIENT.

"Patient? Patient?!" Calhoun growled as the world around them faded into a blur of noise and light. "Up yours! The world is going to shit and you want me to be patient? Who the hell are you?"

A sigh escaped through his bloodless lips, and the Specter nodded his head up again. Calhoun took the invitation and grabbed the loose fabric, finally yanking the mask off their head and revealing the face beneath. The face of the person who had cost him his white whale and the Carrie McDermott, the first partner he thought was worth a damn in a long time. This was a face he already knew he was going to hate. But he hadn't really known exactly how much he was going to hate it.

"Oh, go fuck yourself," he groaned as the world disappeared in a maelstrom of bluish-white light, before immediately cutting to black.

CHAPTER TWENTY-FOUR

A Series of Unfortunate Universes

To say the next steps of Michael and Stephanie's journey were fruitless was an understatement, except for the one universe they found where everything had an apple for a head. They could not escape that one fast enough. But their subsequent jumps brought them to a further array of maddening alternate worlds: a universe where man was slave to an army of nude giants from space, an earth locked in the grip of an eternal World War I caused by a robotic Franz Ferdinand, and, perhaps most horrifying of all, a reality with a "Normal" Al Yankovic. Stephanie's rapid fire touch of death had allowed them to jump through the multi-verse at will, much to the chagrin of Michael's stomach and inner ear, but after a torrent of blood and guts from a diverse selection of universes, they were very clearly no closer to home than they were when they had started out.

Michael finally reached his limit when they materialized on an Earth completely submerged under water. He wanted to voice his displeasure, but could not, as he could not breathe, which, in an unfortunate cycle, displeased him even further. He grasped at his neck as shapes began to swim before his eyes, or perhaps those were fish or merpeople. Whatever they were, Stephanie, also desperate for air managed to grab one and send them once again hurtling into the great beyond, only to land them in the one place least ideal for two people who were sopping wet: the foot of an enormous mountain in a fierce blizzard.

Below them lay a crevasse so deep they could not see the bottom, and above, heights shrouded by the snow so heavy that they could not see the top. Worst of all, the cliffs around them were devoid of people, as was to be expected, preventing any means of escape from this universe, wherever it was. Unless, of course, there were a few bodies hiding in the snow drifts. Were there any, Michael thought, they would soon have to welcome two more.

In hindsight, as his teeth chattered, Michael wondered why he hadn't realized Stephanie's harebrained schemes would lead them down the path through certain death by hypothermia. It was almost a given.

The only way forward was up and, lacking any better plans, the two exchanged silent glances through the howling winds. Michael's glance was more tired and accusatory than anything. Stephanie took note of that and avoided it as they trudged up the snowbanks to the best of their ability.

Michael's foot squished into his socks and sent a gush of water into his shoes with every step, one of his biggest pet peeves (amongst a host of others, to be sure, but this one was up there). Each oversized lunge into waist high drifts of snow caused the water that had logged him so fully to begin to freeze.

"Damn it, Stephanie!" Michael's voice was mostly lost within the roaring mountain gusts. "What the hell? We've been everywhere and we've made no progress! If we weren't going to die before, we're going to now! We don't even know where we're going or what we're looking for!"

"I thought it would work out!" Stephanie called back.

"You always say that! That's not how the world works! Not everything works out!"

Stephanie growled something that was mostly consumed by the biting winds. It sounded like, "Believe me, I know."

As the drops of water against his skin began to harden, and snowflakes began crystallizing around his eyes, Michael squinted, struggling to see straight. This threw the far side of the mountain pass into sharp relief. Most of it was blanketed by a freezing, blinding white, but one spot was untouched: a deep black and purple gash in the side of the mountain. A cave.

Michael yanked on Stephanie's stiff clothes for her attention, and without a word – for opening his mouth might've caused his tongue to freeze to his teeth – directed her toward the sudden lifeline the multiverse had thrown at them.

A few minutes later, they stumbled out of the blizzard and into the dark, dry shield of the mountain cavern. Michael kicked off his shoes and flung his damp socks against the wall, where they hung for a moment before falling to the floor with a squelching plop. The floor was smooth and cold, but it was dry, and it felt a whole hell of a lot better.

"That was lucky," Stephanie removed her wet green jacket and tossed it to the floor with another slimy plop.

"Yeah. At least now our frozen corpses won't be covered by snow," Michael squeezed what water he could out of his shirt and started to rub his shoulders. His loud sneeze echoed off walls. "Great. It begins."

While Michael was fearing for his life, Stephanie had pushed back further into the cave. She emerged back into the light carrying a handful of sticks, "Hey, there's wood here. We could start a fire."

"You know how to start a fire?" Michael sneezed.

"Yeah. I've done it hundreds of times," Stephanie raised three fingers in a salute. "Scout's honor."

"You weren't a girl scout."

"Yeah, but I'll take any chance I can get to risk their honor," Stephanie threw the wood down into a pile. "I'm not going to let you sneeze to death, Mike."

"That's probably the most apropos death for someone like me."

"C'mon. There's more wood back here. Give me a hand."

Much like their attempts to find their way back to their home universe, Michael and Stephanie spent an inordinate amount of time banging two rocks together. Eventually, against Michael expectations, Stephanie managed to make the dried kindling erupt into a steady, crackling fire that the two of them huddled around. And as large snowflakes continued to drift outside the cave's mouth, Michael and Stephanie began to dry nicely.

"Y'know. I think it's my fault," Michael broke the silence that was peppered only by the crackling, popping fire. "I did it again. I just keep following your dumb ideas because I'm too frozen by fear to do anything else. Even though I know you don't care and are just always blindly flying by the seat of your pants. It was fine when we were growing up, because, hell, we were kids, but not anymore.

"You just barrel headfirst into every situation, and treat everything like it's a damn joke. You can't even take care of yourself. And it's always up to me to prop you up, since I'm the only one of us that cares about anything and takes things seriously. It's a crazy feedback loop that just keeps getting worse. I can't be the only real friend in this friendship anymore."

The remnants of Michael's tirade echoed throughout the cave for a few long seconds. Stephanie remained quiet until they dissipated, then spoke up.

"Let me ask you a question, Michael," her tone matched his, but in a more subdued whisper as the fire cast shadows across her face, seeping into every curve and corner, aging her far beyond her years. "What do you know about my parents?"

"I uh . . ." Michael stopped. He hadn't been expecting that. As he searched back through his memories, nothing about her parents came to mind. He knew they had died when Stephanie was young – before they had met – but Michael had never seen a picture of them. " . . .nothing."

"Ellis and Tina," her eyes returned to the flames. "Those were their names. I think. I was a kid, they were always just 'mommy' and 'papa' to me. In the almost fifteen years we've known each other, did you ever even think about asking me their names? Or about what happened to them?"

"Well, no . . . I figured you didn't want to talk about it."

"Of course I didn't!" Stephanie's voice echoed throughout the cave before dropping back down. "But I'd like to have been asked."

"Well, I'm . . . sorry. I didn't think—"

"Yeah. I know. You think I never take things seriously. That I'm all about just making jokes and thinking things will be alright. Well, it's the only way I know how to be."

"What do you mean?"

"After my parents died, you know I lived with my Aunt and Uncle. But I was forced on them. They just . . . never seemed cut out to be parents, y'know? Your mom was always on your back about everything, right?"

"Still is," Michael corrected.

"Yeah. I would kill to have something like that. But my aunt and uncle didn't put in an effort. I mean, they fed me, and clothed me, but that was about it. They turned me loose and let me do whatever I wanted.

"Remember that Friday in 8th grade where we hung out for hours after school? And then I spent the weekend at your place?"

Michael nodded.

"It was when we solved the mystery of who ate the cookies and it was your dog?" A slight smile appeared on Stephanie's face before vanishing.

Michael recalled a young Stephanie tugging on his mom's slacks to ask if it was okay that she slept over. And then she had said something else that Michael could not hear, but he remembered seeing his mom's face turning flat when she agreed. He had been so happy to hear the 'yes' that everything else was immediately forgotten.

"It was because my aunt and uncle took a long weekend away and forgot about me," she continued, "I guess I can't blame 'em. They didn't want kids. But I never had real parents for the rest of my life. I had to be my own parent," Stephanie paused, and leaned toward the fire. "So y'know how moms and dads have to keep their cool - or pretend to - in front of their kid so they don't get scared or worry about stuff?"

"Yeah." Although Michael remembered his mother losing her cool often over trivial things, but she always comforted him through tougher times.

"I didn't have any parents that were there for me, so I was the one who had to put on a brave face for myself after they died. And then all the time. And here I am."

"I didn't know that about you."

"Well, you never asked. So I never told you. Never told anyone. Didn't think it mattered. Figured that life was just a bunch of confusing shit and nothing mattered. What kind and gentle universe takes away a kids' parents?"

"Right," Michael bit his lip, the hot burn of shame igniting the back of his head.

"But even then, you're the only one of my friends who stuck around," Stephanie whispered over the crackle and, for the first time, Michael could not blame the internal guilt that ignited in his chest on his parents' overbearing upbringing nor social anxiety. "It was a real kick in the ass when you said you'd had enough."

"I'm sorry," was all Michael could manage. "I didn't mean that."

"Of course you meant it," Stephanie shot back. "And I know you want me to change."

"Steph, I don't want you to change."

"Yes, you do. And I do, too. But I can't change. I want to be all serious and get my life on track like you. Get a job. Pay the rent. But I can't. It just doesn't work for me. Stuff like that just seems petty and not worth obsessing over. I know it shouldn't, but I'm too set in who I am. And I kind of hate that," Stephanie rubbed her hands together.

Michael slowly began to realize that maybe his annoyance with Stephanie stemmed from how carefree she could be as opposed to how trapped and helpless he always felt, and his guilt quadrupled. He clenched his jaw in an attempt to prevent it from overwhelming him.

"But then we got sucked into this whole multi-versal time-travel shitshow," Stephanie continued, "and I figured . . . if I can't change who I am now, maybe I could change who I was in the past. Or maybe I could find a universe where I still had a family. And then we'd be better friends for it. But instead, everything went tits up like with all of my shit. We don't even know where and when we are now. It's not worth it. Hell, I almost killed you several times over."

"Steph . . ."

"I'm sorry for not telling you all this," she said, finally. "And I'm sorry for not being better. All I can promise you is that if we do get back home. I'll try to be more responsible and do my best to hold down a job. But I don't think I'll ever be as competent as you."

"Good," Michael looked down. The frozen interior he had been cultivating for so long began to thaw with the first crack of a smile. "If you were anything like me, we'd have killed each other a long time ago."

The two did not say another word to each other and, over the next hour, fell into dreamless sleeps. This could have been attributed to the utter exhaustion of finally expressing honest feelings after two decades of friendship, or the carbon monoxide build-up in the cave due to the fire.

CHAPTER TWENTY-FIVE
Sage Advice

Michael shivered himself awake. Light streamed through the cave and cast itself across the warm gray ashes of the fire. A brief gust of wind put out any remaining smolder. Michael pushed himself up off the cold ground and found his now dry socks and shoes by his feet. Donning them once again, he turned toward the mouth of the cave, awash in the blinding combination of daylight and snow. Stephanie's silhouette cleaved the light in two and provided enough contrast for Michael to confirm that it was no longer snowing.

"Mornin', Mike!" Stephanie's voice ricocheted down the cave toward him. Any iota of what had transpired between them last night was gone, and the mask was back on. But she was her usual chipper and upbeat self again, so Michael didn't want to press further.

"Mornin'," Michael grumbled out of the corner of his mouth. "Whatimezit?"

"I was hoping you'd be able to tell me," Stephanie pointed at his hand. "Can your thing ring do its thing?"

Michael had almost forgotten about the ring. After so many jumps it felt as if it was now a part of him. He gently rotated the dial, hoping whatever circuits were inside hadn't shorted out. The red light shot out onto the pure driven snow, and Michael angled it back within the cave to get a less washed out display of their current position.

```
USER_HOME:\\10E63.99873445219
USER_TIME:\\20130913190387235
CURR_UNIV:\\10E63.99873445322
CURR_TIME:\\20630924284015846
INPT_DEST:\\ _
```

The cursor blinked at him again.

"Still not home, but the universe is similar. And we're in the future. Further in the future than we were when we met Matteo. Much further," Michael said.

"Neat!" Stephanie smiled. "Are we far enough for flying cars?"

"How should I know? Hell, I don't even know wher—"

"Himalayas," came a rough grunt off to the side.

Michael jumped and slipped upon hitting the ground. His feet went flying out from beneath him and he crashed to the floor on his tailbone with an echoing yelp.

"Hahaha!" an old woman with a voice as rough as sandpaper, and dark, weathered skin of a similar texture chortled as she shuffled through the snow and into view. "Thank you. I haven't had a good laugh like that in a few years. That's some quality slapstick."

"Who are you?" Michael glared up at her from the cold stone floor while massaging his butt with his hand.

"Oh, right." The woman drew tighter the thick red wool shawls that were draped around her body. Her eyes were frozen into a permanent squint, either to cope with the snowglare or perhaps because they had merged with the deep wrinkles that had carved their way into her face. "We haven't met yet."

Michael and Stephanie shared a look, then stared back at the woman, expecting some elaboration. Whether or not she saw them through the folds of her face was unknowable. No answers came, instead a long beat of silence persisted.

"Well, the universe works in mysterious ways," she cleared her throat. "Now, if you'll excuse me, it's 9am. Or, it would be, if there were still any clocks around. So, time for my morning meditation." Without any further context, she shuffled onwards past the mouth of the cave disappearing around the other side.

"By the way," she called back. "You're welcome for the lighter."

Michael arched an eyebrow and turned toward Stephanie, who had a guilty grin on her face and a lighter she revealed beneath her fingers.

"Hm. Girl scout, my ass," Michael returned his attention outside, but could find neither wrinkly hide nor gray hair of the mysterious old woman. It was only a few minutes later, that he could see her small form making its way up the mountain, a bright red speck in a sea of white slashed by daggers of black that looked like steps.

"Should we go after her?" Stephanie asked.

"Yes! Let's go," Michael leapt to his feet before smashing back down onto the ground, again.

Stephanie chuckled. "She's right. That was pretty funny."

"Thanks," Michael deadpanned while pushing himself up and ensuring a modicum of balance.

*   *   *

The snow was up to Michael's waist at this point and he took comically large steps in order to make any headway. Stephanie followed comfortably in his wake. By the time they reached the pass where they had last spotted the woman, Michael's shoes had again become victims of the insidious melted ice that had seeped in through every pore. Nevertheless, they found themselves staring up a steep flight of stairs that ascended into the morning sun. A crisp, clean portion of yesterday's snowfall lay across each step, which had been meticulously carved into the sheer cliff face. The only disturbance was a set of old lady footprints, the smaller toes gnarled and less defined.

"You've gotta be kidding me," Michael said. "Her damn feet are going to fall off."

"Yeah. Let's find her before that happens," Stephanie pushed past him and bounded up the stairs two by two with such vigor that she had already reached the first landing before Michael started to follow.

It only took about thirty steps before Michael's knees began to ache, and he wondered how Led Zeppelin had managed to make a stairway to heaven sound so appealing. But perhaps he had missed the entire point of that song. Stephanie was still far ahead of him and, though she, too, had slowed down, she continued to propel herself skyward with some unseen source of energy. For all Michael's criticisms of her never caring, she certainly had been giving it her all these past few days. If you could call them days.

Climbing nearly vertical stairs for forty-five minutes was not the scenario that human legs had been designed for, so eventually Michael and Stephanie's arms helped them out. By the time they reached the top on all fours, they collapsed on the soft bed of snow that awaited them.

"How many frickin' stairs was that?" Michael groaned, lying on his back.

"I'm going to say infinity."

"Quit your complaining. You aren't the ones who had to carve them," the woman's scratchy voice droned.

Michael lifted his head up to see over Stephanie's butt – she had flopped face down into the snow and was using it to cool off – to see the old woman sitting cross-legged atop a boulder. She seemed to be meditating, though her constant squint made that more of a guess than anything.

"I was wondering when you'd make it up here," she said, basking in the glow of sunlight that beamed directly onto her. Before her stone pedestal was a precipitous drop into a sea of clouds. "I'm not getting any younger."

"Okay, hold on," Michael pushed himself up. "Who the hell are you anyway? Are we supposed to know you?"

"Well, no," the old woman admitted. "But I know you. I've met you a lot of times."

"What?" Michael took a step back.

"Well, not you specifically. All the others eventually come through here. It's a bit of a pit stop, since you all never seem to know exactly where you're going."

"Listen here, Yoda," Stephanie was up and rushing toward the woman, her hand extended in an angry claw. "You better stop being all cryptic and give us some answers, or I will seriously explode you so hard—"

The woman calmly raised her hand, but didn't flinch, nor did she make eye contact. "Hold on there, sweetheart. I'll give you everything you need to know. Just slow your roll."

Stephanie stood down as Michael sidled up behind her.

"But who *are* you, really?"

"My name is Kiara Hobson," she said with a zen-like tone, which still somehow retained its cranky old person chic.

"Hah! From the list!" Stephanie snorted.

Kiara cleared her throat and turned her gaze out over the puffy white cloudscape and to the tiny peaks of other mountains in the distance. "And this is my world."

"Wait, could we go back a second to the part where you said something about how you met a bunch of different versions of us?" Michael asked. "Because that's kind of freaking me out."

At this, Kiara turned and snapped, "You're going to have a lot more to freak out about if you don't shut up and listen to me. So are you going to keep asking questions or are you going to let me tell my damn story?"

"Sorry."

Kiara turned back to stare at the middle distance. "I used to be a cop here. Pretty good one, too. Until some sort of disaster destroyed all of civilization fifty years ago. Called it 'the Cataclysm.' Hell of a way to end a career, I'll tell you that."

"Cataclysm?" Michael asked. "What kind of cataclysm?"

"Dunno. Nobody lived long enough to give me the scoop. You see, I'm the last person alive on this Earth. I spent the next few decades looking for survivors, but I found none. Do you know how irritating that is?"

"I can imagine," Michael attempted to empathize.

"No, you can't. Have you ever tried to buy booze on a dead earth? You've got to brew your own! Shit ain't easy!" Kiara cleared her throat. "Anyway, I eventually made my way up here to the Himalayas. I'd gotten old by then, and this seemed just as good a place as any to hang around. Nice. Peaceful. Crisp air. So I spent the next decade or so carving out those stairs, and here I sit, serving as a guide post to any wayward travelers of the multi-verse."

"You know about the multi-verse?" Stephanie cocked her head. "Then you know how we can get home!"

"Yes, yes," Kiara waved a disinterested hand. "I know all about this whole space and time travel deal. Mostly because you two wouldn't shut up about it."

"A few years after the cataclysm occurred, the first pair of you popped up. I had no idea what was going on, and after a brief scuffle you," Kiara pointed a gnarled finger at Stephanie, "touched me and I exploded."

"Yeah . . . uh . . . I kinda have a habit of doing that."

248

"But the next thing I know, I pop back into my lonely existence."

"Wait, you come back?" Michael asked.

"What did I say about the questions?"

"Sorry."

"Anyway, yes. I come back. Then I meet another pair of you, slightly different, but the same. Same thing happens, I go kaboom. Then I'm back. Later on I meet another one of you two and the cycle repeats. It's gone on pretty much forever. You guys come in, I explode, something resets and I keep on keeping on. Apparently, I'm the crossroads where all of you guys end up. And don't ask 'why me?', because god knows I keep asking myself the same thing every day. Point is, you two goofballs broke the universe, and now it's up to you to fix it."

Michael had started to zone out about halfway through Kiara's explanation. Something about the true vastness of the multi-verse hit him like a wave. Not only were there other versions of himself and Stephanie out there, but they had all been making the same mistakes and breaking the multi-universe on a daily basis. And not only was Michael a screw-up in his universe, but in every universe. The enormity of his failure doubled back on him and he rushed to the edge of the mountain and ejected the contents of his stomach into the cold air.

"Oh, yeah," Kiara rolled her eyes. "We've got a puker this time."

Michael inched back from the edge, as he realized how high up they were. "Leave me alone. I just got done hearing about how my uselessness transcends the laws of time and space. You think you could give me a minute?"

"What, you thought you were special?" Kiara snorted.

"No one's special," Michael plowed his head into the snow. "Steph's right. Nothing matters."

Stephanie's footsteps crunched toward him. She picked him up by his armpits and sat him upright, dusting off the residual frost. "Don't worry, Mike. We're not screw-ups. I know we can fix this. But we have to do it together, like the old lady with the beef jerky skin said."

"You better," Kiara spat, ignoring Stephanie's jab. "You've got to close whatever loop you two broke. Once you do, everything you've screwed up gets undone. I come back, and all the other missing people that Stephanie's erased from existence come back."

"I said I was sorry!" Stephanie moaned.

"No, you didn't," Michael said out of the corner of his mouth.

"Well, I meant to."

"Oh, no. Are you another pair of them that bicker and bitch?" Kiara sighed and slung her head low. "I miss the two of you from the cowboy universe. They were fun."

"So you're saying every version of us from different worlds has had to come here?" Stephanie cocked an eyebrow. "What ever happened to free will?"

"Kiddo, you'd be better off not getting into this philosophical shit, trust me. 'Free will' is just a concept people yell about when they don't want to do things they have to do. There's only ever a lack of it. Do you think I want to be talking to you right now? I've could be building anatomically correct snowmen."

Stephanie pushed Michael away and moved toward Kiara. "Do you think we could've caused the cataclysm in your world?"

"I've considered it," Kiara rubbed her weathered chin. "Maybe my universe's version of you two didn't have me to advise you with your dimension hopping shenanigans. Couldn't close the loop. No way to be sure. If it's true, I forgive you," she said, then muttered out of the corner of her mouth, "Not much friggin' else for me to do now."

"So how do we fix this?" Michael asked. "How do we close the loop?"

"That's for you to figure out. I don't see any of you after you do," Kiara shrugged. "I'm just here to help you move on."

"Alright, so since you seem pretty used to this, I'm going to just explode you and we'll be on our way back in no time," Stephanie raised her hand again.

"Yeah, no," Kiara raised her hand back. "You might want to step back. You're not going anywhere without my help."

"And why not?"

"Because," Kiara's voice broke into a childish sing-song, "I know something you don't know!"

"Yes," Michael agreed. "You've made that pretty clear."

"Your ass-backwards method of multi-verse travel isn't random. You're supposed to have a little doohickey that syncs with your ring, but since that's gone . . ."

"I said I was sorry!" Stephanie repeated.

" . . .since that's gone. You have to direct it yourselves."

"Right," Stephanie said and reached into her jacket to extract the fragile, bloodstained pieces of the handwritten list of missing people. "We've been using this list to guide us through the universes. And you're the next one on it."

"The list doesn't matter!" Kiara grabbed it out of Stephanie's hand and tore it in half, letting the dried pieces flutter off into the wind and over the edge of the mountain.

"Hey!" Stephanie ran towards the flying papers and stopped just before she toppled off the mountain. She turned and stormed back to Kiara. "We needed that!"

"No, you don't. Haven't you been listening to anything I've said? The list was just a jumping off point to guide you in the right direction. What you need to do is look inside yourselves," Kiara took in a deep breath, emphasizing the gravitas of her proclamation. "See with your minds. With your hearts. You've got to *want* to be where you want to be, and you both gotta agree. You see?"

Michael blinked while taking this in, then raised an eyebrow, "That's a little fairy tale for my taste. You're saying this scientific physics *machine*," he waved the ring on his finger around, "is going to read our mystical auras? That doesn't make any sense. Besides, we still have a few names at the end of our list—"

"Listen, kid. I'm just the messenger," Kiara shook her head. "Some of your other multi-verse doubles told me this, so I'm just telling it to you. You don't want to listen, fine. Have fun when you jump out of here and end up in some crazy nightmare dimension where people have cow's heads and eyeballs for fingertips or some other horrifying shit like that."

"Then what happened to the other versions of us after they came here?" Michael asked.

"I've told you all I know. But as far as I can tell, nothing good," Kiara groaned as she lifted her creaking bones off of the rock. "I can't even guarantee you all ever got back to your homes."

"Or maybe we do and that's how everything resets in the other universes!" Michael stabbed the hair with his finger.

"Yeah, sure. Whatever," Kiara shrugged. "I don't really care. Everyone I've ever known is dead."

"Sorry," Michael and Stephanie muttered.

"Ah, it doesn't matter. Let's get this over with," she hobbled her way over to the two of them. "I'm not as young as I used to be and I feel like I've grown infinitely older just by talking to you."

"Kiara," Stephanie held her hand out ready to do the deed, but Michael noticed a slight trembling in her arm, "before I do this . . . I have a question . . ."

"I know. You always do. But now's not the time."

"But . . ."

"Hold on to it. You'll know when," Kiara's hand shot out and grabbed Stephanie's wrist. With a sharp crack the elderly woman's body jolted and flew back over the edge of the mountain and disappeared into the cloudy depths below, but not before combusting into a fine, bloody mist halfway down.

Michael and Stephanie stepped back after having craned their necks over the edge in order to watch Kiara's macabre demise.

"You think she'll come back like she said?" Stephanie turned to Michael.

Michael could only shrug.

"So what do we do now? Put on our ruby slippers and wish for no place like home?"

"Seems like our only option," Michael said as the rock below them began to crack and splinter and the deep blue light of the universe began to seep out. He took a deep breath, shut his eyes, and reminded himself of Kiara's words, however hokey they may have been. But, peeking out of one, it comforted him to see that Stephanie too had closed her eyes and was silently thinking to herself, no doubt about where she truly wanted to go. Silently, they clasped hands and hoped that maybe they were heading home after all.

CHAPTER TWENTY-SIX
Nightmares of Their Own Creation

Before Michael even opened his eyes, he felt something was wrong. More specifically, he felt his hands bound behind his back and the coarse fibers of rope chafing his wrists as he jostled against them.

"Oh, good," Stephanie's voice came from behind him. "You're up. These guys aren't the best conversationalists."

Michael tried to crane his head around, but had little range of motion. He couldn't see Stephanie, but he did manage to take stock of his surroundings.

"Oh, *Goddammit!*" He shouted when he saw the first creature that had a cow's head situated upon a nude body. The thing stood before them, brandishing a ceremonial staff made of a gnarled branch whose tips ended in naturally occurring teeth. A long shawl of thick, scratchy wool draped over its shoulders and did little to cover its modesty: a set of genitalia that looked like two octopi kissing. Its fingertips, which it refused to stop wiggling, each ended in bulbous, wet, and bleary eyeballs.

Michael and Stephanie had been bound back to back against a thick wooden pole on a raised stony dais. Around them was a vast valley flanked on all sides by towering mountains whose jagged, irregular peaks reached longingly towards the light of an ominous setting black sun. Filling this valley, bathed in the ebony twilight, were a horde of naked cow-eyeball-hand people staring balefully up at them with both their cow eyes and hand-eyes, the latter of which were raised to the sky and brandishing torches that glowed with unnatural green flames. It was, as Kiara had said, their very own nightmare dimension.

"Okay, this is wayyyy too much. Hamburgers were one thing, but cow monsters are a whole different animal."

"Technically, they're the same animal, Mike."

Michael grimaced hard, even though Stephanie could not see him. "I really cannot handle this right now. How did we get here?"

"You tell me. I open my eyes and find myself all tied up like in the last scene of Indiana Jones," Stephanie replied. "Did you let that crazy old lady get into your head? Did you think about that freakish nightmare place?"

"I don't know!" Michael couldn't be sure it wasn't his fault. "Subconsciously, maybe?"

"Well, maybe I let her get to me subconsciously, too. I guess her idea to use our internal compasses to navigate kinda worked."

"Sure as shit looks like it, Steph!" A logistic thought made it through Michael's mania, "How'd they hogtie you without getting blown up?"

"Great question. I asked them about it, but they didn't really want to give me a straight answer," Michael felt Stephanie's head nod over to the shambling masses. "All they seem to be able to say is—"

"ALL HAIL THE MAN-GOD," the closest cow-eye-hybrid – the one with the tooth stick – finished Stephanie's sentence with a deep, bellowing that rattled the necklace of miniature human skulls that hung around its neck. The call echoed off the valley walls and into the sky.

The congregation before it began chanting in response. They repeated the words of the shaman-leader with docile droning as the green fire bathed them in an unholy light. "MAN-GOD. MAN-GOD. MAN-GOD."

"So what the hell is a Man-God?" Stephanie asked.

"Do you really want to find out?"

"Kinda. Don't you?"

"Not particularly!" Michael snapped. "This is not the time to stick around and ask dumb questions. We need to leave, *now.* Can you just, y'know . . .?"

"Fine. Fine," Stephanie turned her attention to the shaman cow. "Hey you! Cow Man Supreme!"

The newly dubbed Cow Man Supreme torqued towards them in a fluid motion that unsettled the cockles of Michael's heart. Although this reality was already surreal, Cow Man Supreme moved like it didn't belong. As if it had been digitally inserted into the scenery after the fact. Its cold, dark eyes blinked with a mucousy slowness that betrayed no hint of complex emotion. Michael struggled not to look at its terrifying genitals to no avail.

"Yeah, that's right," Stephanie continued. "I'm talking to you, Monster Mash. C'mere a minute. I got a question for you."

It began to approach the two of them, with erratic, jerking steps that were somehow still in time with the chanting chorus behind it.

"Yeah, that's it. C'mon," Stephanie said. "I've got your Man-God right here."

The cow shaman stopped and tilted its head, as if its mind had been occupied by another thought.

"THE MAN-GOD," the words drooled off of its forked tongue before it turned once again and staggered to the lip of the dais. It raised its staff high in the air and lead the masses in further chanting that erupted into a loud braying.

"Oh, man, come on! No! Where are you going? Where's it go—" Michael stopped his whining as a shadow swept across the valley, ending the cacophony of moos almost instantly. Michael shivered. A feeling of sheer cold pierced down to his bones. On the far side of the valley, the mountains rumbled. Michael wasn't sure what was happening, but he had never felt the same kind of fear it inspired in him. And he was usually afraid of everything.

"What the hell is going on?" Stephanie swung her head to the side indicating the chaos in the valley as the mountains began to crack and splinter, throwing up fissures of steam and lava.

"Uh . . . I'm gonna guess Man-God."

"BEHOLD THE FURY OF THE MAN-GOD," the shaman shouted. "TOBIAS, PREPARE THE SACRIFICES."

"Oh, great. That's the word I wanted to hear," Michael rolled his eyes as a heretofore unseen guard, advanced on the sacrifice pole, its muscular cow body heaving with blind passion.

"Back up a second. Is this dude's name Tobias? Who names their monster cow child Tobias?"

As 'Tobias' extended his eyeball-tipped hands towards them, Michael yelled, "Steph, could you just shut up and do your thing?"

"Alright. You might want to brace yourself for this!" Stephanie said.

Michael screwed his eyes shut as the entire pole lurched back. Stephanie yelped as her skull thonked against the leathery face of Tobias the cow guard. An ear splitting, pained, but still somehow hilarious 'moo' rang out, as Tobias fell off the dais and onto the ground below with a sickening crack. Before his blood could ooze into the ground, a thunderclap of blue lightning ignited it into another portal. Stephanie and Michael rocked against the pole, causing it to dislodge and tumble backward.

"Here it goes again. Think of where we want to be," Michael said as they leaned into the topple. "Let's try and go someplace that'll help both of us."

"Yeah. That sounds like a good plan, Mike. See you on the other side!"

And as they fell towards the unknown once again, their hands interlocked between the bindings, and together they sang 'kumbaya', but really only focusing on the "yaaaaaa!"

*   *   *

Michael awoke with a face full of dirt and the hot midday sun drawing sweat out of his back. He spit out the dust and rocks that had made their way into his cheeks by some sort of saliva-induced capillary action. Pushing himself up, Michael rubbed his sore, but free wrists. Where the rope and pole had gone, he had no clue, but he was glad to be rid of them. But Stephanie was also missing.

"Steph? Stephanie?" Michael, his heart thumping in his chest, spun around, looking for her. What he found instead were the remains of dusty tire tracks that his fall had disturbed. He had been deposited on what looked like an elevated, dirt road that cut through an empty desert that approached the road from the right with a deep ditch at their juncture, then dropped off with a dangerous, steep and sandy hill on the left that led to yet more desert far below.

Michael pondered his location for a short while, only to have his train of thought interrupted by a wood paneled station wagon that came barreling towards him, horn blaring at the very last minute. Michael saw the car swerve to his right, just before he dove left – the least optimal direction – and tumbled for a full three minutes down the steep sandy hill, occasionally hitting the odd dry bush with his neck or groin.

His sole thought during the ordeal – other than "ow" – was, "At least I'm in a normal universe where they have cars."

Michael eventually rolled to a stop at the bottom, inches before a cactus would have slammed into his face.

Still high on adrenaline, he jumped to his feet, ignoring his potential de-facing, and spotted a thin column of smoke snaking its way up from whence he fell. He could not see the car, or really any of the road from his current position, and attempted to scrabble back up to apologize and offer his assistance, only to be denied by the loose sand and dirt.

Michael staggered backwards away from the hill and cupped his hands over his mouth. "Hey! Hello! Are you okay?" But his words were lost to the desert winds.

As he didn't hear any sort of explosion, Michael hoped the inevitable family of four that had been in that station wagon were okay and just a little irritated that their car was now in a ditch.

They would have been in much worse shape if they'd crashed down on my side, he thought. But Michael's attempts to assuage his own guilt were futile. He needed to get back up there, make sure they were alright, maybe help them if he could.

So Michael set out, trudging through the sand parallel to the steep drop he had fallen down. Perhaps he could find a more manageable pathway back up. Stairs would have been ideal, of course, but he couldn't count on the presence of a Kiara Hobson to have carved them.

As he made his way past dry shrubs and the occasional cactus, the sun beat down mercilessly on his shoulders, and more rivulets of sweat began to escape from every pore in his body, even some pores he wasn't aware he had. He had always been a very poor sweater. As Michael wiped the salt off his brow for the eighteenth time, the hill fell away as he entered a sort of half-canyon between a large cliff face a much less sheer incline covered in rocks the color of the setting sun.

The real sun, still situated directly above, continued to torment him, and as Michael began to crawl his way up the side from rock to rock, he began to reconsider his desire to help these people, whoever they were. He had to find Stephanie. Besides, they must have called a tow truck by now. Or whatever other kind of roadside assistance existed in this universe.

In fact, what universe was he even in? Michael stopped his upward climb, and attempted to rest on a rock. The extreme heat penetrated his jeans and singed his butt, causing him to jump back up. His yelp echoed through the narrow canyon. Sighing, Michael looked down at his hands and rotated the ring, pointing the display end down into the shadow he cast.

The familiar scroll of red text began to appear.

`USER_HOME:\\10E63.99873445219`

`USER_TIME:\\20130913190387235`

But, just as the `CURR_UNIV` field was to pop up, the entire display jittered, fizzled and winked out of sight.

"What the hell?" Michael stared at the ring and began hitting it. "No, no, no! Where'd it go? What's going on?"

He rotated the ring again, but it refused to respond. If Michael had known more about its functionality, he would've known something was causing interference. Something about his presence in this time and place. But he didn't know that, so he just kept hitting it.

"C'mon . . . c'mon . . ."

"Excuse me?"

Michael didn't hear the plaintive question the first time, as he was too busy abusing the ring. The second time, however, surprised him so much that he stumbled back, falling over the burning rock and into the even more burning sand.

"Ow! Jesus Christ! Hot hot hot!" He jumped up and began swatting the sand off of him, as if it were a colony of fire ants. Once Michael was suitably satisfied, he looked up to find a teenage boy looking at him. Early teens, just right at the awkward stage Michael had never been able to escape.

"Could you help me?" The kid asked. And he definitely looked like he needed help. His flannel shirt and jeans were torn in odd places. Michael figured this was a cool fashion thing that he, as a particularly unhip individual, was unaware of. But on second glance, the amount of scrapes and cuts on the boy's exposed skin, not to mention the giant bleeding gash that ran along his forehead and the fact that he was sheepishly cradling his arm proved otherwise. There was something else about him, though. Something Michael couldn't place. But whatever it was took a back seat to his concern.

"Oh, my god. Are you alright?" He cried.

"Yeah. I . . . I'm okay, I think," the kid rubbed the part of his head that wasn't bleeding. "But my family. I think they need help. There was an accident. We ran our car off the road."

Michael winced. His guilt surged as he wondered if it was best to come clean about his involvement in the situation. Honesty was always the best policy, but would it really matter right now? Would it just distract from actually being able to help out? Besides, there were plenty of other policies he could use. He liked his universes better when the biggest issues were strange mountain women, cubist lady cowboys, or literal cow boys. Moral dilemmas were proving to be more of a hassle.

"Where are your parents?" Michael's first thought was that he needed an adult. A real one. They would know what to do.

"They're back at the car. They're really hurt. They can barely move. And my sister's too little. I was the only one of us who could go get help. I'm really glad I found you."

No such luck, then. He'd have to be the adult, despite being emotionally and physically ill-equipped. Michael stood up straight, and took a deep breath and steeled himself against his growing internal criticism.

"Yeah, me too," Michael nodded toward the boy. "Do you have a cell phone?"

"A what?" The boy looked taken aback. "I'm not a millionaire."

Cars but no cell phones.

"Okay, never mind. We'll have to do this the manual way. Which way were you guys heading?"

"This way," the kid indicated the way through the canyon. "There's a small town nearby. We were going to visit friends."

"Good, then we're on the right track," Michael internally breathed a sigh of relief. It wouldn't be long before he got this kid to safety and balance his karmic scales, then he could start looking for Stephanie. "Let's go. We should be able to call for help there."

Michael started walking, and the boy hobbled behind with a slight limp. Michael looked back and bit his lip. "You alright?"

"Yeah," the boy avoided eye contact with a mix of awkwardness and prideful anger. Whatever universe this was, teenagers certainly were the same here. "I'm good."

"Nuh-uh," Michael had to be the adult here. "You're not good. Trust me. I'm the mascot for 'not good.' Come here. I'll help you."

Michael turned around and began to stride towards the boy, but felt an unusual sense of resistance. Not from the kid, but from everything around him. Despite this, Michael reached out his hand and, swallowing his misplaced teenage pride, the kid clasped it.

"There. See? Not so bad. Sorry about my sweat," Michael's tone turned so parental that it surprised him. He braced the kid's body against his own and helped him walk. "What's your name, dude?"

The boy, still avoiding eye contact, stuttered. "It's . . . uh . . . It's-hey. What's going on with your ring?"

Michael glanced down to find that Matteo's time ring had started to sputter and shake, blue sparks ejecting from it like a cheap five dollar firework.

"Shit shit shit!" Michael nearly dropped the kid out of fear. He wasn't sure what was going on, but it wasn't looking good. He began to yank at the ring, but it refused to come off. "It's not safe! Run! Get away from me!"

"Run?" The kid cried. "Run where?"

Before Michael could answer, the unrelenting sun that had been present just a moment ago was inexplicably covered by localized dark clouds whose linings began to glow a familiar shade of blue. A bolt of what looked like lighting streaked out of the sky and struck the ground between Michael and the kid, blasting them backwards and throwing Michael headfirst into a rock and unconsciousness.

*　　*　　*

"Mike! Mike! Mike!" Stephanie's chanting knocked Michael back to life. "You alright?"

"What? Huh?" Michael shook off the intense fog that had clouded his brain. His vision was blurry, but that was normal. He waited it for it to become a little less blurry, then looked around. "Hey, where'd the kid go?"

"Kid? There's no kid here," Stephanie brushed off Michael's concern. "I think you must've hit your head on a rock or something.

"But, just now. There was a kid. Like... thirteen years old."

"I don't know what you're talking about, but we gotta go. Right now." There was an urgency in Stephanie's voice. "There's something wrong with this universe."

"Wrong? What's wrong?"

"Uh, why don't you take a look?" Stephanie jerked her thumb back as Michael's neck craned upward to see that the once empty sky had been consumed by the dark clouds from before, and the entire area was bathed in sickly blue light. The rocks that had once lay scattered across the hill were beginning to slip the bonds of gravity and float languidly into the sky until about half-way up before they began to disintegrate and disappear.

"Oh, Jesus Christ," Michael cried. He didn't want to share the fate of those rocks. "What the hell is going on?"

"I was hoping you'd tell me. Whatever it is. It's not good. You didn't happen to blow someone up, did you?" Stephanie smirked

Michael was in no way amused. The momentary paternalism he conjured for the kid had vanished in a flash – much like the kid – and his usual anxious fear eagerly filled the vacuum. He glanced around, but could find no trace of the kid, nor any traces of blood and guts that indicated a Stephanie-style explosion. "I . . . don't think so."

"So I suppose that just appeared, then?" Stephanie pointed over Michael's shoulder.

Michael turned around so hard he could've snapped his spine. Hovering behind him was the familiar sparking vortex of multi-versal slipspace, almost camouflaged against the color of the rest of the universe. "I didn't even see that!"

"Alright, whatever. Doesn't matter. It's a good thing it showed up. We gotta get outta here."

Through the space between the canyon wall and the rapidly disappearing hill, Michael saw the horizon vanish in a flash of bright light that began to advance toward them. His stomach sank as he realized that the horizon didn't vanish, but was rather curling up, the dry, cracked desert ground becoming an enormous wave that blotted out the sky and was coming right for them.

He had no reason to protest as Stephanie grabbed him by the wrist, dragging both of them into the portal before it zipped closed behind them. A minute later and they would have been toast, or worse. The familiar crackle of the void between multi-verses filled Michael's ears, as the two twirled through the abyss. They nodded to each other, wordlessly and closed their eyes. Each concentrating on where they needed to be. There was no place like home, but, in the back of his mind, Michael couldn't help but hope that kid had made it out safely.

CHAPTER TWENTY-SEVEN

Child's Play

"Ewwww."

Michael jolted upright, opening his eyes. The first thing he felt was the soft burn of sun-warmed blacktop beneath his palms. Then, the harsh stare of a small child. A universe of kids, maybe? That made sense. His last thought before passing out was of that kid, whose image, despite Michael's best efforts, was slowly fading from his mind just as that previous world had disintegrated into the void.

"Yuck! You're all sweaty," a child's tiny voice brought Michael back into the present, passing judgment on his current state of affairs. Quite unfairly, Michael thought. He stared blankly at the small boy that stood above him. There was something unnervingly familiar about him.

"Ugh," the child wrinkled his nose, "and you smell like poopy."

"Listen kid," Michael snapped. He knew he probably smelled like poopy – given what he had been through – but he wasn't in the mood to be chastised for things beyond his control. "You don't know my life. But if anyone smells like poopy, it's you."

"No, you smell like poopy!" The child sneered.

"No, you d—" Michael caught himself before he was stuck in a loop, sucking in a deep breath to quell his frustration. Letting it out slowly, he was overcome by a strange sense of déjà vu. It all clicked into place when he turned around and came face to face with the brick wall of the educational torture chamber he had inhabited from the 1st to the 5th grade. Not a universe of kids, but a leap into an alternate past. And the rotund kid that wouldn't stop haranguing him had the same look and build as Anthony Finster, his childhood bully. Except this kid's hair was a brilliant jet black, rather than Finster's curly, attention grabbing red. Hair color aside, Michael's deep-seated resentment of him still applied.

"Whatever, stupid pants," Anthony slapped Michael on the forearm and ran off.

"Yeah, keep running. I'll show you who's stupid pants, you little bast . . ." Michael trailed off as he rubbed his stinging arm. Shaking it off, he looked around the schoolyard. Children were running hither thither playing kickball and innumerable variations of tag. Some of the boys were just punching each other in the head and laughing. He remembered those kids with a particular fondness. While Michael had never been popular, he always found solace in the fact that he never felt the temptation to fall in with them.

Michael rotated his ring and let the red lit display sink into the crevices of the asphalt playground.

```
USER_HOME:\\10E63.99873445219

USER_TIME:\\20130913190387235

CURR_UNIV:\\10E63.99873445217

CURR_TIME:\\19990917123347168

INPT_DEST:\\ _
```

The universe was similar to their own, but fourteen years in the past. They weren't truly home yet, but they were getting closer. But Stephanie had again been separated from him.

Michael made a note of the date – a familiar one – as he knew what he would be seeing shortly. Rotating the ring closed, Michael walked across the field in search of Stephanie, dodging his way through a particularly aggressive session of Red Rover. Despite his stench and horrific appearance, the kids paid him no heed. They were too busy having fun, as they should have been. It seemed like these were happy, carefree days and Michael wished he remembered them with fondness. When he reached the corner of the wide field, he was reminded of why he didn't. He found Anthony Finster once again, but this time he was whaling on a rail thin boy wearing glasses.

"Well, this is just all my worst nightmares," Michael said as he watched a version of his younger self being beaten up.

"Stop hitting yourself! Stop hitting yourself!" Finster chanted as Young Michael attempted to shield himself from the blows with limited success.

"But you're the one who's hitting me!"

"Man, shut up!"

Adult Michael was about to make a move to break it up, but didn't know what the etiquette was. He couldn't remember whether or not he was supposed to interact with his past self or not, even if it was an alternate universe baby version. Luckily for Michael, he didn't have to consider this line of thinking much further, as Stephanie burst onto the scene. Only this Stephanie was a tiny seven-year-old doing karate moves that she had picked up from television. As a result, it was more of a general flailing about than 'karate.'

"Hey, Finster! Get away from my friend!" Young Stephanie yelled. "Why don't you pick on someone who can fight back?"

At that moment, Finster stopped punching Young Michael, who took the opportunity to run away. Finster looked over, stared Young Stephanie down, his child's eyes filled with a strange admiration for the girl that had confronted him. With a swift pivot, he turned and put Stephanie in a headlock.

"Ow! Ow!" Young Stephanie cried as Finster punched her in the stomach repeatedly. "I wasn't ready. No fair!"

If anything, young Finster had to be commended for his gender-blind treatment of his peers. He may have been far ahead of his time. Stephanie, similarly, should have been commended for her remarkable ability to take a punch and stay standing. Adult Michael smiled. This was the day he and Stephanie had first met. The entire situation warmed his heart in a demented, stupid kind of way.

Before he got too sentimental, the moment was interrupted by a firm hand on his shoulder and a stern voice. "Who're you?"

The hand spun Michael around so that he was now faced with the chubby, dense body and furious glare of his elementary school gym teacher. The one who always made him the butt of every joke. The one who had made him and Stephanie run 20 laps every time they talked or laughed out of turn, which was most of the time, making for an unreasonable amount of laps. The one who happened to be Anthony Finster's father because that was just how life worked. "Oh, uh, hi Mr. Finster."

"I'll. Ask. You. Again," Arthur Finster punctuated every word, as if he were talking to a child. "Who the hell are you? What are you doing on school grounds? And what the hell are you covered in?"

"Thing is . . . I'd tell you but you probably wouldn't believe me. You see, I'm actually from another—" Michael stammered.

"Get the hell out of here." Finster's hair, like his son's, had lost the fiery red characteristic Michael remembered from his yearbook, and adopted the dark black of this universe. His mustache, a similar color, bristled as he ensnared Michael in a headlock. Like father, like son.

"No, no, listen, it's not what you think," Michael attempted to claw free, but to no avail. The kids stopped and stared as his dirty, repulsive body was dragged across the field by a surly man who had no business teaching children to begin with. "There's a reasonable explanation for this. I mean, it requires some suspension of disbelief, but otherwise it's pretty straightforward."

"Save it, perv. I'm calling the cops," Mr. Finster smirked, revealing his chipped tooth. He was enjoying this.

"Hey, Mr. Finster!" a voice called out.

"Oh, God," Michael pivoted along with Finster's arms as he turned to face an absolutely filthy, disgusting Adult Stephanie Dyer.

"Get away from my friend! Why don't you pick on someone who can fight back?" Stephanie planted her feet and assumed a karate-like stance. She was definitely enjoying this. "I'd say 'pick on someone your own size', but given your fat ass, that'd be a long and exhaustive search."

The crowd of kids that had gathered oohed in and mumbled in muted awe. Michael caught several instances of "Did you hear that? Ass! She said 'ass'!"

"Great. There's two of you?" Finster snarled. "I'm goin—"

"Wait," Stephanie held up a finger. "I'm not done with my fat jokes yet. One: I didn't know the movie 'The Blob' was a documentary. Two: If your belt could work any harder, it'd win employee of the year. Three: You look like the kind of guy who would subscribe to Arby's. Oh, that was a real good one. Mike, write that one down."

"Kinda busy here!" Michael forced his words up through his constricted, burning throat.

"Alright, enough," Finster released Michael and rolled up his sleeves with a strange gusto. "I think I can take on two perverts covered in shit. C'mon!"

"Oh, I don't think so," Stephanie grinned. As the children expressed their wonderment at the word 'shit', she turned and nodded to Michael. "We're getting closer right?"

"Yeah, looks like it's working," Michael looked up just in time to see Stephanie barreling full-speed towards their old gym teacher. And now he knew why Finster's wife had reported him missing. He'd been erased from the multi-verse due to Stephanie's oncoming punch. Slightly irritated by this realization, Michael motioned for Stephanie to just get it over with.

Finster narrowed his eyes and dug his heels into the blacktop, confident that he could take the impact. A hush fell over the playground as the kids had stopped their games. Taggers stopped mid-tag and dodgeballs hung in the air. The children fixed their eyes on the impending clash. Young Anthony Finster stopped his beat down of the younger Stephanie to cheer on his father taking on the elder Stephanie.

"Get 'er, Dad!"

"I've been wanting to do this for a real long time!" Stephanie leapt into the air and delivered a flying punch to Mr. Finster's chubby face. Time literally slowed to a crawl as the fat rippled across his chin. The crashing of the waves culminated in a flash of familiar blue lightning and a deluge of Finster fluid. One could only imagine how traumatized Anthony was. But Michael honestly couldn't have cared less. In fact, as Stephanie grabbed his hand and the blue blazes of space-time surged past them, Michael was happy that they'd escaped his childhood nightmare as soon as possible.

* * *

"You have *got* to be kidding me with this. Again?"

The multi-verse had taken Michael's refusal of his childhood nightmare as an order and deposited them back in the living nightmare that he thought they had left behind two jumps ago. Thankfully, this time, they were not bound together. The Cow Man

Supreme looked on in wide-eyed surprise, although that was the default cow expression. Behind him, the green torches of a thousand other cow-people flickered beneath the rumbling mountains that had begun a slow collapse into hell.

Cow Man Supreme thrust his finger – tipped, of course, with a yellow-irised eyeball – out towards them and summoned a high-pitched gargling roar. The assembled hordes echoed that sentiment and the entirety of the nightmare universe began to advance on them in a quick erratic stagger, as if someone was spastically alternating between the play and fast forward buttons on a VCR.

"We better get out of here," Stephanie said as she dragged Michael to his feet. They stumbled backwards to the rear edge of the dais, over which they had once fallen, tied back to back.

"Oh, you think?" Michael snapped. "Or maybe we should lob some fat jokes at them!"

Stephanie paused, "Do you think that'd work?"

"No! I don't thin—" Michael stopped as he caught a flicker of familiar blue out of the corner of his eye. He turned around to find the soft glow pulsing from behind the back of the dais, illuminating the guts, entrails and fluids of the Cow Man guard Stephanie had used as fuel for their passage a few jumps ago. "Steph! Look! We were just here. The portal hasn't closed yet!"

"Well, that was lucky," Stephanie shrugged.

"Don't touch anything else! Let's just go!" Michael rushed to the edge of the dais and peered down, into the still gaping wound in space and time that they had just left. He turned back and called to

Stephanie who was dodging cows left and right. "C'mon! We gotta do this together. I'm not leaving without you!"

"Go!" Stephanie cried back as she ducked and rolled under a muscular, hairy arm, eager to avoid contact with the eyes that hung off the end. "I'll catch up with you! "

Michael nodded and, surprised by his own bravery, stepped into thin air and plummeted down past the barrier between this world and the next.

"Alright! See you later, boys," Stephanie had eluded her captors reached the edge of the dais, staring down at Michael, who was falling quickly away from her. "Make way for Steph!" Stephanie's voice began to fade with distance, but Michael extended his hand when he saw her take the leap. "COMING THRRRRROOOO—"

Stephanie's yell cut out suddenly and, as he fell backwards into infinity, Michael could only watch horrified as he saw the portal seal up before his eyes with a rapid zip that thundered through the void. He tried to scream a frantic 'no', but it left his throat as a whisper. As panic and fear began to set in, Michael screwed his eyes shut and began to hyperventilate, wishing for everything to be as it was before. He barely noticed as everything transitioned from all-encompassing blue to an empty black.

CHAPTER TWENTY-EIGHT
Not The Worst Idea I've Ever Had

Michael opened his eyes to darkness. He blinked twice to ensure he had not gone blind or died. He hadn't died, that was for sure, unless you could blink after death. Plus, he could feel his way around the cramped space that contained him, his knees bent up under his chin. So he was blind then? That may have been an unexpected side effect of traveling through the multi-versal slipspace. He had no way of knowing. Michael blinked again, and a slice of light emerged in the darkness. Not blind either. That was a relief. Moving towards it, his hands rubbed across what felt like smooth wood, while his wet, matted hair brushed against a flat plank above him that further constricted his movement. Knocking his various joints along the edge of this would-be coffin, Michael inched his way toward the sliver of light. It was the seam of a door. He pressed his eye against it and saw something terrifyingly familiar as the door creaked slightly open.

"Aw, crap." Michael was definitely not dead. But, given what he could see through the crack, he wished he was.

"Sir," Michael could see and hear Stephanie clearly as she put her hands up, assuming an air of authority she did not possess. "Please. We'll be working with you today. Firstly, my colleague and I are new to the detective biz, per se, and we were wondering . . . how does one become 'hard-boiled'? I only ask because you seem to be quite hard-boiled yourself, sir. How would we, per se, get all up like that?"

Michael also saw himself, in all his nervous, sweaty unglory, trying to handle the situation.

"Stop saying 'per se'!" His other self yelled. "Ignore her. Please."

"I was planning to ignore the two of you!" The broad-shouldered frame of Detective Rex Calhoun gestured at the slight, hunchbacked frame of Elena Finster, a woman whose husband Michael had just witnessed sublimating into a bloody mist. "This woman's husband is missing and I'm here to investigate. *properly* investigate."

Michael shoved his back against whatever cupboard or storage space he was in. Groping around his hand blindly, he twisted his ring, and let the blood red display light up the cramped, empty shelving space he found himself in. The smooth, polished grain of the wood gave it away. It was Elena Finster's giant living room armoire.

```
USER_HOME:\\10E63.99873445219
USER_TIME:\\20130913190387235
CURR_UNIV:\\10E63.99873445219
CURR_TIME:\\20130913170132416
INPT_DEST:\\ _
```

An excited chill ran down Michael's spine and over his entire body. Everything matched! Or, well, close enough. Being off by a few hours was pretty good. He was home. But Stephanie was gone. He remembered watching the portal seal itself up just before she made it through. She was stuck in the Nightmare Dimension. Well, maybe not stuck, she could always find her way out, but who knows where she would end up.

"You're here for your client. Understood," Calhoun continued, unaware of the man in the armoire. "Then I'll be on my way," he paused for a second, savoring his next phrase, "once you show me your licenses."

A stray thought entered Michael's head. What would happen if he intervened? He could leap out of the armoire to save Stephanie and himself before they embroiled themselves in the oncoming storm. But then, in the off chance they weren't all arrested, there would be two of him existing at the same time. Would that violate the Law of Conservation of Mass – the only thing he remembered from high school physics? Or maybe he'd just disappear, like Michael J. Fox after Season Four of Spin City.

The Stephanie out in the living room cleared her throat and brought Michael's attention back to surreal reality, "So, Detective. What if – hypothetically – we didn't – hypothetically – have P.I. licenses?"

"Well, then that would be illegal! Very. Illegal," Calhoun nodded.

"Right," Stephanie nodded back.

"I would have to arrest you." Michael could feel the dark joy dripping off of Calhoun's every word.

"Hypothetically, of course."

"Hypothetically. Of course," Calhoun confirmed, seconds before whipping out two sets of handcuffs and slapping them onto Stephanie and Past-Michael's wrists. Elena Finster gasped and covered her mouth in shock. Calhoun turned to her sweetly, "Excuse me for a second, ma'am."

"This is horseshit!" Stephanie yelled over Calhoun's rote statement of their Miranda rights. As Calhoun dragged them away, her voice faded out. "I want a lawyer! Is Dick Wolf an attorney? I want Executive Producer Dick Wolf! Am I being *detained?*"

The front door slammed shut, and Michael – Present-Michael – let out a loud sigh that he didn't know he was holding in.

"Hello?" Elena Finster's tremulous voice echoed through the empty living room. "Is someone there?"

Michael cursed under his breath. He started to shake with the supreme terror of uncertainty. Should he exit or stay in? What if he changed history? Did it matter?

But, in the end, as Stephanie was fond of saying, nothing really mattered.

The back of the armoire tore itself open with a blinding blue glow and the deafening crack of broken wood. A dark hulking mass slammed into Michael, throwing him out of the armoire doors and clear across the hardwood floor onto the living room carpet. A thunderous bang and clatter rang out as the armoire itself crashed to the floor.

"Oh my god!" Elena Finster screamed.

"Ugh. I'm . . . I'm alright," Michael pushed himself up, his ears ringing and head throbbing. Shaking off the daze, he found himself face-to-snout with the muscular, heaving form of Cow Man Supreme. It gave off an angry snort, and its nose gas made its way into Michael's lungs.

"Bwah!" Michael cried as he tried to stumble backwards.

"What the hell is that thing? What's happening? Why are you such a mess? Why were you in my armoire?" Mrs. Finster blubbered question after question as the enraged monster shaman clasped its eye-tipped fingers around Michael's neck and raised him three feet in the air. "I thought you and the girl left with the Detective!"

"Great questions, Mrs. Finster," Michael struggled to get his words out, haphazardly slapping at Cow Man Supreme's well-toned arms, "Real great. But I don't have the time to go through all the details right this second. You might want to run away now."

Cow Man Supreme let out a long bellow, and Mrs. Finster scampered out of the living room and around the corner into the hallway, out of sight. Spots swam before Michael's eyes as his struggled to draw breath. To be honest, he was a bit disappointed that his life wasn't flashing before his eyes, although the last thing one needs to watch before their death is a damn clip show.

As the edges of his vision blurred, he saw only his hands clutching at the arm that was clutching him. Matteo's silver ring glinted in the soft ambiance of the living room. Not knowing where the idea came from, Michael found himself using his last ounce of strength to rotate the ring. Hopefully the red display would be bright enough to temporarily blind the Cow Man and stop its incessant choking.

Unfortunately, Michael's last ounce of strength was not enough, and the ring did not activate. His arms fell to his sides, limp, and everything went black.

The next thing he heard was the tail end of a battlecry: "-OOOUUUUUGGGGGHHH!" The pained braying of Cow Man Supreme followed. Michael hit the ground with a loud thud and sharp pain up the side of his body. Most of his vision remained clouded, but a set of hands grasped his arms and helped him to his feet. As the blurriness dissipated, he saw the face of his oldest friend yelling at him as she shook him awake.

"Mike! Mike! Get up! Shake it off!" Stephanie screamed as she started slapping him across the face. "Everything's going to be okay now. I'm here. I'm here!"

This shocked Michael back into coherence. He shook off the bleariness. "Okay, okay! I'm good," but Stephanie continued to slap him until he shoved her away, "would you stop that?"

"Sorry," Stephanie's smile morphed into an expression of faux shock as Michael punched her in the arm. "Ow! What was that for?"

"For slapping me. And because where the hell did you go? I thought I lost you."

"Hah. Not just yet," Stephanie's laugh was distant and entirely unlike her usual chuckle. Michael stepped back a moment and realized for the first time, that he had never seen her so tired before. He had been so caught up in everything that was happening and his selfish desire to get back home that he never realized that it was happening to Stephanie, too. "I uh . . . just exploded another one of those other cow dudes when I missed the first portal, and here I am. Back home, I guess?"

Michael nodded.

"Great," Stephanie peered over his shoulder. "Now, about this guy . . ."

Cow Man Supreme stirred from its resting place beneath the Finster's picture frames in the foyer. Its impact had destroyed the bottom half of the wall and chunks of paint, wood and insulation clung to him. Not to mention a few pictures of Mrs. Finster and her husband. It grunted and rose to Its feet. Before it could get its bearings, Mrs. Finster dashed out of her bedroom, brandishing a large black umbrella and assaulted it with repeated thwacks.

"Get. Out. Of. My. House. You. Monster!" was all she could get out before Cow Man Supreme flung her across the room by the umbrella. She came to a crashing halt near the armoire, unconscious and worse for the wear, but still breathing.

"Oh, boy," Stephanie said. "So that's what happened."

Cow Man Supreme demanded attention by letting out a gargling roar that resembled the bellow of an angry whale more than that of a cow. It had shaken off the shock and now began to advance into the living room, staring down its two most hated enemies. "DESTROY. YOU. DESTROY. INTERLOPERS."

"Okay, so what should we do?" Stephanie glanced at Michael as they both retreated away from the monster's snorting, grunting advances. "Sounds like he's none too pleased with us interlopers."

"Can't you touch him and make him explode?"

"I don't think it works like that. If this is our universe, he's the one that doesn't belong. If I touch him. I explode!"

"Are you sure about that?"

"I don't know."

"What if I take off my ring and we both touch him?" Michael posited. "Would our combined energies from this universe override his and make *him* explode?"

"What are you basing that on?"

"Absolutely nothing!" Michael admitted. He was just trusting his instincts, as he had done when he had shot that hamburger in the forest. God, this had been a crazy couple of days. "I mean, that's what you always do, right? Go for broke with little regard for the consequences? I mean, what other choice do we have?"

"Worth a shot," she smiled a wistful smile. "There's two of us and only one of him. That gives us the advantage."

Michael smiled back.

"DESTROY. YOU," Cow Man Supreme repeated. "DESTROY. INTERLOPERS."

"Yeah, yeah," Stephanie said as she broke away from Michael and strafed around Cow Man Supreme, not breaking eye contact. The creature spun around to meet her. "We got it the first time."

"Is that all you can say?" Michael said. And Cow Man juddered back around to face him. They had it sandwiched between them.

"YOU HAVE ANGERED THE MAN-GOD."

"Yeah, uh, about that. One, we don't really give a shit about your Man-God," Stephanie drew his attention back to her.

"Two," Michael continued, yanking off his ring and tossing it aside. "If he's so powerful, why doesn't he come destroy us himself?"

"I WILL DESTROY. DESTROY. YOU. DESTROY. INTERLOPERS."

"Again with the same ol' song and dance. You really gotta get some new material," Stephanie said. "And that's three!"

On three, Michael leapt forward, as did Stephanie from the other side, arms outstretched. As they grasped his wiry muscles simultaneously, Michael felt warmth on his fingertips as Cow Man Supreme sublimated into a bloody, gory mist that collapsed in on itself before exploding outward in a muffled explosion, throwing him against the living room wall and Stephanie back into the foyer. In place of the monster stood another giant rip in the fabric of the space-time continuum, pulsing softly with blue light and giving off errant bolts of electricity that singed the carpet and the edges of the coffee table. Elsewhere and elsewhen, a Doctor named Coleman Supirn vanished from existence, leaving his wife scared and confused.

"Oh, great. It's this thing again," Michael rolled his eyes. If it had just been him and Stephanie here, that would have simply been the end of it. But Cow Man Supreme had determined it would not end that way. "What do we do? Any minute now, Calhoun is going to walk back in here and find us and the whole thing is going to go to hell."

"No."

"Huh?" Michael turned to face Stephanie. She looked more somber now, more serious than he'd ever seen her before. That, coupled with the bone weariness he had felt in her earlier, made her lack any and all resemblance to that girl he had called his best friend for so many years.

"I'll take care of it. This is my fault."

"What? What are you talking about? We'll figure it out together."

"I'm the one who dragged you into this mess. The rent. This whole detective thing. The dimension jumping. It's been my fault from the beginning. I'm not going to let you keep paying for my mistakes. I'm going alone this time. And I'm going to fix this. I promise."

"No. That's crazy! I almost lost you once. I'm not going to lose you again. You don't know what could happ—" Michael stepped forward, but Stephanie raised her hand to stop him. On her finger was his ring. Michael gaped at it. "When did you – you don't know how to work that thing."

"Neither do you," she snapped. "I guess I'll keep jumping until I figure it out. Or die. Whatever comes first.

"You were right," she continued. "You've always been right. I need to start taking things seriously. So I'm finally taking responsibility, for once. Right here. Right now. Because when nothing really matters . . . then everything matters."

"Steph, don't."

"Listen, it's not the worst idea I've ever had. And it definitely won't be the last," Stephanie said. The energies of the rip in multidimensional space-time crackled behind her, silhouetting her body and casting a blue pallor across the hardwood floor. Silhouetted by her impending fate, she approached the portal, which had begun to shudder and emit a low, angry hum.

"Please," Michael repeated as he leaned against the fallen armoire to steady himself, "We have do this together."

"No, Michael. I need to do this alone," Stephanie looked away. "I started this loop and I need to close it. And to do that, I need you to trust me."

"Steph—"

"I know I haven't given you any reason to, and I'm sorry. I wish I could go back and fix that. But I tried and look how that ended up," she ended with a small chuckle. "So for once, can you just pretend that I know what I'm doing?" Stephanie turned back to him and their gaze lingered for half a minute.

Michael swallowed his words and stayed quiet. The air stood still. There was no movement aside from the constant rotation of the portal that hung in the air next to the silence.

"I'm sorry," Michael continued, attempting to push up glasses that he had lost long ago. "I'm sorry I called you an embarrassment."

The corner of Stephanie's mouth went up in a smirk. "But I *was* an embarrassment."

"Yeah. But you're not supposed to *say* that," Michael returned the smile before pausing and looking away. "But you've always been my best friend. And . . . and you were right, too."

"About what?"

"It was kinda fun to play detective with you," he said. "Just like it used to be when we were kids.

"I . . ." Michael began again before sputtering. "I don't want you to die."

"Neither do I! You think I'm doing this for my health?" Stephanie said with a smile that quickly faded. "You're my best friend, too, Michael. I'm trying to help you, like you always did for me. Just think of this as my way of saying thank you."

"For what?"

"For putting up with me," Stephanie winked at him. She turned and let out a quiet sigh before approaching the portal. Tendrils of blue energy reached out and grabbed at her. Michael reached out a hand, but nothing could be done, and soon Stephanie was gone, sucked into the great beyond with a disgusting blorp. The portal lingered a little while longer before sucking in every bit of Cow Man Supreme's blood and entrails that had plastered themselves across the living room and across Michael's skin and clothes, then finally disappearing with a zip.

CHAPTER TWENTY-NINE

But Maybe It Was The Last

Michael's time to mourn was short, as the bizarre reality of the situation caught up to him. He rushed to the front door and swung it open, eager to beat a hasty retreat, but stopped in his tracks as he saw Rex Calhoun, tailed by the past iterations of himself and Stephanie, making their way back up the sidewalk.

That avenue was closed off to him, and now Michael would have to improvise. He hated being put on the spot, but now he had no choice. In too much of a panic to close the door completely, he made his way back down the foyer towards the living room, hoping a genius plan would come to him. As expected, none did, so he swung himself around the doorjamb and into the bedroom that Mrs. Finster had bravely charged out of before she had been swatted down by a violent cow monster with terrifying genitalia. His back flush against the wall, Michael heard the front door open as Detective Calhoun entered. His heavy clomping footsteps, even when trying to be discreet, matched Michael's pounding heart. Calhoun stopped at the archway between the hallway and the living room, right in front of Michael's hiding place.

"Goddammit!" Calhoun shouted, before picking up his radio and calling for emergency backup.

This was his chance. Michael could escape! But as he peeked his head around the corner, the door creaked open again and he ducked back.

"What . . . what happened?" Past-Michael said just feet away from his future self. Or present self. Proper tenses were the least of Michael's worries.

"Your guess is as good as mine, Dyer," Calhoun grumbled.

"I'm Duckett," Past-Michael corrected. "She's Dyer."

"I don't care."

Michael heard Stephanie walk into the living room and wail an apology to Mrs. Finster's body. He remembered this. It was pretty over the top. Certainly something that would occupy everyone's attention long enough for him to sneak past. Michael peered around the corner to see the backs of Calhoun and himself staring at Stephanie, who had knelt down beside Mrs. Finster's body. He paused for a second, because it wasn't every day that one saw their own backside, and frowned in embarrassment. Clutching the doorframe, Michael swung his body around the corner and into the foyer. Neither Calhoun, nor his earlier self, turned around. So far so good. Michael began to creep forward, careful not to hit any potentially creaky floorboards.

"Would you get the hell away from there?" Calhoun bellowed. Michael froze in place before he remembered that he was yelling at Stephanie. "This is an active crime scene!"

"Sorry! Sorry! Sorry!" Stephanie got up off the floor and spun around, and tiptoed her way around the trashed living room toward Past-Michael and Calhoun. And then, for a fraction of a second, her eyes met Michael's. She saw him standing stock still up against the foyer wall. Even though his vision was blurry, Michael's eyes momentarily focused and he could see her clearly. Stricken with panic, he raised a shaking finger to his lips and broadcast a look of wide-eyed panic he hoped she would pick up on. With a nod of acknowledgement so slight as to be imperceptible, Stephanie broke eye contact, cleared her throat loudly and grabbed onto the frayed edges of her jacket near her collar. "So . . . uh . . . who do you think did this?"

Michael let out a silent breath as Stephanie launched into her tirade, and broke into a quiet run. He was out the front door in a moment, and only then did he notice that he had been clenching his teeth the entire time. Unfortunately, he had no time to relax, as the droning whines of incoming sirens pierced the air. Panicking again, Michael searched around for something he could use. The only thing he spotted was the familiar dented, rusting hulk he called the Garbagemobile basking in the waning evening sunlight. Never had he been so relieved to see that hunk of junk.

Michael once again evaluated his only option and dashed toward it. Of course he couldn't drive it away, but perhaps he could use his limited knowledge of the future to his advantage. He could get his past self to drive him home. Perfect! Michael slammed his fist against the car's trunk which rebounded with a hollow clunk before popping open with ease. Crawling inside, Michael caught a glimpse of his and Stephanie's past asses being shoved out the door of the Finster residence before he clicked the trunk shut from within.

*   *   *

It was about seven minutes into the ride that Michael regretted not getting his shock absorbers fixed. His head bounced between the top and bottom of the trunk in a painful parody of Pong. He was already covered in disgusting goop and human and cow effluents from his travel between universes, but now his situation worsened as he was slathered in all manner of strange automotive liquids and goos that had leaked out of whatever containers he had forgotten to empty. On top of that, he was being treated to the trailing pieces of a familiar argument that he didn't want to relive, now that he had context.

"Jesus, . . .at kind of . . .planet do . . .ou live on, Stephanie? . . ." the noises of traffic and passing sirens obscured some of Past-Michael's rant. "This has been... waste of . . . time."

" . . . at least...out of there."

"Y'know . . . I've had it . . . We're done . . . we're done." The catalytic converter popped and rumbled, giving Michael a taste of only the best quality highlights, along with the occasional raspy snarls of an unmaintained engine. "I'm sick of dealing with you, Stephanie! I've had to cover for you . . .cause you think you can . . . not care about anything . . . at all! . . .That's not how it works and . . . time you learned that. I can't cover . . . anymore. . . . Getting sucked into your black hole of a life is not what I had planned . . .You're an embarrassment, Stephanie . . .omplete embarrassment and I am so out."

Sitting through another garbled rehash of his words just drove the point home of how Michael had completely shat on the best friend who had possibly just given up her life in a final act of selflessness. In fact, everything she had done was just to help him, in her own particular oddball, convoluted idiom.

And that's when it clicked. Stephanie had seen him, covered in filth, trying to sneak out of Elena Finster's house and without a word she put on a distraction for him. A distraction that just so happened to end with her proposing a ghost as the solution to the whole situation. She was usually better at improv.

But, more importantly, she had known, the whole time, that something strange was afoot, despite not having the full context. So Stephanie's repeated insistence on them continuing as they were, why she was convinced it would all work out was the result of an ouroburos she herself hadn't quite untangled. Everything she did was an earnest attempt to save them. She was sharper and more complicated than Michael had ever given her credit for. Perhaps he had bought in to the idea that she was as goofy and absent-minded as everyone had always said she was when they were growing up. And he hadn't made an effort to dig any deeper. That was what Stephanie had said back in the cave. Michael had been a shitty friend.

Between contemplating his past and trying to avoid listening to it, Michael realized that he had completely neglected to notice if Stephanie's final sacrifice had actually worked. He could only guess at what that brave, stupid idiot had done after jumping into the superstructure of the universe, but Stephanie had promised she would fix everything. Somehow. Maybe she had a plan that he just wasn't privy to. Maybe she was aware of some other hidden detail that Michael hadn't bothered to consider.

After rolling possibilities around in his head, which was itself rolling, Michael realized that he could not be sure until after the Duckett and Dyer currently driving the car met up with – and assaulted – Matteo Carrera. That had been the catalyst for all this: Matteo's irresponsible decision to use a machine that could draw on the energies of multiple universes in order to score a freaky threeway with two versions of his wife. If Stephanie had fixed anything, this would be the epicenter of the effects.

As the Garbagemobile lurched to a violent stop, presumably in front of Michael and Stephanie's apartment, Michael resolved to stay on the tail of their past selves up until they met with Matteo. This way he could figure out if everything had indeed been fixed as Stephanie had promised. His resolve was further solidified by the fact that he could not get the trunk to open from the inside. As he heard Past-Michael and Past-Stephanie exit the car and enter their apartment, where they would continue to fight, he kicked and punched and threw his body at the trunk, all unsuccessfully. It was frozen shut and the lock was secure. The one time that the Garbagemobile worked like a proper reliable car and not the junk heap that it was, to Michael's chagrin. He promised himself that he would buy a new car if he got out of this one, but that was a promise that would certainly be forgotten. Now there was nothing to do but wait and listen to time play out once again, like a re-run on a radio. Michael wasn't looking forward to it.

*   *   *

Michael would have been lying if he said he hadn't at least considered drinking the anti-freeze on the drive to the Des Creté Motel. Fortunately, as he reached out to finally sample a taste of the nectar of the automobile gods, the car ground to another screeching halt, tossing him to the back wall of the trunk. A hard piece of jagged metal dug its way into his back, leaving a nasty scratch.

"Dammit," Michael rubbed his back and his fingers came away sticky with blood, but not too much. But he would certainly need a tetanus shot. It had been another three hours in his rusty prison and Michael wondered if it was best to just give up and succumb to the fumes that were undoubtedly poisoning him even now. However, the wilderness near the Des Creté Motel allowed some actual air to seep in through the cracks of the trunk, keeping him alive for at least a little while longer.

He heard himself and Stephanie bicker back and forth before deciding to move amongst the bushes. A little while later, he heard Stephanie approach and let the air out of the Garbagemobile's tires by mistake. Michael rolled his eyes and waited for Stephanie to open the trunk for him. It wasn't until he heard her bound away that he pushed past the fog of his addled mind and realized that while she knew he had come back in time, she didn't know he was in the trunk of the Garbagemobile.

Michael slammed his head against the side of the wall in frustration, which helped nothing. The only way out now was if any of the other patrons of the motel wandered by, and he banged on the trunk loud enough to get their attention. That is, assuming people being locked in trunks wasn't the norm in the world of the Des Creté Motel.

Five minutes later he heard the familiar crack of the universe tearing in two, and shortly after that, the rapid zip of the universe doing up its fly. Now everyone was gone and all Michael could do was play the Waiting Game. Or, more accurately, the Please Don't Drink Poison Even Though You're Thirsty Game. It was a pretty terrible name for a game. Then again, it was a pretty terrible game.

Another thunderous crack broke through the air, this time closer, in the parking lot. The body of the Garbagemobile shook and shuddered, and Michael along with it. Michael heard a telltale 'glorp' noise, as well as another hasty zip. Once the sounds of the universe subsided, he could also make out the frantic, heavy breathing of another person. Was it another time traveler? Or maybe it was Stephanie coming back to save him.

"Hey! Hey! Hey, hey, hey, hey!" Michael pivoted his lower half and bicycle kicked against the trunk lid, his legs rebounding against the metal with every impact. "There's someone in here! Let me out, goddammit! Let me out!"

"Hello?" It was the person outside, still breathing heavily. His voice was muffled, but distinctly male. Certainly not Stephanie. "Is someone in there?"

"Yes! I just said that," Michael yelled. "Let me out!"

"But I don't have a key. Should I . . . should I go get the manager?"

"No, you idiot! Just hit the trunk with your fist."

"Will that work?"

"Yes!"

"It doesn't seem to have worked for you."

"Just do it!" Michael's parched throat screeched.

The stranger's fist slammed against the top of the trunk, and it popped open with remarkable ease. Michael pushed himself up and leaned out, grabbing every bit of fresh untainted air that he could suck into his lungs. After coughing for a good minute, he stared up at his savior and their eyes met: Michael's in a mix of tired fear and rage, and Matteo Carrera's in wide surprise.

"Holy shit, it's you," Matteo said and broke into a run.

Michael, despite his weariness, leapt out and managed to grab Matteo by the collar of his shirt. "You're not going anywhere," Michael twisted him around to meet him face-to-face.

"What . . . what're you going to do to me?"

"Oh, a lot of things," Michael nodded. "But first, I'm going to ask you politely for a drink of water."

Matteo Carrera may have been an interdimensional sex pervert, but he was nothing if not accommodating. They walked over to his car, where Matteo offered Michael a spare water bottle and some clothes to replace his that had been stained beyond repair.

Michael stared down at the pink shirt and blue sweatpants in his arms. "These are women's clothes."

"Yeah. Sorry. They're my fiancée's. She keeps her gym stuff in the car. Hope you like the Jonas Brothers."

"I don't."

"Neither do I. But if I have to deal with it, so do you."

Despite reservations, Michael put on the t-shirt and was working on the pants. He looked up at Matteo, "What happened to you after we chased you through the portal?"

"Well, I landed in an alternate universe. Three years in the future. I looked around for you guys, but didn't see you. Since the coast was clear, I was about to use the base unit to come back home," Matteo dug around in his pocket and extricated the stopwatch-like base unit that Michael remembered being destroyed. "Then I felt really sick. I think I blacked out. Next thing I know, the universe spits me back out here where I came from."

"What about the other missing people?" Michael asked.

"What missing people?"

"Arthur Finster, Carrie McDermott, Kiara Hobson. Terri Bradshaw?"

"The football guy? No. I don't know what you're talking about."

"What about Coleman Supirn? He was a doctor. His case was on the news?"

"I haven't heard anything about anyone missing." A slow realization worked its way across Matteo's face, "Wait . . . did you guys touch some people in other universes without a dampening ring? Did you touch me?"

Michael let the silence answer his question.

"Jesus Christ," Matteo ran his fingers through his hair and began dancing around like a scared madman. "What happened?"

Michael tried to piece together what the other Matteo told him. "Well, apparently, without a dampening ring, we . . . uh . . . violently erased people from existence."

"How violently?"

"You don't want to know."

Matteo started feeling up his body in shock. "Then how . . . how the hell am I still alive? How did you fix it?"

"My . . ." Michael paused. A lump in his throat. "My friend did. I don't know how. But now she's gone. Wherever she is, do you think she'll be okay?"

"This kind of emotional support really wasn't covered in my training as a theoretical physicist . . ."

"Hey!" Michael snarled. "Just throw me a bone here, okay?"

"Well, in all likelihood, she's dead. With the erratic way the multi-verse behaves, we wouldn't even be able to find her body if we tried."

"You're right. You're really not good at this."

"I'm sorry. But the multi-verse is just a big roiling mess, when two opposing universes touch, it creates some sort of nexus, where things can happen in both universes simultaneously. But just because the things are simultaneous, doesn't mean they happen at the same time."

"What the hell are you talking about?"

"Like I said, it's a mess. But it looks like Stephanie's plan worked. The multi-verse is pretty elastic, and if she found some way to snap it back into place, it will have self-corrected and ironed out any causal inconsistencies or 'existential errors' as I call them." Michael didn't care what Matteo called them. He wasn't following any of it, nor did he care. Stephanie was gone, and that was all that mattered. Yet this guy kept yammering. "I don't know how she figured it out. Everything seems to be stable and I don't think I lost any memories, either. Mild brain damage is a common side effect. And I feel pretty okay there."

"I wouldn't go that far," Michael muttered. "So now will you stop risking the safety of the entire universe in order to have some perverted hook-up with your wife and your alternative wife?"

"Hey," Matteo smirked. "You can't blame a guy for trying."

"What the hell do you think this is, a goddamn game?"

"Actually, I think it's a breakthrough. I've just got to run more tests. Maybe another universe with a totally different Dorabell."

Michael slammed the side of Matteo's car with his hand. It hurt, but he grit his teeth and yelled through the pain. "My best friend is dead and you didn't even learn a goddamn lesson? Give me that!"

"Hey!" Matteo yelled as Michael snatched the base unit from his hand and dashed it to the ground. Next, he wrenched the ring off Matteo's finger, hopefully taking some skin with it, and did the same, before stepping on it for good measure. The ring didn't break, but it felt good to do it. "What the hell, man?"

"I'm not letting you risk any more lives. Wait three years and build a better one. Because I have a feeling we're going to be coming back," Michael turned around and stormed away dramatically, or as dramatically as one could storm in a Jonas Brothers t-shirt, yelling over his shoulder. "And if I see you before then, I will tell your fiancée everything and then I will punch your face off of your head."

Michael stormed away, as Matteo's called out to him, "Wait. How am I supposed to get home if my tire's flat? And why is my tire flat?"

"I don't care," Michael grumbled to himself as he marched into the motel office, and demanded that the sleeping owner call him a cab.

CHAPTER THIRTY

Goodbye and Good Riddance To Bad Luck

Calhoun jolted up in bed. That is, if you could call a collection of loose springs and stuffing shoved into a fabric casing to approximate the bare minimum of a mattress a "bed". Every muscle in his body sang with the fierce song of an angry old woman falling down the stairs and his head didn't fare much better. A cold sweat trickled down his face and the back of his neck. Calhoun blinked a few times in rapid succession, attempting to clear what felt like a deep sleep out of his eyes as they adjusted to the dimly lit surroundings. Thin streams of light that pierced the cracks between the venetian blinds on the far side of the room—and he could only really make out the aged wood paneling of the walls.

"What . . . the hell?" Calhoun attempted, but the words slid out of his mouth in a slur. He had no idea where he was, or what he was doing there. His memory of the past few days, if they had been days, was a quickly fading blur. He could've been drunk and it wouldn't have been the first time.

Tearing off the thin bed coverings and looking down, Calhoun found that he had stripped to his undershirt and boxers, hopefully by himself, although he struggled to remember even that. As his vision became clearer, he saw his coat, hat and other clothes hung haphazardly on a set of hooks by the door. They were crumpled and not at all in decent shape. That leant some credence to the drunk theory.

Calhoun smacked his lips to dispel the odd chalky taste that had invaded his mouth and swung his rubbery legs over the side of the bed and directly into the nightstand.

"Ow! Son of a bitch," he bit his lip and grabbed his knee. It'd swell up in an hour's time guaranteed. The nightstand was solid enough to put a dent in him, but, upon closer inspection, one more good hit from Calhoun's leg would cause it to collapse. As if on cue, the drawer slid out and crashed to the floor, leaving only pieces of wood and a Gideon Bible that had been assaulted by crayons. Calhoun bent over and picked up the Bible. He had never been a religious man and didn't intend to start, but he found a matchbook peeping out of the top, wedged in between some nonsense he didn't bother to read.

Ignoring the piercing pain in his knee, Calhoun turned the matchbook over in his hand. The purple text popped against a splotchy yellow background: 'Des Creté Motel. 1 Inconvenient Location. 7113 Spruce-Pine Lane.'

"Hm." Spruce-Pine Lane was way out in the sticks. Calhoun wondered what he had done to himself to end up all the way out here. He stood up and immediately realized that that was a mistake. His head swum and a searing pain pierced through his temples. This was one hell of a hangover. He could barely keep his busted knee from buckling. But, then where was all the booze? Maybe this wasn't a hangover. Maybe he'd had a stroke. That'd be a new one.

Calhoun stumbled his way over to the blinds and – in another mistake – pulled them open. Daylight flooded the room and his eyes, causing him to emit a pained yelp. It was a good thing no one was around to hear it. Squinting into the light, he could make out a seedy parking lot with a few scattered cars parked at odd angles. These hunks of junk had seen better days, including one that had a replacement door from a completely different colored car. Oddly, all of their rear tires were flat. But, thankfully, Calhoun did not see his old Crown Vic among them. If he had been drunk, at least he was smart enough not to have driven himself here. Thank heavens for small miracles.

Calhoun shrugged and turned back into the room, ready to shit, shower and shave, when he was confronted by a slightly larger miracle. The unconscious human being chained to the motel radiator he had blindly shambled past caused him to jump. Once he collected his bearings, Calhoun squatted down and pressed his fingers against the man's neck, his slumped head making it a bit difficult. He was alive, but unconscious, and dressed in a familiar blue letterman jacket. As the man's features resolved in the warring mix of daylight against the motel's inherent dankness, Calhoun recognized him as Tobias Wilkes, the goon that he had been chasing.

"Huh," Calhoun was stunned. He ripped what appeared to be a yellow sticky note off Wilkes sleeping face.

FOR YOUR TROUBLES: 1 TRICK PONY. It said in unassuming black marker.

Something prickled at the back of Calhoun's head, making it past the pounding of his eardrums. The note was oddly familiar, but he couldn't quite place it, or the handwriting. It definitely wasn't his. But maybe an angrier, drunker version of him had sarcastically scribbled it before passing out. Anything was possible. He wasn't even sure how both he and Wilkes had gotten here.

Calhoun felt like he was missing something important. Something that he had forgotten. He remembered botching his operation to tail Wilkes, and then chasing him down the streets of Squalor's Wallow in the rain instead. And then . . . nothing. But why did the note seem so familiar?

Then he had it, for just a slip of a moment, everything rushed back into his head, completing the elaborate confusing jigsaw puzzle of the last few days. The notes, the lightning, the Spec-

The motel phone rang, shattering Calhoun's revelation into a million little pieces. He leapt at it and yanked it off the cradle, hoping to keep Wilkes asleep.

"Hello?" Calhoun whispered into the phone.

"Yeah," a flippant voice came through the handset. "Someone ordered a wake-up call for 6:30?"

Calhoun glanced across at the digital clock on what remained of the nightstand. "It's 9:45."

"What do I look like, a clock?" The line went dead.

Now what was he thinking about? Oh, yeah. Wilkes, while not the entire Trick Ponies enterprise, would definitely be the first step in pulling down their house of cards. And Calhoun had bagged him. He crumpled up a sticky note he found in his hand and tossed it toward the wastebasket, missing by several feet. Calhoun wobbled his way over to his hanging coat and fished out his cellphone. He had a few bars and a bit of battery left. Good enough for a call to the station. After requesting an officer pick him up, Calhoun took another look at the unconscious drug dealer in his motel room, and set about having that shit, shower, and shave. As far as he was concerned, he'd earned it.

*   *   *

Calhoun's return to the station was nothing short of triumphant, at least from his point of view. He strutted in with Tobias Wilkes shambling out in front of him, hands cuffed behind his back and hangdog expression on his face. Handing him over to a pair of uniforms for processing, Calhoun strode up to the bullpen where he was hoping for an ovation, but only got a curt nod from the others and the unwanted attention of Detective Brook.

"Eh, Rexy. Where've you been?" Brook asked from his cubicle.

"Brook," Calhoun leaned over the cube wall, "I just bagged Wilkes after the better part of 2 years. So nothing you can say today is gonna chap my ass."

"Well, if I was there last week," his eyebrows raised an excruciating amount of times, "you wouldn't have lost him in a thunderstorm and we would've brought down all the Trick Ponies."

Calhoun grimaced. As loathe as he was to admit it, his ass had been well and thoroughly chapped. But something Brook said caught his ear.

"Hold on, Brook. Last week?" Calhoun hadn't thought to check the date. "What day is it now?"

"It's Friday. You've been out for a week. We all thought you were on vacation."

"A week?" Calhoun was blindsided by this information. How could it have been a week? He just remembered fighting Wilkes in Squalor's Wallow. Other faint echoes of memories popped up in brief glimpses of a week unlived, but were suddenly silenced. Unsure of the truth, he opted to press forward, making his "No, I was . . . tracking Wilkes!"

"Well, good for you. Thanks for letting me in on your little plan," Brook scoffed. "How'd you catch him, anyway?"

"Well, I—" Calhoun stopped. His eyes darted around the floor, as if his answer would be found on the grubby tiles of a police bullpen. Alas, they were not, so Calhoun returned to what he knew best: aggressive standoffishness. "I just did. Blow it out your ass."

"Whatever, buddy," Brook flipped his pencil in the air. "Just let Lieutenant Lin know that thanks to you, we only have one of the Ponies in lock-up while the rest are still running free. We're gonna be working this task force together for a while longer, if you don't utilize the full scope of my talent."

Calhoun bit his lip to avoid saying exactly what Brook's talent was good for, and began to slouch toward his office. Brook called out to him before he could reach the knob. He froze and shuddered angrily as he turned around. "What?"

"Oh, yeah, by the way. You have a visitor."

"Visitor? What visitor."

"I dunno. Some girl from the 35th. She's cute. Didn't know you liked 'em young," Brook went back to clacking away at his keyboard, "said to tell you she had something for you on the Finster Case? Whatever that is."

"Finster Case?" Calhoun muttered to himself as he turned the knob, shoving his door open as far as it could go before it jammed up against the rickety chair that sat next to the wall. He needed to get rid of that damned chair. Slipping in through the crack in the doorway, Calhoun found a young girl wearing an oversized CSI windbreaker sitting on his desk. The girl's overall presence rang a faint, far off bell, but he couldn't place her face or name. He hung up his hat on coat on his rack, which was leaning perilously against a rusty filing cabinet. "Uh, hello?"

The girl stood up, careful not to topple or muss up some pile of important papers. Joke was on her, none of them were important. She cleared her throat. "Oh, hi. Detective Calhoun, right? I've been waiting for you. I work CSI crosstown for Detective Hobson."

"CSI? You look like you're twelve," he grunted, as a strange flash of déjà vu distracted him for a bit before depositing him back into the moment. "What do you need from me? Hobson not keeping you busy?"

"Well, since we weren't slammed with work, she loaned me out as part of the team that scrubbed the Finster house after you left," she cocked her head. "I think."

"You think?"

"Sorry. I've just had a weird couple of days. It's like not all of me is there. Might've partied too hard this past weekend, I guess, haha."

"Yeah. I know what you mean," Calhoun nodded in solidarity. "So what do you got for me?"

The girl picked up a folder from behind her and handed it to Calhoun. How she had found the right one out of the manila chaos atop his desk was beyond him. "I thought you might want to look at the results."

"Oh yeah." The memory of the Finster Case finally caught up to him . . . for the most part. The old woman. Someone had come in and wrecked her up real good. But he couldn't quite recall why he'd been over there in the first place. It was part of his missing week and a half that he'd need to look into. But for now, Calhoun opened her folder and glanced down at the assessments. The old Finster lady seemed to be okay – recovering, at least. But according to the CSI results, they'd found three sets of DNA in the living room. Two were human with no matches in their database, and the other was . . . "Cow?"

"Bovine DNA," she confirmed. "Yeah. I thought it was weird, too. Figured it could just be a prank. Local kids breaking in and wrecking up the place with some cow blood they bought at a butcher's shop."

"Pretty shitty prank if you ask me. Back in my day, we used to stuff phone booths." Stuffing phone booths was a little older than

Calhoun's time, but he found it amusing. "So you think the other two matches are just some local college dipshits?"

"Yeah, probably. Unless you know anybody else who was at the scene that day."

Calhoun jolted as a sharp intake of breath filled his lungs and a memory of a memory that he could not remember asserted itself.

YOU MIGHT JUST WANNA KEEP AN EYE ON THEM.

A faint anger bubbled up behind his eyes. Calhoun couldn't quite understand why, but somehow he knew that he was entirely justified.

"Hm," he flipped the folder closed. "I might know a couple of people worth talking to. So, if you'll excuse me," Calhoun sidled past the CSI and made his way out the door, hat and coat in hand, "I've got a bit of business to attend to. Nice to meet you . . . uh . . ."

"Carrie," she responded. "Carrie McDermott."

"Thanks for the help. Maybe I'll see you around," Calhoun slipped back out of his door. Because if one thing was certain, it was that he needed to pop those two little pimples before they stuck their noses into any more of his goddamned business.

CHAPTER THIRTY-ONE
Dawn Of Eviction Day

Michael sleepwalked through the next week, stumbling around arbitrarily while carrying a numbing weight on his shoulders. He attempted to bury himself in his work, but since his work consisted of mindlessly staring at screens and punching numbers into blocks so that other numbers could flow through and interact with more numbers in different blocks, there was only so much depth in which he could be buried. He hoped Ravi Shah would swing by with a tone-deaf grin plastered across his face. Michael would lash out and punch him, then get fired from this godforsaken hell hole of a job. That would've livened things up a bit. But no, Ravi kept his distance, preoccupied with some mundane task or another, and Michael was allowed to keep his job, for now.

Michael took the bus home after work every day, at least until he could afford to hire a tow truck to drag the deflated Garbagemobile back home. Being surrounded by burnouts, old ladies, and the occasional hyper-obese man with narcolepsy issues caused him to lapse into idle thought once again. He had wondered what he would tell Stephanie's aunt and uncle. He didn't even know how he would get in touch with them. And if Stephanie was right, perhaps they never cared about her anyway. But Michael couldn't believe that to be true.

In order to shake the constant reminders about Stephanie, Michael had also taken to visiting Elena Finster in the hospital on his way home from work. She had not died, but rather endured a very severe heart attack brought on by what the doctors called "excessive stress," but what Michael knew to be "interdimensional cow attack." But he never told them that.

Michael would sit by Mrs. Finster in the bed, sometimes talking, sometimes mumbling. The doctors and nurses merely stood by and watched. They assumed he was her son. Michael, again, knew the truth, that her son – childhood bully Anthony Finster – had been living in California for some years with his boyfriend, but Michael wasn't in the habit of telling people things that didn't really matter. Especially when nothing, objectively, really mattered to him anymore.

"Who're you?" A gruff voice followed the open and closed swing of the hospital suite door. Michael looked up to find the chubby, but sagging face of his middle school gym teacher. Arthur Finster's hair had seen better days. It was now a graying orange blonde instead of a fiery red – or jet black for that matter – and there was a whole lot less of it.

"I . . . uh . . ." Michael stammered as he stood up, his chair squealing against the floor.

"Wait a minute . . . I know you," Mr. Finster pointed at him with a slow nod. "You were one of my kids . . . weren't you?"

"Uh, yes, sir. That's right, sir," Michael avoided looking at him directly, as if his wisps of remaining hair were solar flares.

"Duckett, right?" Mr. Finster actually smiled a bit as Michael peered up. "Yeah. You used to be a lotta trouble. You and that other one. The girl. Dyer?"

"Yes, that's right."

"That brings back memories," Arthur Finster moved to his comatose wife's side and placed his hand on her shoulder with a tenderness that Michael would have though foreign to him. "I'm sorry if I was hard on you back then. Elena and I were going through a time. I was a bit of a hothead. Drank a lot. Then I blacked out one day. When I came to it was just an hour later, but it scared the hell out of me. Couldn't remember a damn thing. Doctor said I had minor brain damage due to a stroke. It was a real wake up call. So I hope you'll accept my apology," Finster paused as he looked at his wife. "Wait, how'd you know Elena was in the hospital?"

Michael had left long before Mr. Finster had finished his rambling apology, leaving only a swinging hospital door in his wake. But before he left the hospital entirely, Michael made an additional stop to a room on the first floor, which held two patients who suffered from sudden onset amnesia. Michael did not dare go through the door, but merely peered through the glass porthole to see that Terri Bradshaw and her brother Jacob were up and alert, answering their doctor's questions. That was good at least.

As their attending physician exited the room, Michael ducked out of sight, then ran to catch up to him, attempting to act casual.

"Uh, excuse me, Doctor . . ." Michael looked down at the man's name tag, and his words stuck in his throat. He coughed to dislodge them. "Doctor Supirn. I'm a family friend and I didn't want to bother them, but I was wondering how the Bradshaws are doing?"

"Oh, quite well. Quite well," Doctor Coleman Supirn nodded as he stared at his chart with an expression of almost bovine nonchalance. "A serious case of memory loss and time loss. They can't seem to remember anything for months. Looked like a stroke, but they're both incredibly healthy. No sign of permanent brain damage."

"That's good," Michael muttered, cursing Terri's loss of memory. Maybe this was the universe's way of punishing him for daring to dream. Stephanie would have made fun of him for literally suffering the worst case outcome. "That's good. So they'll be okay?"

"Yes. Just a few more days of rest, I'd say. Weird coincidence, as I suffered from something similar not too long a–" Doctor Supirn turned to find that Michael was no longer next to him.

As he speed walked out of the hospital, Michael's phone rang for the twentieth time that day. He let the Mighty Ducks theme play for a short while before picking up.

"Hello," he said, monotone, knowing what it would be. He was right, another person asking for help from the now defunct detective agency. Despite his attempts to purge the ad from the internet, callers still streamed through the alternate universe cell phone he had removed from the Garbagemobile. All he offered the callers and emailers was a curt "Sorry, we don't do that anymore." And this one would receive the same. The only call that differed was from one Dorabell Underwood. She got a "Your husband wasn't cheating on you. Big misunderstanding. Forget about it. No charge."

Michael's general malaise did not lift, even when he returned home. "Home", of course, being a temporary word, as today was the day he was due to be evicted for his multiple missing rent payments. Mr. Doupolous smiled angrily as he watched Michael trudge up his stairs for the last time. The only way Michael's situation could get any worse was if he were to move in with his mother. Thankfully, since she was all the way down in Boca Raton, he didn't have to consider that option. Instead, he only had to contend with the aggressive rental prices in this city and the possibility of being homeless.

The one speck of joy in his otherwise dreary existence was the brief moment before the lock clicked open and his apartment door swung in. Each day, a sliver of hope bloomed in his chest that Stephanie would be there, lounging on the couch watching a stupid movie or playing video games, and each time this hope was dashed.

But this time . . . this time . . . the hope turned to fear. As the door swung inwards, Michael found the imposing figure of Detective Rex Calhoun hovering around his towers of cardboard boxes, and peeking in each one. He turned around just as Michael remained frozen in the doorway.

"Hello, Michael," Calhoun said, his voice dripping with false saccharine.

"Oh my god. How'd you get in here?"

"Window was open."

"What? Again?" Michael rushed to the opposite wall and slammed the window shut. This really had to stop happening.

Calhoun jerked his thumb in the direction of Michael's moving boxes. "Going somewhere?"

"No!" Michael blurted out without thinking. "I mean, yes! I mean, sorry. I'm being evicted."

"Hm. That's a damn shame," Calhoun gestured to one of the smaller, waist-high towers. "Mind if I sit?"

"Yeah. But not on that one. It's plates. Use the other one. The one marked 'pillows.'"

Calhoun nodded and shifted to the other box. "So why're you getting evicted?"

"Couldn't pay the rent." This was not a lie and Calhoun could not arrest him for it. At least, Michael hoped not.

"Makes sense. This area's getting expensive. Even though it's a bit of shithole. You tofu-farming hipster millennials are gentrifying me out of my own damn city," Calhoun gazed out the window, before snapping back toward Michael, who stiffened. "Geeze. Relax. I'm not here to arrest you."

"You're not?"

"Believe me, nothing would please me more. I would have you downtown so fast that your head would spin off of your neck."

"Could you just get to the point?" Michael had tried to think of some joke Stephanie would say, but all that came out was irritation.

"Easy there, Touchy," Calhoun raised his hands in mock offense. "No. I'm not here to arrest you. I'm just here to give you some friendly advice."

"Advice?"

"Yeah," Calhoun advanced on him in a way that was incongruous with the words "friendly advice". Towering over Michael, he jabbed a finger into his chest, but it felt more like the barrel of a gun. "Leave the detective stuff to the police. Just because you and your friend somehow conned your way into licenses doesn't mean you're real detectives. You might think this is all fun and games, but it's not. Right now, you're just indulging a senile old lady who thought her husband disappeared, but next time lives might be on the line. This isn't some sort of fancy playground tea party. This is real life. Do you get me?"

Michael paused. "You think kids have tea parties on playgrounds?"

"Don't test me," Calhoun scowled at Michael, who could not remember if he was capable of other facial expressions. "Now you keep your nose clean. If I see you again, it'll be too soon. And let your little girlfriend know, too. Where is she, anyhow?"

"She's not my—" Michael stopped mid-protestation. It wasn't worth it. "She's moved out already. We had a bit of a . . . falling out."

"Huh. Probably for the best. She wasn't very bright."

Anger stirred up in Michael, but he stopped himself when he realized he was about to scream at a cop. "She meant well."

"I'm sure she did."

"She was a good person!" He insisted.

"Well, if she was so great, why did she bail on you?" Calhoun raised an eyebrow.

"She didn't bail on me! I bailed . . . I bailed on her," Michael looked down at his feet. "I took her for granted."

"Alright. Whatever. I didn't come here to listen to you learn a life lesson," Calhoun rubbed his eyes as he got up off his cardboard seat and dusted off his lap. "You two knuckleheads just watch your step," he moved to the door. "If I ever see or hear from either of you two again, it'll be your asses! Are we clear?"

Michael nodded. "Crystal."

As the door slammed shut behind Rex Calhoun's coattails, Michael decompressed and sulked over to his room, to continue packing up what little he had left of his life. Most of his things resided in the boxes in the living room, and aside from some trash and a mattress shrouded in garbage bags, Michael's bedroom was nearly empty. The only major remnants lay in Stephanie's room, behind the door he had closed weeks ago and refused to open. The movers that would come later in the afternoon would have to deal with it. Better them than him.

Michael moved past the blank white door and into his own room. In the center, just by the upturned mattress, lay the yearbook Stephanie had slid underneath his door. He stared down and the open pages and black and white pictures of times past. Michael was about to crouch down and pick it up when he was jarred by a repetitive banging that shook the walls of his room. Jumping up, he dashed out of his room into the hallway, following the sound. He did not have to move too far, as the pounding resonated in the door to

Stephanie's room. Planting his feet, Michael pushed past everything in his mind that warned him against opening it, and embraced the parts of himself that expressed the hope he so needed. Now, more than ever, he needed a mark in the win column of his life, and he clasped the cold, vibrating knob and with a slow turn, pushed open the door.

Stephanie was crouched on her haunches, bashing a giant wrench into the baseboard of the wall, sending splinters and chunks of wood flying. Michael stood silently agog until the door slammed into the wall, breaking Stephanie's single-minded destructive focus.

Tossing the hammer aside, she smiled as she lifted up the pair of dark goggles that covered her eyes. They were more suitable for operating an industrial arc welder than for someone destroying a wall. "Hey, Mike. What's up?"

"What . . ." Michael stared at the ghost for a long time before he found his voice, " . . . the shit, Stephanie?"

"Oh, this?" She pointed at the hole in the wall, then grabbed a familiar gray pneumatic gun that had been sitting behind her. "My grappling hook got delivered a while back, so I decided to stash it in this wall, just so any alternate universe versions of us know where to look for it three years from now," she stood up and twirled around, her arms outstretched as the long dark trench coat she had draped around herself flowed through the air. "You like the detective's coat I bought? It came with a free scarf. Heck of a deal."

"I thought you were dead!"

"Oh, that!" Stephanie chuckled. "I lucked out and landed here two months ago and basically hid under my bed until I was sure the past me was gone. Didn't want to cause some sort of weird paradox. Psht.

I'm not stupid," she mimed shooting herself in the head with the grappling hook gun.

"So you've been hiding out for two months? You know we're getting evicted today, right?"

"Oh, that's today? Cool," she slicked her hair back over her head. "Perfect timing. Our fancy new digs are signed and good to go."

"What?" Michael asked. "What new digs?"

"This fetching trench coat and scarf ensemble isn't the only thing I bought," she got up, kicking aside a small stack of yellow sticky notes that had been under her butt. "C'mon. I've got something even neater to show you. You'll see. I took care of everything."

"You . . . did?" Michael softened. He may have even been holding back a smile. All the other shit be damned, Stephanie was back again. Nothing else mattered. "Alright," he said. "What is it?"

CHAPTER THIRTY-TWO

Dicks For Hire

At Stephanie's direction, Michael hailed a cab outside their apartment.

"Well?" Michael asked a few moments after they had gotten into the back seat.

"Well what?"

"Where are we going?"

"Oh, right!" Stephanie leaned forward over the driver's shoulder. "271 Ball Street."

"Lady," the cabbie responded with an accent Michael could not place, and a very phlegmy grunt. "You sure about that? That's in—"

"Squalor's Wallow. That's right," Stephanie confirmed. The cabbie shrugged and hit the gas.

"Squalor's Wallow?" Michael hissed. "Why the hell are we going there? That place is Crimetown, USA!"

"You'll see soon enough," Stephanie's knowing smile was an irritating, but pleasant sight.

The drive downtown was a quick one. The familiar, yet ramshackle homeyness of midtown faded into a blur as they merged onto the highway. The cab finally slowed down as they entered Squalor's Wallow, an area of town that sported, according to national crime statistics, a murder rate of 200%. Logistically, more people had to move into Squalor's Wallow every day to replace those lost in the previous 24 hours. Given the low rent rates, this wasn't entirely impossible. And today, Michael and Stephanie were two of those people.

The cabbie sped away to arguably safer pastures, dumping Michael and Stephanie in front of a brick building that looked like it was struggling to keep itself upright, and would have preferred to collapse atop the fledgling convenience store beneath it. Without a word, Stephanie grabbed Michael's wrist and yanked him toward the green door just adjacent to the convenience store. She smiled as she turned the knob and walked into the ground floor, which consisted only of a lobby somehow more narrow than the one from their previous apartment. The two of them shimmied through the empty, musty corridor.

Michael looked over his shoulder constantly as he followed Stephanie up two flights of dark and not entirely stable wooden stairs, leaving his footprints in the thick layer of dust and cobwebs that had accumulated over the past fifty years. The top floor was another, slightly wider hallway with multiple doors, each of which had belonged to a now abandoned business. The logos – or the remnants of them, anyway – on them told tales of failed law firms and courier companies. At the end of the dank hallway sat a stained wood door that was newer than all the others. Its glass pane, a wavy frosted variety that distorted the light that streamed through it, had a logo emblazoned on it in a classic, art deco style. Six gilded words hung there.

DUCKETT & DYER
P.I.s FOR HIRE

Of course, some enterprising young artist native to Squalor's Wallow had already found their way into the building and, using a can of bright red spray-paint, supplanted the word P.Is with the word 'Dicks' in all caps. The paint was still fresh and dripping down the glass.

"Ah? Eh?" Stephanie presented the door with gusto.

Michael wished he was surprised, but only one thought occurred to him. "Why is my name first?"

"Because otherwise it doesn't rhyme," Stephanie said, opening the door. "Also, certain liability issues."

Despite the ghoulish neighborhood and dilapidated building, the office was actually quite nice. Better and bigger than their former apartment. Wood paneling ran halfway up the elegant dark blue walls, and the crimson rays of the evening sunset streamed through the windows and glanced off a single hardwood desk. The office was beautiful. It was the premise that was ludicrous.

"How'd you afford this place?" was Michael's obvious question.

"Oh . . . yeah. I forgot to mention. While I was waiting around for the past few months . . . I just moved some money around," Stephanie walked the perimeter of the office, looking everywhere but at Michael. She ran her fingers along the walls. No flakes of loose paint fluttered to the ground. "I hired some guys to do the renovation. Had to pay them extra to come here, too."

"Yeah, let's back up," Michael said. "Whose money was it that you moved around, exactly?"

"I dunno . . ." Stephanie scratched her nose and looked away. "Some guy's, I guess."

It took Michael five seconds to discern the truth, "You were the one who stole the rent checks, weren't you?"

"Yeah . . . well . . . uh . . . I figured that since they were already stolen, you wouldn't miss them." The gears in Stephanie's head may as well have creaked aloud.

"Wonderful. And the ads? And the P.I. licenses we didn't apply for? I assume that was you, too?"

"Uh . . ." Stephanie bit her lip in absent thought, "Yeah. That was me too. In order to fix the multi-versal spasm, I figured I had to force past us into that situation to close the loop. So I had to make you broke and tell Terri she was going to be kidnapped. You should've seen her reaction. Lots of crying. It was a whole production.

"Anyway, I wrote up that list we found, too. Didn't know all the names of the people I exploded so I just put some fake ones in the middle. One of them was H.N.R. Pufnstuf. I'm just surprised neither of us noticed."

Michael realized he wasn't as upset as he should have been. As a matter of fact, he was impressed. Stephanie was retroactively trying to get her life in order, in her own chaotic way. It was a valiant effort that Michael had to appreciate. He waved his hand around the "detective agency." "So you arranged all this?"

"Hell, yeah. And I found some time to mess around with Calhoun a little bit. That was fun," Stephanie clapped. "By the way, don't worry about moving all your stuff, I talked to your movers and they'll be bringing it here. Nice guys. But, again, I needed to pay them extra to come here. It doesn't matter, though. This place is even better and cheaper than our old one! There's a murphy bed in the wall. Aren't murphy beds awesome?"

Michael just smirked.

"They are," Stephanie banged her fist against the wall and a fully made murphy bed hit the floor with a clang. "They are awesome! There's even a full bathroom. It'll be just like home. I'll run the detective business on the side to start paying my share. You don't have to cover for me anymore," Stephanie twirled around the office in a goofy faux ballet. "You and me, together again. It'll be fun! Trust me," she opened her arms, inviting Michael to say his piece. "Ah? Eh? Yes?"

"This is dumb, Steph. Real dumb." Michael said. "Probably the dumbest thing you've ever done."

"Oh," Stephanie's shoulders slumped.

"But I think I need a little dumb in my life. It's really good to have you back," Michael grabbed Stephanie in a long hug. Things weren't exactly like they had been before, like Michael had wanted, but with a little work on both their parts, maybe they could be better. But there would have to be limits. "One condition, though. I'll let you do the detective thing as long as you keep me out of it. I've had enough trouble for one lifetime."

"I promise," Stephanie said. But both of them knew that Stephanie had never been very good at keeping promises.

EPILOGUE

So This Is How It Begins . . .

"Alright!" Stephanie yelled as she peered over the stone dais, into the electric blue tunnel as Mike's falling body receded into infinity. "See you later, boys," she took one last look behind her, as a legion of cow-faced monsters shambled angrily towards her. She had seen better days, but this was getting ridiculous. That being said, she liked ridiculous. It kept things interesting. "Make way for Steph! COMING THRRRRROOOO—" Stephanie's yell was cut short as the portal consumed itself and she landed face-first onto wet dirt.

"Oof." Stephanie sat up and spat a clump of dirt out of her mouth. The ground rumbled with the impact of three cow men and their illustrious, orange and red shawled leader, as they jumped down to engage her, but not in the good way. "Hello, boys."

Cow Man Supreme roared a mighty roar and directed his lackeys to advance on her. Their clawed feet gouged deep into the soft dirt.

"Okay, this time we're gonna do this for real," Stephanie grit her teeth and lunged forward, pushing off the ground and barreling into a cow man's torso. Immediately, the offending monster exploded, covering the area with the requisite blood and guts. Another portal opened up with a thunderous crack and again Stephanie was on her way across time and space, screwing her eyes shut and hoping against hope that she would land in the right universe and the right time.

Stephanie's eyes shot back open as the familiar bellowing of Cow Man Supreme echoed down through the blue void. Flailing her arms in a mediocre approximation of swimming in zero gravity, Stephanie managed to rotate her body around to confirm that the cow-headed eyeball-fingered monster was smarter than she thought and had managed to follow her through the portal.

"You just don't take a hint, do you?" Stephanie grunted, but there was nothing left for her to do, except let this monster follow her to her next destination. Wherever that was. She swum back around and, resigned to her fate, streamlined her body and closed her eyes once again, rushing like a bullet toward whatever lay before her. Suddenly, she began to drift right, or what she thought was right in an infinite, unchanging blue void. The snarls and roars of Cow Man Supreme began to fade away as Stephanie was yanked violently out of the slipspace between universes and into reality, crashing into something made of wood that splintered and cracked upon impact. It was a few moments before she came to with a massive headache. She groaned and sat up, rubbing her head as the space vortex zipped shut behind her.

"Ugh. What the hell, man? Where am I?" Stephanie winced as she pulled a coffee table leg out from under her. Her eyes widened as she recognized it. It was Mike's old coffee table. A cheap, particle board number that could not handle the full force impact of a 137 pound woman. She looked around at the peeling mint green paint and general familiar mustiness of the living room she had found herself in, once again. She suddenly felt at ease.

"I'm home. I'm home!" Stephanie shot to her feet and began celebrating. "Mike!" She called out. "Mike! Are you here?

"Michael's not here, Steph," Stephanie Dyer – a second Stephanie Dyer – walked out of the hallway that led to her room.

"Oh, goddamn it. Is this another alternate reality?" Stephanie yelled.

"Relax," the second Stephanie said, her voice still and calm. She rotated the silver ring that adorned her middle finger. A bevy of red lasers shot out and formed a display on the wall above the TV.

```
USER_HOME:\\10E63.99873445218
USER_TIME:\\20160914170186221
CURR_UNIV:\\10E63.99873445219
CURR_TIME:\\2013071719228432
INPT_DEST:\\ _
```

"This is your home universe," the other Stephanie continued. "Just two months before you left. I made sure your Michael wasn't home. And your past self is at a John Hughes movie marathon."

"Oh, yeah," Stephanie nodded blowing aside the hair that had fallen in front of her face. "That was a good weekend," Stephanie squinted. She did not recognize her other self. She was basically identical, but Stephanie noticed a few faint wrinkles around the eyes. Other than that, she just lacked energy, drained of all the manic reserves Stephanie was currently drawing on. "You're not from around here, are you? You're me. But you're not me."

"I'm from the universe you first jumped to. Three years in the future."

"The one with the white Beyonce?" Stephanie raised an eyebrow. "That shit was weird."

"No!" The other Stephanie protested. "Your Beyonce is weird! It doesn't make any sense."

"You don't make any sense!"

"I don't—" The other Stephanie stepped forward, but caught herself before going on. "This isn't productive. We're just going to have to agree to disagree."

"That's because you know I'm right," Stephanie crossed her arms and pouted.

"Would you drop the shtick?" Other Stephanie sighed and ran her hand through her hair. "I'm you. I know what you're feeling right now and blocking it out with jokes isn't going to help. I'm here to tell you something important. We need to do something."

"You sound like Mike," Stephanie turned back to what could be her future.

"Yeah, well, Michael's not an idiot. You should learn something from him."

"And I will? Three years in the future?"

"Hey, I'm an alternate you," Other Stephanie shrugged. "Whatever happens to you in three years is your problem. All I can give you is my advice. It's up to you to listen."

Stephanie moved to sit down on the couch, but realized she was still covered in oozing cow-person detritus. She opted to remain standing. "Okay. I'm all ears. Why am I here? And why two months early?"

"Because you're going to need prep time," Other Stephanie paced back and forth across the creaking wooden floor. "Now listen carefully. You need to steal the next two months' worth of rent checks that Michael writes out. There's an old office down on Ball Street that could use some renovation. That's where you're going to set up Duckett & Dyer: D—" Other Stephanie caught herself. "P.I.s for Hire."

"Ball Street?" Stephanie cocked an eyebrow. She'd recognized the street name from news reports. Not good ones. "That's in—"

"Squalor's Wallow. Don't worry. You'll get used to it. The next thing you're going to have to do is—" Other Stephanie paused and thought. "Y'know what? Why am I wasting time? You're not going to remember. Here's a list of stuff you have to do and a flashdrive with some pictures and other things you might need to know some day," she reached into her pocket and presented a small rolled up piece of paper to Stephanie before reflexively jerking it back. "*Don't* lose it."

Stephanie grimaced and grabbed the paper out of her doppelganger's hand, wrapped inside was a flashdrive, as promised. Holding the paper by its edges, as to not stain it with too much cow man juice, Stephanie skimmed some of the bullet points. "Buy sticky notes. Take P.I. Exam. Ads: Internet and Radio. Picture on the flash drive. Use the right Phone Number," Stephanie looked back up. "Which phone number?"

"In your pocket. You took a version of Michael's cellphone from another universe, right?"

Stephanie fished around in her inner pocket and retrieved a small black and silver flip phone she had pocketed from the universe where she had kissed Jacob Bradshaw. She had remembered the kiss – it hadn't been great – but did not remember taking the phone. She placed it gently next to the ruins of the coffee table, as if it might explode. "Oh."

"Yeah. When you're done, shove it in the glove compartment of the Garbagemobile."

"So you're telling me that Mike was right? That I was responsible for all of this?"

"You, and me, and every other Stephanie across the multi-verse," Other Stephanie stated, as if this were a well-known phenomenon.

"So where were all of you when we were jumping around like a couple of dicks?"

"Because . . . well . . . I can't say," Other Stephanie turned away.

"You came all this way, across *universes*, and you can't say anything. You're just going to tell me what to do and jump away somewhere?"

"I–"

"No, you listen to me, sunshine," Stephanie yelled. She had never gotten angry at anyone. Always, she had tucked her nascent fear and anger away, never forcing it on anyone else, and subjecting only herself to her own guilt and shame. Now, she was standing right in front of herself, and this was possibly the only time she would get to express it on someone that could take it. "I have traveled too far and gone through too much! And suddenly you coming barging into my universe telling me that I have no free will outside of this list?" She threw the flashdrive at her doppelganger's head. It bounced off and hit the ground with an impotent click. "You better believe I deserve a straight answer. Tell me everything."

Other Stephanie sighed and slumped, resting herself against the TV stand. "Something's wrong. Something's out there."

"Out where?"

"I don't know. In between all these universes. It's coming and it's coming for us. Trying to erase us from existence," she paused. "And it's winning."

"Why us?"

"I don't know. And I don't know where or when it started. Probably when the first pair of us got dragged into this. But now we're all in trouble. The only way we've been able to stave it off is making sure that every universe stays alert and picks up their slack. That's why we instruct each of us to start a detective agency in every universe. You know as well as I do that it's an idea you can resist."

"No, no. This isn't what I signed up for. I just wanted to have some fun."

"I'm not stupid. I'm you. We both know that's not the real reason you thought this was a good idea. You know what you really want," Other Stephanie turned grave. "And what your reasons are."

Stephanie shut up, afraid to ask the question that had quietly haunted her for years. The question Kiara had told her to hold on to. The question which, in hindsight, caused her to drag herself and Mike into all of this out of some vague, misguided hope that maybe they would be able to answer it as detectives.

"Go on," Other Stephanie's question needled under her skin, prickling her with a faint pain she hadn't felt in years. Not until recently. "Ask. I asked when I was like you."

The words just fell out. "Do we ever find out what happened? Do we find out who killed our parents?" Stephanie did not look up. If she had, she would have seen that the Other Stephanie did not look up either. "And what happened to my brother?"

"I'm sorry," Other Stephanie said to the floor, "but traveling through the multi-verse doesn't help. It just . . . hurts," she trundled over to Stephanie and put a comforting hand on her shoulder. Due to her dampening ring, neither of them exploded. "You have to stay aware of anything strange that happens on your doorstep. Because it's your turn, now that we're gone."

Stephanie met her own gaze. Even though they were the same height, it felt like her other self towered over her. "What do you mean gone? Where are you going? Where's your Mike?"

"It's too late for my Michael. He's . . ." The Other Stephanie began to choke up as she walked away, fiddling with her ring. "He's gone now. But I'm going to go help yours." A stable crack in the space time continuum unfurled before her, exuding the same royal blue, but instead of the violent crackling abyss Stephanie was used to, this one marshaled itself with a sense of tame decorum. She inched closer to the portal, and Stephanie could only watch.

"Don't make the same mistakes I did," she said. "Keep your Michael safe. Please keep him safe."

"Wait. If we're all being erased, how come we're still here now? Shouldn't we all have disappeared?"

Other Stephanie smiled weakly. "Steph, just because things happen simultaneously doesn't mean they happen at the same time."

"Wait!" Stephanie blinked. "What the hell is that supposed to mean?" But it was too late.

With a quick, offhand salute back to her, Other Stephanie breached the surface of time with a warrior cry, "COMING THROO—"

As the multi-verse portal swallowed her other self with a satisfied glorp and a demure zip, all was quiet. Stephanie looked at the cell phone and the flash drive on the floor. Her hands were wracked with a trembling that had not been there moments ago. An uncountable amount of time passed before she sucked in a gulp of air and went to take a shower.

For the first time in her life, she had a job to do.

DUCKETT & DYER

Dicks For Hire

Will Return In

"The One-Hundred Percent Solution"

ACKNOWLEDGEMENTS

If you have read this far, I bet you're expecting something funny or dumb out of this acknowledgements section. Something in the ballpark of:

"It's true what they say: It takes a village to write a book. So, I'd like to thank the village of Clent, southwest of Birmingham, without which, this book would never have been possible."

But, no, this is my time to be serious. A lot of work went into putting this book together and not all of it was mine. There are a lot of people I need to thank for their unconditional love, support, and willingness to review the terrible drafts I shoved at them. So here we go.

Andrew Cannizzaro, my friend, my roommate, and writing partner in so many damn things. Thank you so much for always being up to listen to and seriously consider my completely insane ideas. It's hard to find someone who jives so well with me creatively, so it's been a genuine pleasure working with you on my book, your book, and our potential TV show.

Emily Spear, my girlfriend. Thank you for your continual love and support and willingness to put up with my endless barrage of terrible jokes. While I don't have a filter for what comes out, you're always there to point out the ones you like, so I can write them down and save them for later. I know dealing with me is tough, so I appreciate your dedication.

Tareque Powaday, my fellow writing teacher, and one of the most amazing artists I've ever had the pleasure of meeting. Thank you for being so great and quick with the pen to address my ridiculous nitpicks and demands. And thanks for having an encyclopedic knowledge of comic books and art styles that I can easily reference.

The Panera Collective. Thanks for slogging through my early drafts with me and pointing out the logical inconsistencies and just plain bad writing. It was always great to know that I wasn't the only person struggling to complete a novel. I will be forever in your debt for helping me eliminate 90% of my adverbs.

Jackie Dinas, thank you for being one of my loudest champions and always being willing to chime in with your book and publishing industry expertise. I would be completely lost without your helpful, informative and enthusiastic guidance.

To the Clip Show crew who indulged me and helped with my beta versions, Kevin Froleiks, Patrick Reilly, Ryan Stanisz, Logan Lampton and Rae Rossi, thank you for bringing keen comedic and stylistic eyes to this book that would otherwise just be full of fart jokes and nonsensical onomatopoeias.

Thank you to Roman Levant, my best friend, who's always around to trade jokes and memes and esoteric references that only we understand. That kind of relationship is key to my relative sanity and don't you forget it.

Thank you to my friends Samuel Kaminsky, Mikhail Karadimov, Mallory Gordon, Ed Pabey, and Laura Transue who are amazing friends and have always enthusiastically supported my ideas and efforts, no matter how dumb they may be.

Thank you to Kelly Aldridge, of Dancing Quill Editing, who offered to edit my book and did so while pregnant! You're an amazing superhero and I wish you the best.

Of course, thanks to my mother and father. Although they probably won't read this book, since it's not their speed. They always were insistent that I "could do whatever I want." Which I do appreciate. Because that means they believe I can do anything I dream up. It's incredibly freeing.

And a final thank you to my grandfather. He may not be alive to read this, but he was a continual source of inspiration in my formative years. Without him I would not have gained compassion, drive, love of the written word, and my good humor.

Oh, and you, too! Thought I forgot about you, eh? No such luck. Thank you for buying – or obtaining through [il]legal means – this book, and for supporting independent authors such as myself. In this day and age, there are so many entertaining things competing for your attention and I'm grateful that you chose to spend a few hours with my book. I hope you enjoyed what you read, and if you did, I'd love to hear from you. Again, thank you from the bottom of my cold, cold heart.

CPSIA information can be obtained
at www.ICGtesting.com
Printed in the USA
BVHW030935090619
549760BV00012B/14/P